SILVE

STILE

OVER 100
GREAT NOVELS
OF
EROTIC DOMINATION

If you like one you will probably like the rest

NEW TITLES EVERY MONTH

All titles in print are now available from:

www.adultbookshops.com

If you want to be on our confidential mailing list for our Readers' Club Magazine (with extracts from past and forthcoming titles) write to:

SILVER MOON READER SERVICES

No 2 Granary House
Ropery Road
Gainsborough
DN21 2NS
United Kingdom

telephone: 01427 611697
Fax: 01427 611776

NEW AUTHORS WELCOME

Please send submissions to
Silver Moon Books Ltd.
PO Box 5663
Nottingham
NG3 6PJ
or
editor@babash.com

Silver Moon is an imprint of Shadowline Publishing Ltd
First published 2006 Silver Moon Books
ISBN 1-897809-72-7
© 2000, 2006 Caroline Swift

BEAUCASTEL

BY

CAROLINE SWIFT

ALSO BY CAROLIN SWIFT
ELISKA
THE SUFFERERS
CASTLE OF TORMENT
SILVANA'S QUEST
PURITAN PUNISHMENT
PARISIAN PUNISHMENT

PRELUDE

Emerging from his shower after returning home from a strenuous game of squash, Mikhail felt relaxed and there was a clear hour before him prior to cocktails and dinner with Claudia, his new mistress. From his study in the palatial apartment on the Quai d'Anjou, he watched the ripples of the sunlit Seine reflecting on his latest acquisition, a blue period Picasso. He always found Paris in the spring a delight, particularly when his faithful Gemma, the best maid he had ever had to serve him, opened the French windows and the breeze stirred the papers on his crowded desk. He stood still for a moment, clad only in a towel round his hips.

Among the papers, unfortunately, lay the fax received a week before from the dour Principal of the exclusive and appallingly expensive finishing establishment in England for 'young ladies of high birth and background', announcing the sudden dismissal of his ex-wife's stepdaughter for what was described as disreputable and unacceptable behaviour. Apart from frigging herself almost constantly, she had been found fucking behind the cricket pavilion with the ground staff. It added that some psychotherapy might be useful or, better still, 'stern corrective measures' which were, alas, not within the purview of an English institution such as hers. The finishing school, for its part, had finished with Verenka.

The event could not have come at a less propitious moment. Having installed the vivacious Claudia in his home and in his bed, Mikhail needed time and tranquillity for her to accustom herself to the place. Whereupon, this drama had occurred, encumbering the couple with the abrupt return from abroad of the dark, moody girl just out of her teens already dogged with scholastic failure at the Charlemagne lycee; her heavy presence irritated him and exasperated Claudia. In addition, Gemma was complaining.

In her starched apron and black, mezzogiorno garb of domestic efficiency, Gemma hovered at the study door with

5

whatever was on her mind. Mishka—as most people called him—looked at the woman's grey hair drawn back into the traditional, tight bun. She resembled someone waiting for confession with a priest.

"Is something wrong, Gemma?"

"It's the girl, Signore. She's at it again." Mishka groaned as he heard the rest. "Yes, Signore, not only regularly at night but frequently during the day," she confirmed, her gnarled, peasant hands clasped low before the region to which she was referring. "I have to change her sheets almost daily. They're always stiff with her cum, if I may use the term. As it may have occurred to the Signore, I believe a really sound thrashing would help. With the riding crop."

Basically, Mikhail had no objection to an idle girl masturbating; at least it kept her busy in her room, out of trouble and clear of Claudia. But trouble was brewing.

"Oh, hell, not again," he sighed, looking out at a barge charged with gravel chugging downstream towards the Cite. The prospect of losing Gemma's support was unthinkable. Claudia couldn't cook an egg. Nor could he. It was clear that something had to be done and quickly.

"I believe," the domestic went on - the woman's aggregate of beliefs always amazed Mikhail who had precious few - "I believe it is not right for your Signora to be disturbed by the groans the girl utters when discharging in bed—her squeals and yells, I mean, when she pleasures herself. It's not right," she repeated solemnly. "Your gracious Signora, and you too, Signore, have the right to rest and calm."

Luckily, Mikhail realized, as the maid's bedroom lay at the far end of the apartment, she was spared the moans generated by Claudia's frantic orgasms... But Gemma's existence centred on service to her employer and on nothing else.

He thought for a moment. Strangely, the attractive if doleful Verenka began to provide an enticement, stimulated by Gemma's proposal. He had spanked her a few times but had dismissed the temptation of using the riding crop. After all,

6

she was his ward now her stepmother had run off and left her.

"You think a beating with the crop would solve the matter, Gemma?" As he said it, he felt his cock under the towel stir like a one-eyed ferret disturbed from rest. He did not really require an answer or the maid's opinion; his mind had suddenly been made up for him by the thought of the slender crop with its chased silver handle. Since Ellen's departure there had not been much chance of using it.

"Has the Signora Claudia retired for her siesta, Gemma?"

"Yes, she's asleep in her own room at the end of the corridor. She needs her siestas."

Mishka agreed. She deserved all the rest she could get after the orgies in the master bedroom. There was a full hour before him.

"You're right, Gemma," he conceded. "A good thrashing might well teach her a lesson. But the Signora must not be disturbed. I'll administer it in my study rather than in the girl's room. On the table. So, take her there right away and be so good as to pick up my riding crop as you pass by—the one that used to be in my bedroom but now must be hanging with the coats on the hall stand, if I'm not mistaken."

The woman knew very well where it was to be found. Had the problem been left to her, as it would normally have been back in her village, she would already have used the murderous length of plaited leather twice daily on the degenerate young slut.

She gave a jubilant smirk that was also lethal. Yes, it took a Calabrese peasant to convince these rich, urban sybarites how to deal with a fractious, young masturbator.

Verenka assumed from Gemma's look that another dressing down awaited her, with the usual long, moralizing harangue. Yet somehow, the grey figure at the door of her room, standing like a living indictment, spelled real danger. The culprit pulled the sheet up to her chin, trembling.

"You're wanted in the Master's study, Signorina. No need to dress. Just come as you are."

7

Barefoot, in her silk negligee and flowered nightdress, Verenka followed the maid down the long hall into the sanctum. The shutters had been partly closed, darkening the familiar area; instead of displaying the chaos of papers and bowls of peonies, the polished stretch of the table was ominously bare. As the door closed behind her, Verenka saw the man.

Mishka confronted her, still with only the towel, as a vision she had never encountered before. The tanned body gave her a shock; it was hirsute, matching the pointed beard, and seemed to be made of brawn and sinews, maintained in perfect trim, she knew, at the Montparnasse squash club and Rolland Garros where he played tennis. What turned her rigid was the thing he took from Gemma: the riding crop creaked between his hands as the braided leather curved. The scene boded badly, particularly as under her shift Verenka knew her tiny, lace-bordered panties, no more than a string buried in her crotch, would be stained dark with the residues of the tremendous, thrilling orgasm she had treated herself to just after lunch.

"Strip her naked, please, Gemma," Mishka said nonchalantly. "I need her flesh fully accessible for what she's about to receive," Gemma noticed with pleasure that the towel was jutting out over the erection.

The domestic handled the girl almost as an object and an objectionable object at that. She tore off the diaphanous coverings with determination, the nightdress passing over the long, sable hair with a crackle of silk. The well-fleshed body stood trembling as Verenka crossed her arms over the rich, over-abundant breasts. Cold sweat seeped from the armpits.

"Hands behind your neck, Verenka," Mishka ordered, using the Russian diminutive she hated, while the maid laid the flimsy garments over the arm of the couch. "And take off that disgusting rag you have over your sex. In future, I don't want to find you wearing things of that sort. They only excite you unnecessarily, especially tight, narrow strings like that. Just look how it saws into your cleft. No wonder you're drenched

8

down there. I suppose you've just pleasured yourself."

Verenka hesitated a moment, her flesh crawling with fright yet flushed with exhilaration, before inserting her thumbs behind the elastic border riding the hips. Slowly, the damp triangle was peeled off, dredging the gusset out of the viscous slot. Bending forwards, Verenka slid the silk down, the heavy hunks of the breasts lurching and swaying from the roots. The man again noted lasciviously how the swollen cones of the areoles were smooth, devoid of pimples which he disliked on a woman; the bulges held the nipples firmly erect. No doubt they were puckered with apprehension as well they might.

"Pick it up, like a good girl, Verenka."

The girl stooped again to retrieve the rag. Again the fabulous mammaries swung like the bells of the Kremlin, the mass of buttock flesh turned towards him; his eyes browsed over the wealth of meat. At first Mishka had found the rump to be out of proportion with the remainder of the body, with its sleek but powerful thighs and narrow waist. But it was not so; the nude was exquisitely proportioned. The rump was merely far heftier than Ellen's and certainly larger that Claudia's—that was all. And more attractive than the flesh of most women he had enjoyed.

Verenka's hand had closed over the wet rag where it lay at her feet.

"Give it to Gemma." Then he turned to the maid: "Gag her with it. We don't want unnecessary noise out of her. And you, Verenka, stay like that, bent forwards."

Mishka pressed down on the spine to raise it and part the buttocks and then screwed his thumb deep into the anus. The insertion made Verenka jerk as she let out a low, guttural cry. At the same time, Gemma seized the rag, held the head back by the hair and crammed the thing, smelling of sex musk and discharge, into the throat.

"I think, Gemma," her employer remarked casually, sensing the pressure of the girl's sphincter around his thumb, "this orifice will need considerable enlarging if it's to be profitably

9

employed." He withdrew, watching the muscle close. "In my bedroom closet, you'll find some of the instruments I used on Madame Ellen. I think a Number Five dildo, the rubber one with the internal retention flange, is needed here. Verenka should wear it for a couple of weeks, until her sphincter learns to relax for use. Plug her up tight and remove it only when nature calls. I'll check her enlargement at the weekend after she's had a few relaxing flagellations."

"It shall be done, Signore." Gemma was elated at the prospect and at the humiliation being visited on the trollop.

"Now stand erect, Verenka, and let's see what we have in store for the crop."

The girl's eyes widened in terror, her face paling, framed by her long, dark hair. The two onlookers indulged in a close scrutiny of her nudity: Both spectators were fascinated by the sight. The body, to Gemma's expert eyes, constituted excellent whipping flesh and clearly submissive into the bargain. Santa Maria, how the slut needed flogging!

"Now, Verenka, as you persist in frigging that outsized clit of yours"—Mishka flicked the tongue of his crop over the stump of throbbing gristle, "I'm compelled to whip you, this time with this." He curved the thing again between his hands. "It will sink deep into your flesh and, I trust, into your obstinate nature. And I just cannot have you bringing yourself off several times a day and god knows how many times a night. Once now and then, Verenka, may well be tolerated. But you must control your lust. Therefore, I'm going to flog it out of you." He paused, only to add: "And you'll be whipped every second day until I'm satisfied you've grown up. Lay her over the table and hold her wrists."

Verenka put up a short, feckless fight that earned her a sharp, mezzogiorno slap across the face. Then her superb body slammed down on the table like raw meat, her crotch allowed to jam up into the angle of the mahogany surface—a concession Mikhail decided to grant. The vast breasts flattened, surging sideways on the table top, the head turned in profile between the extended arms. The victim braced her toes against the base of the table legs, the whole erotic length of nudity shuddering in expectation.

Suddenly, Mishka stripped off the wet towel and freed the enormous length of stiff cock, making sure Verenka saw it. Gemma nodded to herself; yes, that was the way a man should deliver a scourging. Stark naked, like the victim.

Before raising the crop, the man ran his hand over the girl's sumptuous buttocks.

"Verenka, you must learn not to clench your arse cheeks when you're going to be beaten. They must hang flaccid and slack. By all means let the flesh quiver when the welts start to rise," he authorized her. "But I want you limp. Otherwise, I'll have to double the ration of strokes. Do you understand?"

The victim nodded desperately between her taut biceps. It was poignant to behold.

To increase the tension, Mishka drew the square tip of the crop down the girl's anal cleft, past the puckered rosebud, to the fluttering labia of the vulva. The perfidious flap of leather explored the mouth of the cunt carefully, unclogging the umber lips and flicking the clit. Mishka noticed the fleshy pinnacle standing completely free of its protective sheath of skin. She had a prodigious stump and it was in full erection. Evidently, the girl was nicely excited by the prospect of flagellation. The prods he distributed over the labia and clit caused the quivering nude to heave upwards and fall back with a slap of the belly.

Already she was grinding the crotch into the corner of the table. Mishka withdrew the crop to peer at its extremity. It was coated with pre-cum. The girl's totally nude body was sexually ready for punishment. Mikhail also was ready.

The crop rose suddenly and sliced into the crown of the buttocks. Six strokes followed rapidly, with extreme accuracy, bringing the welts up in parallel lines, the girl bit hard into the rancid rag gouging her throat. The stifled groans began to fill the study.

Then the crop began to fall less impetuously but more at

11

random, with pauses between the strokes, to allow the effect to penetrate well into the nerves. The unintelligible moans told Mishka he was taking the girl to the limit of her resistance; the rest would be the pure pain a slave body always experienced during its first real thrashing until it was taught to orgasm under flogging. In time, Mishka knew, the girl would grow used to it, and handle the climax as it gathered and exploded. While lashing into the upper thighs, he ran a fist down his cock, lubricating it for penetration.

The strangled, guttural yells behind the gag then drove him to scourge harder, as the head lifted pathetically only to thud back to the table.

"Keep yourself open, Verenka," Mishka ordered her, his breath beginning to shorten. "Don't keep jerking… like that." Shlack! "You'll come… only when I say you may." Shlack!

Still far from placated, the man lashed again and again into the butt. The girl's body began to shudder spasmodically, recalling to Mishka the scores of females he had seen mounting to crescendo as he put them to the whip, Verenka was obviously no different.

Then the flagellation ceased abruptly. Thirty-five strokes—Gemma always counted—seemed to have devastated the victim but without sapping all her energy. Although the trunk lay almost immobile, the loins continued to convulse. The flogged body was on the brink of coming, the stupendous clit grinding away into the protrusion of the table, dribbling with juice. The man fingered the outsized stalk; it was throbbing in total erection and ready.

"I think that… will do for today, Gemma," he grunted, as the maid hopefully began to roll the body over to present the breasts. "No, I'll take her as she is. Hold her still."

As the huge Cossack prick approached, the maid moved round to splay the girl's labia, separating the hot flesh for the penetration. Her diligent fingers opened the girl's vulva and, admiring with pleasure the thick, blue veins on her employer's cock, guided the shaft into the congestion of bright sap. Mishka went in deep. Verenka lurched as if struck by lightning. The cock slammed in for a long moment and then withdrew to thrust its way into the anus. After dozens of plunges, it was back in the vagina. The cock was sliding smoothly in and out, the man's hands hooked round the girl's pelvis, as he sank in up to the hilt, his belly slapping against the flogged butt. To Gemma's amazement and despite the exhausting flagellation the girl had received, or maybe on account of it, Verenka had reached the final slope before the Everest of her orgasm. Mishka was now holding the thighs braced over his own, lifting her belly off the table to fuck faster. Her fists white with her grip now on the table edges, the girl had locked her ankles behind the table legs as Gemma watched the wet, matted head of hair bobbing distraughtly, the chin jarring against the polished surface of the table with each thrust of the cock. Gemma hoped it hurt.

Suddenly a muffled yell filled the room as the orgasm shattered and destroyed the flogged loins. Mishka let her writhe and come freely several times and then sent her to float into outer space where fucked, whipped females disintegrate when they have no more to squander.

Gemma saw him withdraw to send the hot wads of spunk up to and beyond the head of the shuddering body. Verenka slowly came back to earth and lay still.

Wiping his cock on her thigh, Mishka too expressed surprise to Gemma. The girl had, he murmured, the makings of a gifted SM subject, sexually and psychologically, despite her sluggish spleen.

"Someone who can orgasm as powerfully as that after an exacting flagellation, may well have quite a future before her. The bitch is servile to a degree, Gemma, erotically responsive to pain and, above all, she rides cock well—admittedly better up the cunt than the anus, but that too can be gradually trained." He paused a second, staring at the girl's tear-stained face. "No doubt the gullet will prove equally responsive. But that we'll see in her future sessions. I'll put her to the whip again,

13

Gemma, on Thursday after my board meeting. Make sure she's ready, gagged and bound, please."

As Verenka slowly suctioned her sweating body off the table, staggered upright for the maid to prise out the gag, she did something she had never done before at the Quai d'Anjou. Through her tears she smiled at Mishka and then at the domestic. It was a smile of complicity mingled with a strange leer of sexual lust. For Verenka, it was one thing to be whipped nude, but to be whipped and fucked by her handsome guardian before the maid was quite another. It had given her, the expression said, exultation for the first time since her return to France after her disgrace.

"Thank you, Mishka," she blubbered, her hands slithering over the welted rump, "that was... what I've always wanted... To come like that beats frigging, any day."

Her guardian nodded. "Take her back to her room, Gemma, and see to it she cleans herself up. Rub whatever you used on Madame Ellen into the damage and lock her up until her supper's ready. She'll eat in her room tonight. And kindly wipe off the table before Madame sees the mess. And replace the whip on the hallstand. Thank you again for your support. It was just like old times."

"It's only natural, Signore," came the reply. "I'm sure the session taught the little lady a lot and did her a world of good. Shall I serve Bordeaux or burgundy for dinner? There's sirloin. Perhaps your Chateau Courtet 69."

"Of course. And help yourself to a bottle, Gemma. While I shower and change, ask the Signora to come for aperitifs in the lounge when she's ready."

The maid held out his bathrobe and picked up the towel. She thought of everything.

His hand on the door, Mikhail turned before heading for the shower again.

"And Gemma, throw away that dirty cunt string or whatever it's called she had in her mouth. I don't want to see it around again. From now on, I wish to have her stark naked, her wrists

14

tied behind her, when summoned for whipping. And of course firmly gagged. I think I can rely on you to keep the slut out of sight and away from Madame, at least for the time being. Oh, yes," he added, "and perhaps tie her somehow to her bed."

The maid nodded. That was an order she fully endorsed. She had already thought of it herself. There was a dog collar and leash in the kitchen, a remnant from Madame Ellen's time when she was led around the great apartment on all fours, carrying between her teeth the whip to be used on her.

With a respectful bow to her employer after grabbing the girl by the hair, Gemma hauled her out swiftly towards entombment in the bedroom. Even in her modest role as an assistant, she had enjoyed the pre-cocktail hour; it had been something of a curtain raiser, a foretoken of the dramas about to be staged.

15

CHAPTER 1

Nude, Claudia lay exhausted on the huge bed. She stared out at the plane trees beyond the windows that stretched to the ceiling. It was now just over a month since she had moved in to live with Mikhail and at thirty-five she felt her cool golden beauty fully in keeping with the palatial residence where she was now the energetic mistress in both senses of the word. She ruled the household with a serene authority and diligence and was happy.

Elongated naked in the disorder of the black silk sheets, the curves of her slender white body were set off by the dark surroundings that lent the long limbs an unreality that fascinated Gemma every time she brought in the breakfast on its silver tray; Claudia was almost always nude. Gemma had seen others in very much the same state after rigorous nights in the same bed. And, despite her Catholic origins from the Italian Mezzogiorno, still betrayed by her austere black dress and the grey hair drawn severely back into a bun, she accepted it without question. She admitted moreover that this one was particularly attractive, infinitely preferable to the unpredictable Signora Ellen.

"The Master has gone to tennis, Madame," she announced, gazing unabashed at Claudia's slightly upturned breasts and still engorged nipples—indeed the woman must have had a hard night of it and dutifully Gemma made note to change the soiled sheets again. "Will Madame take the lunch here? Shall your bath be run?" Gemma then drew back all the other heavy brocade curtains to let the summer in. It blinded Claudia. She shifted on the bed, adopting the pose of Goya's Maja desnuda, her hands behind her head, and gave the requisite orders for the day. Then she asked, looking towards Verenka's room: "And the girl?"

She lifted her eyebrows over the blue pupils to share her despair with the maid who understood her concern.

"She's working in her room, Signora." Gemma said.

"Or pretending to work, you mean, Gemma. She's probably masturbating again over more love letters from this woman teacher of hers." The maid nodded with an uncharitable smirk. "See to it her room is locked and she is given lunch there. I have no wish to have her sulking around the house. After all she has everything she needs there—her bathroom, table, books, and even her girlfriend's photo by her bed."

Claudia raised her knees and crossed her smooth thighs imprisoning the sex between them.

"Really, I think the Master should take the lazy slut in hand. This can't, it just can't go on. The girl's a burden on us all. You know, Gemma," she confided with a sidelong glance at the Louis XV cabinet where Mikhail kept a number of interesting objects, with some of which she had already become acquainted, "I think a spot of corporal punishment would do her no harm."

"But the Master does beat her, Signora. Quite often. This you did not know?"

Claudia sat up against the pillows. Her surprise was genuine and she did not try to hide it. "Well, no, Gemma. That I did not know. But now you mention it, yes, I sensed something of the sort was afoot. It's done in her room, I suppose?"

For the first time since she had seduced her Cossack at the Auteuil races, always a promising locality to be introduced to likely partners by friends, Claudia felt a sting of annoyance at being excluded from a secret. After all, her Mishka was aware of her experience, not only as a bisexual but as a dedicated dominant—as well as a compliant submissive when circumstances demanded it, as long as she was not damaged by sex torture and the scourge. She had declared her various proclivities quite clearly to her new lover.

"Listen, Gemma. We shall say nothing of this conversation. I shall get Verenka herself to tell me so I can broach the subject with her guardian and persuade him to do the beatings in the drawing room or somewhere more appropriate. More overtly Gemma. In fact I should very much like to watch." Then, after a pause, she added: "And even participate myself. There's little more I should enjoy than castigating the wretched slut."

She paused as a thought crossed her mind. She rose from the black bed and stood up. Her nudity was startling as Gemma caught the customary stale odour of semen, feminine discharge and sweat lingering round the gorgeous svelte loins. What a golden goddess!

"I presume, Gemma, you are called to assist sometimes, are you not?"

"I do not think I should be speaking of this, Signora. But, yes, I hold the girl's arms when the Master thrashes her. Shall I run the Signora's bath now?"

"I see," Claudia said pensively. "Yes, you will run my bath. Now, we agree, not a word of this to the Master." She slipped into the silk kimono Gemma held out to her, and changed her mind. "Tell Verenka she will lunch with me today as a favour, instead of in her room. She need wear nothing more than that brief dressing gown with those ridiculous, hideous flowers all over it."

Before stepping down into the sunken circle of emerald, Claudia examined herself closely in the mirrors completely surrounding the room. Apart from some sombre mottling where the breasts had been hurt through the extravagant copulations and the residues of the fucking seeping sluggishly down between the furled sex leaves, Claudia found herself more elegant than ever. The clitoris had long since withdrawn into the shelter of its agile protective hood of which the woman was so proud; the stub too was exhausted after hours of erection, stimulation and orgasm. The memory of the multiple spasms Mikhail had brought about, sometimes in towering, destructive succession, sometimes solitary and far more devastating, compensated for the throbbing that lingered there and also around her sphincter.

Compared with the cocks of the countless males who had impaled her in the past, her Cossack's was a monster. And he was fully aware of it. Over the last month, she had known it

18

in every orifice, many times a night and frequently during the day whenever she or her lover, or both, could hold back no longer. One night Mishka had even taken her abruptly against the railings of the Palais Royal, her arms outstretched, grasping the gilded spears of the ironwork, riding the erection as if her last minute had come. And come it did and she with it; Mikhail had to clap his hand over her gaping wail of pleasure. The walk back home she clearly remembered, clinging to his arm, the clots of acrid semen slithering down the inner thighs, the curd congealing in the evening air. Her natural lust could hardly ask more of a man. Yet, deep down, she yearned for a great deal more.

Delicately in the bath suds she slipped back the sleeved hood off her point of pale flesh; it was too sensitive to endure a masturbation and moreover she had not the will. But it caused her to revert to the girl locked up in the room at the end of the long passage. Claudia knew the slut pleasured herself frequently; the moans were audible in the corridor itself and on one occasion when the girl had to be summoned to take a call—naturally from this blonde lycee teacher who seemed to be infatuated with her. She had issued forth flushed and disgustingly dishevelled. Yes, Claudia decided, I shall put a stop to these clandestine games. If the wench needed orgasms, she would make her frig herself openly before them. And then she would see to it that she be soundly thrashed after coming, hopefully by Claudia herself. The prospect stirred the lurking spirit of dominance within her and, to her surprise, raised the dormant clitoris.

She was about to direct the shower jet directly and deliberately over her sex when a further query made her refrain. Did Mikhail fuck the girl? The renegade thought made Claudia lie back wistfully in the bath to stare with half-closed eyes at the ornate ceiling and its floral clusters and stupid putti perched on billowing clouds. Perfidious bastard, she mused with a smile. If indeed he's been fucking her all this time, I'll have to reprimand him sternly. She would do so as a joke, for after all he was the guardian... He'll most certainly claim it as his due recompense for the trouble of disciplining the bitch. What does it matter as long as he beats the hell out of her? Claudia sank voluptuously into the foam. I'd like to flay the young bitch, she consoled herself. And somehow get shot of her. Quel fardeau! Quelle merde! The whore was in her way. Unless, of course...

Lunchtime came and the 'whore' in question was led quietly by Gemma into the dining room where her place was already laid amidst the silverware and flowers. Deferential was hardly the term for the spiritless humility of the girl; she was more subdued than ever in her short cotton smock, buttoned down the front and reaching just to her thighs, far more strongly muscled than Claudia had expected. She studied the young woman's features attentively, offering a welcoming smile that, like the straight whisky she sipped, had a chunk of ice in it. The slut was definitely desirable. And with a bit of training...

"Sit down, Verenka dear. We have melone con prosciutto and those nice coquilles Saint-Jacques a la nage which Mishka says you like so much. Gemma will serve you the biggest slice of melon, won't you, Gemma?"

The maid smiled insipidly as she pushed the chair under the girl's rich, fleshy rump, still nicely striated.

The meal consisted of a bright monologue from the new maitresse de maison, eliciting only a few terse replies from Verenka regarding her studies. Already Claudia knew of her catastrophic shortcomings and hopeless failures at the nearby Lycee Charlemagne and the finishing school in England Her return to Paris had been, for some reason, as precipitous as it was degrading for all concerned. A private tutor seemed the only course open, Claudia hardly relished it for it entailed having the frustrated student still sulking about the house but, in sympathy for her lover, she had held her tongue. The girl hardly left her room where she brooded and was frankly farouche.

Somewhere in the hinterland of Claudia's imagination, a

novel perspective began to take shape, a prospect so unorthodox as to appear unworkable. Stubbornly however the thought remained there in Claudia's mind.

She looked critically at the mournful, beautiful girl. In fact, she was faced not with a youngster but with a fully-fledged young woman, mal soignee true but with exceptionally fine features, robust and sexually attractive in a certain way.

Verenka's dark locks were long, parted down the middle, framing a delicate face, sombre eyes and a well-fleshed sensual mouth. Claudia was aware that the love the girl bore her was as scant as the nightdress the taciturn slut wore sitting there before her, fiddling with her bread in torment.

"Verenka dearest, you are really extremely beautiful. You must brighten up. Your attitude worries me." The courses dragged by until the cheeses and the dessert Gemma had prepared Verenka's favourite, an omelette soufflee normande.

"Do me a favour, will you, Verenka darling?" Claudia's voice was pure honey. "It would please me immensely. Take off your silly housecoat or whatever it is, now our little meal is over and let me admire you as you really are. Don't worry, Gemma's gone to make the coffee.

The face at the other end of the table paled under the sultry complexion at the invitation. She dabbed the Bruges lace napkin to her lips after wetting them nervously.

Slowly she unbuttoned her gown. It slipped behind her.

The spectacle made Claudia catch her breath. The oversized breasts swung free as the torso, to which they had adhered on the underside, bent forward. To Claudia the things were like proverbial fruits, ripe, soft and exquisitely shaped; the capacious umber areoled teats protruded as if they had just been sucked; they resembled hazel nuts, no, the tips of her own thumbs. Yes, that would do. The surrounding skin was tight and smooth. Claudia gazed. Amazing, quite amazing. The breasts were probably the finest she had ever studied.

"Please stand away from the table, Verenka dear. You are indeed very lovely. How shall I say? Well, luscious to an extreme." Her eyes travelled down over the midriff and the flat belly pierced by the nicely whorled navel. It was then she saw within the curled hairs the salient pinnacle, the summit of the clitoris. Claudia, who had fingered and drawn her lips along the length of so many female erections, could not trust her eyes; the organ must be huge, almost salaciously obscene, it protruded there, long, gracious and expectant.

Claudia swallowed hard. What must it be like in febrile erection when the slut masturbates it with her delicate fingers, twisting it, elongating it, crushing it? She tried not to think.

As Claudia took in the sight, her own sex contracted along the soft tunnel of her entrails. Then, as they always did, the labia relaxed deliciously, unfurling gently and parting to allow the first liquids to slide down inexorably. Rarely had she reacted so directly to a nude body—and never at a luncheon. Heavens, what a figure the girl had!

"Turn round, my dear, if you please." Her bland request was hoarse with gathering lust beyond her immediate control. Her breath shortened suddenly again as the girl turned away. The effulgence of the heavy, perfectly moulded buttock meat struck Claudia dumb. Across it, a network of welts blazed; some of the damage was very fresh, the crimson marks melding into streaks of mauve, pricked here and there with dark spots where the blood had accumulated under the surface of the skin. On the contour of the right cheek the tip of whatever Mikhail had used on her had imprinted an irregular column of rectangular purple bruises; there was no doubt— the riding crop. Claudia stared for a long moment at the sight: the twin volumes of flesh stood high on the strong thighs; there was no sign of sagging. The masses were firm and rich in all their damaged magnificence. Rapidly and to bridle her thoughts, Claudia tried to gauge roughly how many strokes the girl had suffered but it defeated even her experienced scrutiny. All she knew was that the girl had been lashed very competently and often, some of the weals being recent enough to be still painful.

Claudia pulled herself together after a brief skirmish with the churning want aching in the depths of her vagina. She took a pace towards the nude and ran her hand irresolutely at first and then firmly over the welts. Instantly the meat clenched, prompting Claudia to release the ridged surface, surprised how much residue of pain still survived. Instead she felt for the rear verge of the cunt and drew the edge of her manicured hand up the length of the anal crevice, hot but perfectly white and pristine, untouched by the beating.

Then she felt it.

The object was flat and circular, pressing laterally on the inner face of each buttock but firmly plugged into the rectum. Claudia bit her nether lip with a jolt of surprise.

"What's this, my dear?" The discovery made her voice husky. "Bend over. Let me see. Get down, girl. And open yourself up. Wide open, please."

Verenka leaned forward and spread the cheeks apart with her hands. "Mikhail, I mean Mishka, wants me stretched so it won't hurt so much when… when…"

"When what?"

"When he takes me there. He's very solid, Claudia."

"And how long have you been plugged up like this?" She tested the tight retention and girth of the immersed plunger. She had seen and used on girls many similar ones but this rubber stopper was larger than any she could recall offhand.

"About two weeks, I think. Gemma removes it when I need… when I need…"

"I understand. And tell me, how often have you been getting the whip? Your behind is in a fine mess, my love."

Claudia eased the girl erect, turning her round to face her.

"Twice or three times a week."

"I see," Claudia hesitated to press her enquiry too far. "Now, you will tell Mishka, if the question arises, I saw your bottom while you were dressing. Do you understand? Otherwise I'm afraid I'll have to see to it that you get the whip far more often than twice a week."

"It's not a whip. It's Mishka's crop, the one he goes riding with at Chantilly."

"Verenka, a whip, a crop, a quirt, a lash: they're all the same, they're all things to be used on difficult young girls. Like you, Verenka. Now go and get dressed."

Verenka gathered up her sole garment. "Thank you for the lunch, Claudia. I enjoyed it," she lied, avoiding Claudia's sharp blue stare. The woman was more honest: "So did I, Verenka. It revealed a lot to me." After a pause, Claudia sat down. "Something tells me you don't object to being beaten," she said, as if it were an afterthought.

Verenka lowered her head. "I have to do what I'm told. Sometimes it hurts more than at other times but I'm getting used to it. In fact, Claudia, to be truthful, there are moments when I look forward to it. It excites me terribly and…"

The woman listened with her instincts alive. "And what?" she insisted.

"Well, after the whipping, Mishka always takes me in one way or another. And that I look forward to. Very much." A short silence followed, Claudia finding herself unable to summon up anything readily after the admission that had come so naturally.

Claudia began to feel well-disposed towards the female. She liked her frankness. But she chose not to answer.

When Gemma had escorted her back to her room, leaving the coffee before Claudia, a strange restlessness disturbed the beautiful hostess, not only mentally but between her thighs. Her dominant longings exacerbated in her a need for a sexual fulfilment she had been deprived of for several months; now there was promise, very real promise, if she played her cards astutely. Claudia recalled the instant when she had touched the girl's scorched bottom, the sudden shudder and clenching… Yes, it was within her grasp.

Her throat was parched but her thighs were very wet. She went to change her sopping panties. As she peeled off the minute triangle of clammy black silk and dropped it on the bedroom floor, she thought the lunch had been more than intoxicating; it seemed to constitute an integral part of her efforts to regain her legitimate sexual role in life. Beside being the spoiled, adored mistress of an admirable—and unspeakably wealthy—lover, she needed a submissive slave, as in the past, someone, preferably a female, whom she could dominate totally and unscrupulously and rely upon to give her wild, uninhibited delight.

She passed her finger between the wet labia; her sex was on fire. A shy slut of a girl had ignited her; not only had she displayed her scourged buttocks with ingenuous unconcern but admitted to anticipating the crop with pleasure. Claudia knew from experience that often it took months of judicious and discerning training to bring a body slave even to that stage. Verenka was already submitting with good grace and, it appeared, with fortitude—for the lash marks were not those of a beginner.

Claudia's spirits rose; she was certain Mikhail could be convinced to go further—or rather let her go further—with the girl. To own one's own slave under one's own roof without so much as exerting oneself was almost too good to be real. The girl seemed perfect material and the cavernous apartment on the Quai d'Anjou a suitable site, for the maintenance of a sex slave in residence. She swore not to fail herself.

Turning matters over excitedly in her mind, Claudia wandered down the dark corridor lined with Mikhail's polo and tennis trophies. Her stop before the library door was unpremeditated but she let her instinct always guide her; she entered the darkened place with its distinctive smell of must and old books.

No one used the room much with its shelves of books mounting to the ceiling, but Claudia had taken a particular liking to the soft atmosphere, the stillness and intimacy, enhanced by the rich carpets and green-shaded lamps. Rarely were the blinds drawn up; Mikhail, who had inherited the library along with the rest, maintained that sunlight was deleterious for the spines of first editions which should show but not necessarily be read.

Claudia settled comfortably in a leather armchair and surveyed the long beamed room.

On the far side of the cumbersome reading table, covered with racing magazines and newspapers, opposite the fireplace, Claudia stared at the gallery above, a mezzanine reached by a curved oaken stairway. Up there were the rare books, the precious first editions and, Claudia had already discovered, a vast collection of erotic and pornographic literature devoted, for the most part and apart from the usual de Sade classics, to incredibly explicit accounts and scenes of female and male flagellation, incarceration, sexual torture and bondage of naked bodies. Claudia admitted being out of her depth as she studied some of the works; but she often climbed the stairs, always ready to learn.

But it was not the books and revues that tempted Claudia this time. Her attention was suddenly drawn to the four oak columns supporting the gallery. How was it she had never really observed them before? Probably because she had had no real use for them? With florid, carved capitals, the two pairs of pillars formed a concave semicircle, each smooth column a couple of paces apart from the next. Claudia's mind began to work rapidly and constructively.

She rose from her chair to walk round the columns, feeling their firm girth, gazing up at the summits and gauging the distance between them. It was as if the eighteenth century architect had anticipated the strange thoughts and desires of a beautiful, blonde woman two centuries later, a woman who saw that the space between any two of the pillars could well accommodate the stretched naked body of a slave... Claudia smiled and patted one of the columns with her delicate ringed fingers. Flawless! Nothing could be more perfect for what had suddenly entered her mind.

She was enchanted; Mikhail could do with more space and, moreover, the room was far from the main body of the apartment, lined with books and tapestries, and thus, she whispered, it must be relatively soundproof. Very promising!

Claudia examined the columns once again; a body standing on tiptoe on the plinth, arms upstretched would, she saw, reach to just below the carved capital while a body extended between two of the pillars could easily be attached by the four limbs. Claudia thought of Mikhail's Louis XV piece of furniture. So far she had given its contents only a cursory glance but now their relevance became important to the scenario sketching itself out in her imagination.

Hurrying to the bedroom, she unlocked the cabinet. Compared with the equipment and appendages she had learnt to use and enjoy in the two or three prestigious institutions in Hamburg and Brussels, where she had worked for a short time as a dominant mistress, Claudia found the array meagre. Yet there was a pleasing selection of whips, canes and leather paddles and other items, including gags, hoods and harnesses, some of which she had worn to please her lover. To the side, she found coils of rope—some of red silk—and the thongs she sought. Deliberately selecting the longest and testing them for strength, she tied the leathers securely to the head and base of each library column, concealing the loose ends by winding them about the oak.

The fact that her crotch was bare was recalled to her by a steady oozing between the lips; she sat down in one of the leather armchairs and looked at her handiwork. The cords were practically invisible. It was now for her to convince her devoted Cossack that firmer methods were required if Verenka was to benefit. She knew it would not be hard to tempt the man for she, as his mistress, obviously did not satisfy his whims; but she would see to it that Verenka did, and not only Mikhail's needs but her own. For her part, Claudia envisaged clearly what she aimed at: a sex slave.

Staring at the four vertical shafts rearing to the gallery, Claudia snatched her Dior skirt back from over her hips. She spread her labia and started to circle her fingers over the clit;

closing her eyes, she imagined Verenka's rich, delicious body, bathed in sweat, writhing between the pillars... Then, suddenly, the dark head was crushing her clit, then dragging it outwards with gleaming teeth... The images converged and overlapped, for there was Verenka bucking under Claudia's thin lash - the one she adored - the one whose handle she used often, the one she... The alcoves of the library suddenly filled with the muted cry of ecstasy as the woman climaxed, the liquid soaking into the morocco beneath her thighs.

Her whimpers had died away but she was still sprawled in her chair when Gemma, tapping gently but not awaiting an answer, entered with hushed steps. She advanced to the chair, took stock of Claudia's circumstances and the wide-open, wet crotch gaping before her, and announced that the Master was on the line. She handed Claudia the portable with a soft, Calabrian smile of intrigue. Apart from the cloying discharge over the leather, Gemma had also caught sight of the dark thongs at the base of one of the columns; very little in life missed her peregrine eye.

Languidly, Claudia heard her Mishka's voice. She was glad to have company.

"I've just frigged myself off, darling. I came voraciously. I'll tell you why tonight. Oh, such a surprise I have for you, Mishka. Now, tell me, what's new at Roland Garros or wherever you bash those yellow balls of yours."

Claudia was amused at her Cossack's fabricated fury at having lost his match in what had been the last tiebreak. As in everything, he had been determined to win.

"I'm sending Antoine for you, my beautiful woman, at seven. He'll drive you to that pleasant restaurant in the Bois that you like so much - you know, where one takes the ferry across the lake. Wear that pale blue dress with the wide black sash, Claudia darling. And gloves, of course. Look your best. I want to introduce you to someone special friend."

Claudia somehow she guessed it was a woman. Mikhail knew a great many women.

CHAPTER 2

As Claudia stepped out of the ferry, she saw Mikhail, tall and precisely groomed, his short beard neatly pointed. He was very handsome in his white suit. She caught sight of the raised glass he held high in greeting. Then he was kissing her extravagantly near the Cartier diamond in her ear, not to spoil her lips that shone sensuously in the restaurant lanterns. He led her by the waist to the reserved table by the water's edge under the fairy lights. Claudia was already glowing under the sheen of candlelight; she knew just how attractive she appeared and looked forward to the evening.

"When you stepped off the ferry, my darling witch, you were in profile." The man held Claudia's hands across the table. "You have the most delicious and desirable bottom in all Paris. Only Africans could compete. It's perfect!"

After the aperitifs had been served Claudia seized the chance offered.

"Talking of behinds, Mishka, I happened to catch sight of Verenka's when Gemma was helping her to dry off after her bath this morning," she lied with aplomb. "It was terribly marked and welted. She had been flagellated, Mishka." She pretended to look pained.

The man hesitated a second. "To tell you the truth, darling, I didn't want you to be disturbed and worried by the girl. It is a fact that I have to beat her. It's the only way to deal with her. She is my ward not yours and there's no reason to make her a burden on you."

"But I should like to have known this was going on, Mishka. And share your concern, my dearest. I'm sure I could be helpful, supportive and even share the burden."

"Well, now you know, sweet love. I just didn't want to upset you."

Claudia was on the point of proceeding further and even of stressing again and more directly her interest in the punishments, when Mikhail suddenly rose, looking across at the landing stage through the roses.

"Ah, here she is, Claudia. At last. Always late. But worth waiting for."

Claudia watched the woman approach through the muted colouring of the garden lights. She was more than handsome; she was splendid. Her somewhat masculine slenderness gave her a beauty that Claudia recognized as close to her own but different. Probably a few years older than the fair-haired mistress she was so anxious to meet, the Comtesse de Frejaviole knew how to handle herself. She flashed a friendly smile at Claudia. Juliette was, to Claudia's mind, exactly what a manifestly dominant female in the rich, exclusive society of Paris—and its sister cities of enjoyment—should look like: sparsely built and lithe like an animal one should beware of, the woman seemed to know her strength of character and power of attraction. The dark hair, drawn tightly back from the high brow, lay neatly across the nape of a fine neck and was secured, as was Claudia's, with a broad velvet ribbon caressing the bare shoulders.

When they had ordered, the woman leaned back in her chair to survey Mikhail's new mistress. Claudia enjoyed the scrutiny and instinctively sensed that Juliette was—and probably still remained—one of Mikhail's mistresses.

"So here you are at last." Juliette's voice, deeper than her own, pleased Claudia just as did the sensuous lips that uttered the words. The woman had truly something very special about her.

Suddenly and to Claudia's surprise, Mikhail returned to the subject they had been discussing before the guest's appearance. "Claudia here is all upset to discover that I've been giving that lazy little ward of mine a taste of the whip…"

"I'm not upset, Mishka. Just a trifle hurt you haven't let me in on the secret and invited me to participate."

There was a silence before Juliette opined that Mishka had probably only been trying to spare her feelings.

"Spare my feelings!" Claudia laughed. She decided to affirm

her predilections openly.

"You know well enough, Mishka—since I've told you often already—how I relish a whip over a young pair of female buttocks. Fancy keeping it to yourself, you selfish darling!" The waiter served the meal, a little surprised.

"Surely you've gathered by now I can be very versatile with or without a whip. In fact, I'd welcome a moment with this ward of yours, or can I say, ours? The chance glimpse of her incredible rump and what you'd done to it yesterday stimulated me you can't guess how completely, how profoundly." She sipped calmly at her Chateau Margaux, admiring its bouquet.

"Claudia darling I have absolutely no objection to your taking a hand in the correction Verenka has to receive." He cradled Claudia's hand in his own, raised it adoringly to his lips and kissed the fingertips. "In fact, I would welcome it."

Juliette watched the younger woman's smile of pleasure; to her mind it confirmed that the new mistress was astute enough to handle her man with consummate control.

The restaurant lights scrawled their coloured graffiti on the rippling water and a few moths endangered themselves around the candles on the tables. The meal had by then become a source of jubilation to Claudia: Mikhail had accepted her discovery with elegance; moreover, she saw that she was making progress. The conversation was just provocative enough to excite her. But, above all, it was undoubtedly this Frejaviole woman who lent significance to the evening. Despite her having been Mikhail's mistress—the fact was obvious really from the start of the meal—Juliette seemed to share with Claudia something else. Something thrillingly secret.

As the coffee and liqueurs were served, Juliette decided it was her turn to be frank. How gratifying it was, she declared, to discover the dominant also in Claudia. Who would have expected it?

"A slut like this Verenka needs proper, serious flagellation

31

if she is to be disciplined and brought to heel." Claudia said, taking her chance and added: "The girl should be reduced to sex slavery. She should be used violently, even cruelly, in order to train her up. There's nothing better for a body slave than to be given vehement, naked strappings from neck to knees from the start. The bitch should be reduced to total whip-slavery, to be used entirely as we wish and to service us sexually under the continuous threat of punishment, meted out to her stark naked." Still impassive, she turned to her lover: "I presume you fuck the girl or make use of her somehow, Mishka, each time you put her to the whip?"

"Of course, Claudia. It's only natural, as part of, let's say, the flagellator's compensation."

"Mishka, darling, you're right." Claudia said. "You deserve to be compensated for all the trouble this girl is causing. And what's the objection to using her? After all, she's just flesh and there for the taking. But I'd like to go a step further and break her down into a pliant, unmurmuring body slave-in-residence."

Juliette attempted to make her offering. "Then surely, Mishka, Claudia should have her sessions too with the girl, as I do with my Tansu. And get the slave to service her just as you force the slut to service your rigid cock, and that's no sinecure for anyone's mouth."

No one seemed to notice Juliette's language or insinuation, as the man replied: "I don't force her. She goes to her knees willingly, sucks like a glutton and swallows promptly. The slut shows promise and I'm quite certain will excel herself, given regular and graduated encouragement through flagellation. You are quite right, Claudia dear. The girl should be subjected to constant sex, quite apart from whipping. All the more so in the light of what Gemma reports—Verenka must be weaned away from this relentless masturbation she practises. Gemma tells me the girl drives herself half-crazy, writhing and heaving on her bed. Even after being whipped and having come already under the scourge."

"There's nothing amiss in her frigging, Mishka," Claudia declared, "only let her do it before us, I'm sure, darling, you wouldn't object to a hardened dominant like me dealing with your ward. You'll be the first to taste the morsel when I've prepared it." Her lover laughed, kissed her hand and surrendered.

Juliette sat bemused. There was no doubt. Mikhail had this time picked a genuine, determined dominant, just like herself.

She looked into Claudia's blue eyes that changed to violet under the veil of night; the eyes were, she felt, both cold and hard as sapphires and yet smouldering with flickering lust. She saw that it was time to go.

Before separating into the two cars awaiting them on the water's edge, Juliette turned to the fair-haired woman, now holding her lover's arm.

"Claudia, this has been a magical evening. I insist on seeing you again, my dear. Who knows, maybe I have a few hints you might find precious? Call me before or after I go to Rome." She slipped a visiting card into Claudia's hand. "You are always welcome to come and watch my darling Tansu in session when Marcus and I are in town." Once again she kissed her on the mouth with undisguised affection which Claudia reciprocated. Juliette would be very useful. Then the cars moved off softly.

"I like your friend, Mishka," Claudia said as Antoine drove them over the Seine. "She rounded off my day!" She reached into Mikhail's crotch, feeling the cock shaft hardening, thrusting obediently into her grasp as her own sex began to throb amid the seepages. Shifting on the leather, she pulled up her dress to remind her lover that she wore nothing whatsoever over the matted auburn triangle with its jutting clit and carefully shaved labia below. She was ready and had been for nearly an hour, barely able to restrain her flow. Yet she refrained from touching her craving erection between the hairs.

Hastily they entered the sleeping building by the river,

panting with want.

The great bedroom had been made ready by Gemma, the black sheets turned back and a leather-strapped gag placed beside the pillow—should her employers need it.

Several lighted candles threw the shadows of the two tearing off their clothes. Then Claudia stretched her pale, trembling limbs out to the corners of the bed, her hips raised on pillows, the flanges of her sex fluttering almost imperceptibly as they parted and gaped; above her, the man's thick, congested length of meat throbbed, a thread of bright liquid joining its slit to the woman's indrawn belly.

"Mishka, tie me down… if you want to," Claudia whispered hoarsely, "and take me as you fuck that slave of ours across the corridor. One…one condition…"

She was interrupted by Mikhail searching among the cords and sex accessories in the cabinet. "Strange. Plenty of short ones. The long thongs seem to be missing."

Claudia responded quickly, unhesitatingly. "Use my stockings, darling, and take some more from the drawer. Tie me tight!" Her man spread-eagled her nudity and began to bind her to the corner posts; there was little he liked more than a beautiful woman straining in bondage. The stricter the better.

Almost breathless with need, Claudia lifted her head, shaking the strands of golden hair from her eyes. "Promise to give me a free hand with this little bitch. You're too lenient with her. Give her to me to work on."

As he tightened the nylon round the left ankle, Mikhail would have given her half Paris. "Do what you like with her… whatever you want…" And he bent his erection downwards to friction the labia for a moment until his mistress was imploring, begging for pity. Then he plunged in deep; Claudia moaned with relief. She resisted for as long as she could before scuttling her frail defences to welcome the clotted onrush. She orgasmed massively once and rode out the storm, sensing every knotted vein along the straining penis rippling within

34

her pulsing vagina; the secondary waves of climax broke over her again and again. 'How could the man keep up the fucking like this?' She wondered, as she always did before receiving the answer: the jets of scalding semen slogged against her cervix; they never seemed to end. Then she collapsed, still arched and sweating, over the soiled pillows.

Claudia lay awake after Mishka had released her, pondering the favourable events of the day. She would enslave the sensational slut and abase her to the level of Juliette's Tansu; then train her relentlessly—absolutely relentlessly—to the level of a body slave before the girl could comprehend what was happening to her. Yes, I must stir myself, Claudia decided. Starting tomorrow, yes… yes… strike while the branding iron's hot… and sensuously gathering up Mikhail's balls into her moist, tacky grasp she fell asleep.

CHAPTER 3

During the week that followed the dinner with Juliette, Claudia and Mikhail spent a great deal of their time considering the problem Verenka's presence at home was causing to the household. In between beatings, still administered by her guardian for the moment, she spent most of her day in reverie or moroseness, brooding in her room. Only when her tutor was present, did she manifest interest. Mikhail decided to question the teacher on one of her thrice-weekly visits; they needed to know how things stood between the girls before proceeding with Verenka. He suggested that Claudia speak with both girls.

It was after her siesta when Claudia decided broach the matter using, as a pretext for intruding, the redecoration of Verenka's suite and the best colour for the new drapes. As there was no sound from within, Claudia tapped lightly and entered. What she saw stopped her quite still, her hand grasping the curved, bronze doorknob. Her knuckles were white with the pressure; her spine had straightened.

The sheets had been ripped off the king-size bed, pillows thrown over the floor in disorder and in the shuttered half-light of the late afternoon the room seemed to swelter with heat and odours. Marina and Verenka lay naked, entangled in a glistening contortion of sweating flesh, the tow-headed elder girl's face crushed against Verenka's black fleece and the viscous vermilion gash of her sex. Verenka was moaning between Marina's thighs, straining to keep level with the frantic licking, sucking and distension of her own cunt. Reversed over her, Marina's crotch was above the girl's mouth; Claudia could see that Verenka was beyond recall, about to collapse into the boiling cauldron of her orgasm.

Both females were heaving in the crater of some Stromboli, in the surging lava of an Etna within each other's loins. Claudia could only think of volcanic images, of magma, of steaming, viscid extract slithering from the cunts and mouths. She let it happen.

The affection linking pupil and tutor, to judge by the slick bodies jerking and thrashing on the bed, was not just sexual; Claudia knew that from experience. Moreover, both girls were running an enormous risk but probably considered their love was worth it.

They realized they were no longer alone when Claudia closed the door and took a step into the room. Marina was the first to gather herself together; she swung off Verenka and sat, panting, on the edge of the bed. Without trying to conceal her sex, she stared at the intruder, at the same time taking Verenka's hand in her own. Claudia perched herself on the arm of leather chair and crossed her arms.

"I see," she remarked softly. "So, this is what is termed a refresher course! I think, Marina, you'd do best to get dressed and leave."

"No! Claudia, no! Please, I beg of you," Verenka cried. She had lifted herself up on to her elbow. "Don't you see, Claudia, we're in love?" Her voice was trembling pathetically.

"It's true," was all Marina could muster. But she walked calmly towards her clothes lying crumpled on the carpets and began to dress.

"Well, perhaps," Claudia replied, "but it comes as something of a surprise, Marina. You were not engaged, you know, to suck the living guts out of your pupil. You're here to educate her, if that's possible." She paused, irresolute as to what exactly to do in the absence of her lover. Things had gone much further than anyone realised. "Well, we'll see what the Master has to say. Come back on Monday after we've had the chance to discuss the situation. Believe me, Marina," Claudia added archly, "I've nothing against lesbian affairs but surely not in working hours. And stark naked. Recklessly naked."

She watched the woman dress neatly and meticulously.

Her body was slender, almost athletic, the arms dusted with golden down not unlike Claudia's own; the pubic growth, far from covering the tidy triangle, flourished as a narrow swathe of bright, thick hair, now flattened and sodden with discharge.

The breasts were relatively small but sharp, crowned with ample nipples still erect from excitement; as Marina leaned forwards to slip into her high-heeled shoes, Claudia stared, fascinated at the pleasing droop of the extraordinarily white breast-flesh beneath the blouse. Yes, they were tempting; they would throttle well at the base. Then, as the girl drew up her slip, the neat, round buttocks fitted in perfectly, positioned trimly and firmly above the thighs and leading down to well-proportioned legs and ankles that lent the whole body a balance Claudia herself envied.

When the girl's blue-green eyes turned to her, the flushed cheeks on either side of the pretty nose made Claudia study the face closely—something she had never done on the previous encounters; the lips were sensuous, gleaming as she moistened them with the tip of her tongue. In her attractive, whorled ears there were tiny golden rings. She had liked the way in which the older girl had endorsed the love binding the pair; the female had spirit and seemed to display not the least sense of guilt at being found buried between her lover's thighs. Claudia had expected her to be crestfallen but the frank, open features merely indicated mild surprise. Her composure, under the circumstances, intrigued Claudia. Yet there was a trace of fear somewhere, fear mixed with ductile compliancy. What if this female too was basically amenable to the whip?

Marina stepped over to the bed to take her companion into her arms. Then she kissed her passionately on the mouth. "It was as marvellous as ever, darling. It's just such a pity we can't be left in peace. Take care of your precious self whatever happens. On Monday, we'll see."

As if the mistress of the house were not three paces away, Verenka hugged the girl.

"Oh, Marina, I love you. You were exquisite again. I've never, never come like that. Never! Don't ever leave me. Claudia and Mikhail understand love. They're madly in love too. Whatever happens, don't abandon me now. If you do, I'll let them kill me."

38

As she passed Claudia, still seated and dumbfounded, Marina stopped.

"I suppose you'll whip her for this, as you usually do," she said, without animosity.

"Probably."

"Well, it's me you should whip. Or at least let me share it. Because we have made love every time I've come here. You two can do what you like to me—the same as you do to Verenka. You'll never make me leave her. If we have to we'll leave together."

The threat of them stealing away from the Quai scared Claudia; two months earlier she might have welcomed it but to risk anything at this delicate juncture was an ominous challenge. She would have to negotiate carefully.

"Oh, Marina dear, let's not become dramatic, please! I'm sure there is a way of settling all this pleasantly. Let me talk to the Master in my own way."

With this concession, Marina nodded and left. They heard Gemma closing the door.

Claudia gazed at the fabulous naked body on the bed, noting the scarred rump was healing fast. No, she would let nothing allow the girl to escape her grasp, least of all now that events were crystallizing so promisingly.

"Well, I must say, Verenka, this is a surprise. A pair of little milkmaids tossing each other off in bed in the middle of the afternoon! If only you had told me, you silly darling! But, you see, as a potential body slave, you can't do this sort of thing without the consent of your Master and your loving Mistress." To make her stipulation clear, she sat down beside the girl and caressed the weals over the left buttock, as if to underline her point. "I don't know how Mishka is going to react. You'll certainly get a double flogging for this anyway, my dear. And, I should add, in new surroundings, which will be very different from those you have been used to. You see, you have to be educated both in mind and body. There's no other way and also it provides us with great pleasure, as you

39

know." She paused. "Of course, Verenka, if Marina shared the sexual duties you carry out…" She was aware she was treading on thin ice, so she added: "But she would be very averse to living in a household that carries out whippings, leave alone participating by sharing it with you, Verenka.

"How do you know?" The girl summoned up all her mettle to question her mistress. "She would share anything with me as long as we can stay together and make love together. She will accept a great deal, Claudia. She told me so."

"Did she, indeed! Tell me more."

"We've discussed it, Claudia. She knows I get whipped. She tends to my welts just as Gemma does and she admits they excite her as they excite me. She's not used to the crop but for me she'll put up with it. Oh, dearest Claudia, you and Mishka won't prevent us from seeing each other and making love, will you? Say you won't, Claudia."

"It rather depends on Mishka, doesn't it, sweetheart? We expect you to love and respect us, Verenka, but as the body slave we have decided you shall be henceforward, you must obey. And having lesbian fun with one's tutor without permission is hardly obedience, is it?"

The girl rolled over on the bed, displaying to the full her startling pair of whipped buttocks and crying softly. The sight only hardened the blue eyes looking down on the nakedness. The superbly dressed woman rose from the bed and smoothed her pleated skirt over her sleek hips. The progress accomplished astonished her.

"Verenka, I'll discuss it with Mishka and we'll see also how Marina reacts, shall we? Only I really can't imagine a prim private tutor stripping to receive the lash."

Anxious to reassure the implacable blue eyes, Verenka protested that, as far as she knew, her lover, in earlier days before coming to the Quai, had experienced almost everything that Mikhail demanded of her.

"In addition to cunnilingus, as we know. And talking of that," Claudia went on, "I think it would be most pleasant,

Verenka, if you and I had a moment together. I'd like to see how you perform, my sweet slave. Get up and come to my bedroom. We have a clear hour or so before us before drinks, don't we? You needn't put on any clothes. Just come as you are, dear."

On the black sheets, the girl performed as never before, even with Marina. She worked with assurance on the abrupt assignment, bringing her mistress to the primary and then to three rushed, successive secondary orgasms. Claudia was enchanted and generously she masturbated the long, pulsating clit into the sixth spasm Verenka had enjoyed that day.

Stroking the dark hair, wet with sweat and discharge of her liquids, the blonde mistress felt constrained to congratulate her slave. This was certainly no beginner.

"Well, I must say, that tongue of yours works wonders. But it still requires a lot of training, like the rest of your body, and we'll be seeing to that shortly. In the library."

"Why the library, Claudia?"

"Oh, that's where you will be whipped from now on. It's quite special, you'll see, and I'm certain you'll enjoy it even more." She paused. "By the way, from now on you will address me as 'Mistress' and your guardian as 'Master'. I hope that is clear. The same rules would apply to your little friend if and when she agrees to share in our delights."

"Oh, Mistress, I'm sure she will!" Verenka sought eagerly to confirm the prospect, however vague. Claudia, lying naked and replete, smiled, her pulse quickening again. And she held out the prospect of days and nights with Marina, well worth the occasional flagellation, tied between the library pillars.

"I used to spend hours up on the gallery in the library, browsing," Verenka told her, "among all those wonderful sex and pornographic books… They're just spellbinding… There was one I especially liked. She looked down and began to play with her lengthening clit among the black, dripping hair, parting the plump labia ostentatiously. A pleasant, pungent demulcent transposed its odour to Claudia as she watched the delicate fingers sliding absently over the wet, crimson sheen of the vaginal membranes. Her recounting, stimulated by Claudia's mention of the library, was churning her loins into renewed readiness.

"You see, in the book there was this astoundingly beautiful Venetian woman being sold naked as a slave, along with her serving girl. They were in chains, so lovely and proud. But their owner had not found a buyer…" She stopped and clasped her thighs together to halt the surge descending slowly down the channel of the vagina. Her breath was short and shallow, the nipples hardening on the bulge of the areoles.

"Well, go on." Claudia urged, "masturbate your clit while you talk and use the other hand on me. Gently! I'm very tender and raw down there after that rasping tongue of yours. That's more like it. Smooth and gentle. Don't forget you're also a naked slave servicing your Mistress. Now, tell me more."

"Well, they were taken down to a sort of slave dungeon, to a cellar and bound between huge columns and whipped from neck to knees… Then…" The voice had become slightly hoarse as it struggled for words. "Then they were staked out, beautifully naked, and scourged terribly. And afterwards…" Verenka was panting; she tried to stay Claudia's hand that had joined her own between the swollen labia and at the base of the clitoris. Claudia thrust deep and suddenly into the palpitating vagina.

Verenka gulped in an attempt to continue her images. "Then they were flung on to square stone slabs and chained down for the owner's guests to fuck… At least, that is what the book said…" Her words dried up as her cunt began to drip on to the black sheets.

"Go on. Don't stop. Did it excite you?" Claudia knew it had done; she saw it in the young, dark irises.

"It excited me so utterly that I used to go up there to read and read and stare at those pictures over and over again… the slave owner torturing the women… the Venetian female's breasts… whipped and tortured… all crimson… Ahh,

Mistress, don't stop… My cunt's coming!"

The nude body arched back, the hand twisting the clit ruthlessly. The moans became sharp cries. Then Verenka gasped. She came with all her force, far more violently than at the earlier climax. She thrust her flesh against her mistress and sobbed tears of relief.

"I love you, sweet Mistress. Never let me go… nor Marina. I need her so much."

"So do we," came the gentle reply. "I'll do what I can for your golden-haired Madonna, I promise. Now, move over and stretch out, head over the edge of the bed and get to work on me, properly."

She drew the girl towards her, thrusting the head downwards, the black hair trailing on the carpet. Then she knelt before the reversed face, cramming her sex on to the waiting mouth; within the swollen flesh folds, the vagina was already clogged with gluten. The pale stem of the clitoris sought the girl's tongue. Claudia dug her fingers brutally into the breasts as though she required purchase for the cunnilingus; she looked lasciviously down the superb sweep of the nude before her—beyond the sharp ridge of the ribs, the midriff curved erotically down to the contracted belly and the matted bulge of the pubis between the elegant projections of the pelvis bones. And beyond lay the strong legs, parted wide. Verenka's arms encircled the woman's white thighs, gripping the buttock cheeks with force as the fingers distended the puckered rose of the sphincter. Claudia ground her tumescent flesh lips against the face.

"Suck, slave! Suck the erection. Get your whore tongue deep into me. Yes, yes," the voice was gravely and hoarse with wanting, "Suck the cum into your gullet, slave, and service me deep. Better than that, you lazy whore-slave!" The woman slapped Verenka's left breast savagely, watching the heavy load of flesh roll and tremble. The nipples had by then gained their full distension and, as she slavered against the face, Claudia began to twist the taut nuggets of umber flesh; a modicum of breast torture enchanted her, enhancing the pure pleasure spreading from the yearning cleft, craving for assuagement.

She excited herself with blatant, heedless phrases that she knew the girl could hear above the slapping and grinding. "Suck deeper, slave! Flick the clit with that hot tongue of yours. I'll flog your crotch until it's swollen. Hung by the ankles and gagged... stark naked, you whore of a slave! Ahh..." The climax began to burgeon, the discharge flushing down copiously, pouring on to the sweating, straining face, half-hidden between the sinuous thighs undulating and crushing the clotted mouth; lips against lips. The slave had talent.

As the orgasm burst, Claudia continued to utter incoherent words. "I'll beat you into red meat, slave! Nude and lashed to the pillar... Whipped... Ahh!" The climax came in a series of spasms, each overlapping the next, until the ecstasy was fulfilled throughout her body, radiating out from the tip of the clitoris to the extremities of her being.

She allowed the girl no respite, mangling and squelching the soused sex over the face that strove for breath.

They remained clogged and clinging for a long moment.

"Lick me clean, slave. Drink up all that saliva and the cream of my cum. In future you will suck faster and use your teeth more. Do you understand?"

"Yes, Mistress."

"You require a great deal of training, my girl. And probably the same is true of your work on your Master. We shall see to it, don't worry. Inadequate performance will, from now on, earn you a spirited flagellation with the six-thonged dog whip, not just with the crop. Get this into your head, once and for all. You are a robust, mettlesome girl and can take plenty of whippings to the limit of your resistance. I hope this is clear."

"Yes, Mistress." Verenka slowly peeled herself off the sheets and stood deferentially before Claudia. "Thank you for letting me service you, Mistress."

"Now go and get cleaned up. Gemma will bring you supper. And maybe tomorrow night we can enjoy the library together."

"You mean, look at those books together, Mistress? Oh, yes…" The voice was that of an extenuated, utterly submissive, abject body slave, ready to be handled, abused and hurt as long as she received sexual pleasure.

"No, I mean our own whipping columns."

And Claudia turned the girl out, having enjoyed an hour that was beyond her wildest expectations. There was no doubt the slut had the makings of an unimpeachable sex slave. But she called for intensive education, very intensive, and Claudia realized that she had yet to see the body under the scourge. She could hardly wait to get to work.

In her suite, Verenka showered in the luxurious bathroom, pondering. And as she dried her body before the mirrors, admiring its breathtaking curves, Verenka thought once again of Claudia. Claudia was her Mistress and she was now her body slave. At long last, the most perverse, secret and illegitimate of her dreams was coming true: to be a beautiful, docile and loved sex slave in the service of two wonderful dominants. If only Marina would concede her own body also…

She felt strangely akin to that magnificent nude Venetian woman treading the stone steps down to the whipping chambers below—accompanied by a fair-haired companion whose name might well have been Marina.

CHAPTER 4

The crucial confrontation took place the next Monday, which had given Claudia ample opportunity to discuss the project with Mikhail, who appreciated the prospects but doubted Marina would agree. Nevertheless, he gave his mistress a free hand. "Who knows?" he remarked, "She may well concur. Tell her she can have her salary doubled and put into a bank meanwhile and live here without a problem. As long as she obeys."

Cancelling his appointments with the Credit Lyonnais, he agreed to attend the interview Claudia envisaged.

"If the woman cannot do without Verenka, then I agree we should make our conditions quite clear. And I believe some sort of protocol should be drawn up to tie her to her obligations." The man stressed the word 'tie'.

During the evening, in response to Claudia's urgings, they duly drafted the protocol for Marina, by which she consigned herself to Verenka's same guardians. The terms were straightforward. Mikhail read out the draft from his processor and Claudia added only a word or two. She had seen other agreements of the same sort elsewhere.

Marina arrived promptly on the Monday to give her lesson. Claudia asked her to stay on for a moment in the drawing room.

Mikhail and Claudia were ready for her.

The man explained the situation simply and clearly. "Now, either, Mademoiselle, you leave immediately, fully paid for the month, or you stay. If you stay, then I'm obliged to ask you to agree to certain conditions. You have seen the state of Verenka's body—since, I'm told, you are given to sleeping with her, and therefore you readily understand the punishments she is obliged to receive. I gather that such chastisements do not surprise you, knowing the obdurate nature of your pupil. However, if you are determined to remain with her then you must join her. And submit likewise."

"I agree to whatever you want, as long as I can remain with her." The statement came without hesitation and sounded irrevocable. Claudia could not believe her ears.

"Well, in that case, I must ask you to agree to this paper. It merely endorses your choice."

Mikhail extended a printout from the computer and read it out slowly.

"I, Marina Sylvia Messery, hereby consign my body as a sex slave (hereinafter called the "Slave") to service my owners, Mikhail Alexandreivic Karossof and Claudia Patricia de Clesson (hereinafter called the "Owners"), as they deem fit, throughout the duration of this contract which shall extend over one year, renewable. It may be revoked by either party with one month's notice.

"The following provisions shall apply:

"1. The Owners' obligations shall cover the full maintenance of the Slave, including food, appropriately luxurious lodging (two further rooms being added to the Slaves' suite), all travel expenses, clothing (to the extent required), medical attention, domestic service and all necessary accessories, including bondage facilities, flesh rings (if and when fitted), hoods, harnesses, chains and limb manacles. The Owners shall make provision for all instruments of flagellation and sex torture.

"2. The Owners shall transfer to the Slave's numbered account in Liechtenstein a monthly emolument of US dollars 5000 (five thousand) as compensation of loss of income while in the service of the Owners.

"3. The Slave's obligations shall cover full submission to her Owners' demands, including free access to all body orifices, incarceration, naked flagellation and strictly graduated sex torture. Exhibition of the Slave at special sessions and gatherings at home and abroad shall be included under this agreement.

"4. The Slave shall protect her body against pregnancy at all times, full facilities being provided by the Owners. During menstruation, the Slave shall be incarcerated for restricted

47

use.

"5. Under this agreement, the Slave shall enjoy free social and sexual access to the Owners' permanent Slave (Verenka Lucia Aurelia de Courton), including cohabitation.

"6. During all outings, excursions or travel beyond the confines of the domicile, the Slave/Slaves shall be accompanied by at least one of the Owners or a domestic."

Below the text were spaces for the signatures.

Marina stood elegantly apart, neat in her roll-neck sweater that displayed the outline of her breasts perfectly and a tight navy skirt; she wore no stockings but expensive high-heeled shoes that gave her slenderness an unexpected height that again pleased Claudia. Marina's blonde hair was cropped and brushed attractively behind the ears. The sole ornaments Claudia could see were a minutely fashioned gold chain round the left ankle and a similar one round the beautiful neck, cresting over the fine contours of the collarbones.

The woman took the paper and read it through. After a pause and in the silence of the huge sunlit room, she said: "I'm not sure of what is meant by 'sex torture' nor by 'flesh rings'. Otherwise, I have no objection."

Mikhail looked across at his mistress, raising an eyebrow in interrogation. Claudia was equal to the question.

"Oh, that's just a way of putting things, Marina. You'll find out in the course of time. It's nothing to worry about. You'll be in safe hands, I assure you. But it has to be there. As part of the bargain."

Mikhail came to the point. "In coming here, you must share everything, even what we term as torture. I assure you it isn't as terrible as it sounds. You will relish it in time."

Marina hardly moved but the knuckles of her hand clenched and blanched.

Suddenly Claudia posed a question. "You have been whipped, I believe, Marina, or so Verenka tells me, but probably you have not experienced what we call sex torture, it's fairly mild. At least to start with."

"It's a high price to pay," Marina murmured. Then she added: "But as long as I'm not damaged… I'm not prepared to lose Verenka," the lovely blonde said softly, peering at the paper again… I don't happen to have anything to sign with," she muttered. "I suppose a teacher should have a pen." For the first time she smiled coyly.

The couple seemed to freeze for a second until Mikhail handed her his gold Waterman that had signed so many contracts—of a different nature. Casually, the girl signed her name, a tidy little signature with a line beneath. She handed the paper to Mikhail who scribbled his name next to hers. Claudia was asked to append her signature.

"Welcome to the Quai d'Anjou, Marina." The man used her first name for once. "Please feel free to move in when you wish. The suite will be enlarged tomorrow and Antoine, my chauffeur, will help you move."

As she left the drawing room, Marina heard the Russian accent calling after her.

"Oh, by the way, tomorrow night Verenka will be whipped and used in the library. I should like you to be present, naked for servicing. We shall not call upon you to undergo the lash just yet. We shall see how you perform on Verenka."

Recognizing the predominance of her newly found Master, Marina bit her lip and left. A long silence fell over the drawing room. Finally, it was Claudia who broke it.

"So it's to be the library at last," she smiled in her moment of parochial success.

"Yes, darling. The library. I saw the care you had taken to fix the thongs—my missing long thongs—and I fully agree. Of course, the gallery pillars are ideal, of course they are! How stupid I can be on occasion. There are advantages in having a dominant mistress around the house." He took her lithe body in his arms to kiss the mouth.

Claudia felt under her hand the heavy shaft of male flesh rising stolidly beneath the zip. Unzipping her man, she grasped the massive cockshaft and slithered back the prepuce to bare the head. His hand meanwhile separated the viscous lips of Claudia's bare sex under the skirt, while she was sliding her clenched hand smoothly over the vein-ribbed penis from head to base adroitly, lubricating the thing generously from the oozing slit. The shaft did not require her own seepages. Mikhail seized the erect clit between thumb and forefinger to test its stiffness then broke the kiss.

"If Madame will kindly lead me by the cock she is soon going to suck dry, into the library, Madame will be roped to the table and fucked first."

Accordingly, the pair stumbled along the endless passage towards the library, shuttered and secret. As they entered, they paused, Claudia now grasping the man's weighty scrotum at its root, dragging him onwards. Opposite, in the girls' suite, groans and whimpers announced that Verenka had received the good news and was either in an ethereal ecstasy of joy or busy licking the only thing she loved and desired in the whole world, the quivering cunt of her sister lover-slave, drinking its grateful gluten into her throat.

As Claudia closed the door and approached the great, polished table-top to be roped down over its end, she suggested that the girls should participate in the celebration—not, she added quickly, in what was about to take place there in the library, there would be time for that later—but be invited to dinner with their delighted owners. Mikhail readily consented, as he began to strip Claudia of her few clothes, laying her lavish nudeness over the edge of the table and securing the splayed limbs to the widely spaced oak feet. "But, Claudia, my love, only if they are naked."

The man guided his penis to the gleaming sex slit, rubbing the gently fluttering lips and firm clit to prepare the cunt for fucking. He did so mercilessly and slowly until Claudia was pleading with groans of need. Then he plunged into her and a few minutes later filled her with scalding semen as she rode the copulation with repeated paroxysms, the major, prodigious orgasm transcending anything she had known with Mikhail;

its vehemence seemed to blast Claudia's brain into jagged slivers of blinding light.

It was only after an hour that she convinced her lover to unbind her aching limbs and lay himself in turn upon the polished surface, now thickly stained with sperm and her own discharge. Claudia fellated with all her ingenuity the blue-veined, jolting erection, ripping down the foreskin to concentrate on the stamina of the tensioned dome. She knew precisely and maliciously through long experience how to make a man linger on the threshold until the sperm could no longer be bridled back. She did just that to her lover, denying him his second orgasm, until she let the shaft have its way in her mouth; she bit firmly into the taut flesh, inserted her tongue tip deep into the slit and masturbated the entire length of the cock, urging the spunk out of the sac. Although she wanted to swallow, she let the jets pulse upwards before her eyes. The ejaculation came in grey spurts, arching over the belly.

When she had milked the cock to emptiness and lapped up the gobs of pungent sap from the loins and the belly, she continued to suck insatiably until Mikhail stayed her. It was the finest shaft of male flesh she had sucked for a long time.

During their baths and dressing for dinner, Claudia gave her orders to the maid.

"We desire them both stark naked, perfumed, powdered and correctly made-up. Be so good as to place a quirt—the black one with five fingers—on the table among the flowers to remind the slaves of their…" she sought for the word.

It was Gemma who politely supplied it. "Of their destino, the Signora means."

"Exactly, Gemma. Thank you."

Once seated in the dining room, Marina, in her twenty-seven years of labour at the university, the lycee and in various beds, had never come across people like her new owners and the graceful manner in which they toasted her first step into the labyrinth of sex slavery. She was not only excited by her contractual future with Verenka and her guardians, but by the champagne of which she had drunk several flutes in joy, thrilled by her nakedness next to Verenka's at table, with the meal and the compliments she harvested regarding her body. Playfully she had dabbed wine on Verenka's nipples and, in front of her owners, kissed the teats passionately.

A trifle drunk with the wines and with Verenka's caresses beneath the table, Marina even dared to rise and lean towards Claudia to deposit a vivacious kiss on her hostess's mouth. As she did so, Claudia ran her hand between the girl's thighs and for the first time felt the curls of hair over the sex; it was soft, softer than her own, and restricted to a neat swathe narrowing to the clitoris. How different from her own, Claudia reflected absently, and from Verenka's, both wide reaches of growth, covering the pubis entirely. Claudia had seen hundreds of female genitals and made love to them: each was specific, different. The form of the pubic hair seemed either to spread like her own or Verenka's, even requiring depilation or careful shaving at the groin creases, or it was gathered neatly in a furry strip, central above the clitoris and down each margin of the labia. Claudia was one who required the lower reach of the labia to be smooth.

She had watched the girls toasting each other and found herself considering whether she should not have both shaven cunt-clean. A pristine, denuded vulva was so much more pleasant to beat and obtain erotic results—weals over the swollen labia. And Marina's buttocks and breasts, would they endure the usual twenty lashes of the German breast whip that she, Claudia, had learned to employ in London? Time would tell, yet strangely, Claudia was uncertain of the situation.

She now, by her own design, had succeeded in marshalling two sex slaves into her house. Both needed training and neither Mikhail nor she was truly competent to bring sex slaves to the famous pain/pleasure level where slaves took the whip or torture with equanimity and confidence in their owners. Claudia realized that a great deal of work was on her hands but she was determined to drill these girls.

Finally, when the two nude slaves had tottered to their bed, Claudia thought suddenly of Juliette. Yes, she would seek her wise counsel; she made a mental note to call her as soon as possible.

Mikhail escorted his mistress this time to the black-sheeted bed and there she and he enjoyed the residue of sex energy that remained within their reach. Mikhail's beard was stiff with her acrid cum and Claudia swilled his gobbets of smooth semen in her mouth before swallowing—she always believed that male seed was replete with proteins and vitamins and served to keep her young. One swallow may not make the spring, she used to tell her friends, but one swallow of salty, piping hot sperm will keep one healthy for days.

Mikhail fell asleep quickly while Claudia's mind continued to assess Marina: would she react as delightedly as she, Claudia, had to Mikhail's thrust into her? Did the girl have the tongue to burrow deep into an open vagina and lick the silky membranes? Judging from the cries from the far room, Claudia felt the girl had promise. How had Juliette brought her present—and earlier—body slaves to that eminent level where pain and pleasure intermingled, where the female accepted sex, flagellation and indeed torture, with such delight?

Claudia could still hear the groans and muted cries from the room across the corridor as her lesbians orgasmed freely. If only they would control their shrieks of joy, Claudia thought and decided to insist on less abandoned lovemaking. Yet, no; her own orgasms were wild enough and Mikhail's also. Let them suck and lick themselves into euphoria. They deserved at least that, to ready themselves for what awaited them the next evening. The thought harassed her need for rest. Softly she stroked her pouting nubble of clit flesh and then crushed it beneath her fingers. She came rapidly and urgently, sliding up into the heights and then plunging into quietude.

CHAPTER 5

The next night, Verenka and Marina were made to kneel in the library and wait, side by side, their breasts heaving with anxiety. Though desperate to talk, neither dared.

"Spread the thighs out wide," Gemma advised, "and the breasts out. Yes, like that."

They waited for an endless moment, trembling but excited, facing the familiar but now ominous pillars supporting the gallery with its shelves of erotic books.

Marina knelt rigid with terror; her body sweating beneath the warm oil that seemed to hem her in like a second skin, diaphanous and ready to be whipped off. But she held herself erect, conscious of Verenka's taut nudity next to her, the obedient slave, waiting.

That morning Claudia had announced to Gemma that they would be requiring the two slaves—as well as Gemma herself—that evening after the performance at the Comedie Frangaise and supper at Maxim's.

"Around midnight, Gemma," she said, placidly. "I should like the library tables to be prepared with ropes as well as the pillars to be ready with the leather thongs for bondage. The Master and I wish the whole range of whips to be laid out upon the side table where the library catalogue stands."

"Would the Signora wish for the hoods and gags to be ready also?" Gemma enquired.

"Not tonight, Gemma, thank you. But there is one item I should like you to see to: kindly ensure that the new girl's sphincter is securely sealed with the medium-sized anal plug. She requires persuasive enlarging if she is not to be damaged. Maintain it in place for the next few days and nights, releasing only when physically essential. I presume I make myself clear?"

"It shall be done, cara Signora"

"And see to it that the slut Verenka is flushed out for the Master's use."

"D'accordo. It shall be done, Signora."

In the course of the evening, the servant duly readied the girls. They bathed and were oiled from top to toe, the pubic hair being meticulously combed to its full, lush reach. The nipples and areolas received minute attention as they were given their carmine hue, while Verenka's long hair was tied back with a scarlet bow. It was late when the bodies were finally ready.

Marina endured the premeditated preliminaries with solemn foreboding and yet she experienced a thrill of sexual stimulation as Gemma's gnarled hands touched, smoothed and penetrated her flesh. What exorbitant care! Never had she been manipulated in this manner and never felt so helpless. But that was, she knew, a cardinal factor in reducing her to total submission. She had agreed to sex slavery and was about to grasp its fullest significance. Thus, for the first time, Marina allowed herself, along with Verenka, who was accustomed to it, to be cleansed, perfumed and oiled and she had to concede that the old Gemma performed the task to perfection. In complete silence the girls' armpits were checked for stubble, the anal channel inspected and rendered totally pristine, free from the slightest hair. Meanwhile the girls chatted between themselves. They were unaccountably excited but Verenka recognized that it was the joint preparation that gave the long moment its flavour. And, as she stared at her lover's splendid, supple body, she wondered how it would, when the time came, stand up to the fucking, fellatio and beatings, strung aloft or bound down naked. She encouraged her again.

"Don't worry, Marina, my love. You will survive and anyway, I doubt they will hurt you tonight. They want you to see me tied and whipped but you will certainly have to participate somehow. I just hope they make you kneel to suck me off. But don't worry; they'll probably let us off fairly lightly tonight. And then, darling, we can fuck ourselves silly in bed afterwards."

While the owners were sitting in the lap of culture at the

theatre, the slaves were not permitted to sit, being freshly oiled; so they performed a graceful pavane in their room to the tune of some medieval music that Marina had brought with her on discs. Gemma cleared away the basins and sponges and, taking her leave for her kitchen, complimented the two nudes. "Ecco! You are very, very beautiful."

Events took place slowly on the return of the slave-owners.

First, the two girls were duly led into the cavernous, candle-lit space of the library, each pair of arms tied by Gemma to the nape of the neck, a slender rein encircling the throat and wrists, left to trail over the buttocks and then they were left to wait.

Claudia entered the library first. Marina could hardly trust her eyes. The woman was half-naked, clad in thigh length leather boots; her sex was splayed open with slender thongs, gripping her labia apart and revealing the glistening, sepia oval of the vagina. Her thorax was meshed with further thongs, holding the breasts taut and uplifted. She wore elbow-length crimson gloves and in her hand she grasped a long lash of several plaited leathers. As she walked, her heels resounded in the room until she stood, legs apart, before the two naked slaves. Aghast, Marina began to think the situation implausible, unreal, until the woman lifted the slave's chin with the extremity of her whip haft.

"Head up, slave. Eyes down."

Marina obeyed immediately.

Behind her, Mikhail appeared, also wearing riding boots but only to below the knees. A thong encircled his genitals, allowing the erect penis and scrotum to ride against the curled hairs of the flat, muscular belly; his thorax was also criss-crossed with black leathers, leaving the midriff bare, except for a broad belt of studded hide, from which swung a slender riding crop that appeared to have been greased. It was the massive, elevated erection that frightened Marina most; she had seen many cocks in her life but not of that dimension. Her cunt tightened at the thought of its penetrating power.

"These naked sex sluts seem to be begging for immediate attention," the man remarked dispassionately. "Which of the two, Claudia, do you consider worthy of my cock and of your cunt before this beautiful thing is put to the whip?" He dragged Verenka's head back by the hair, his bound penis throbbing over her face.

Marina gasped in anguish. She began to realize that she was probably to be used by one or the other or both and—her heart raced—possibly flogged, despite the earlier insinuations that she was temporarily to be spared; from the corner of her eye, she saw Claudia inspecting the whips and crops on the nearby table. Yet for Verenka's sake—who certainly was to be thrashed, that was obvious—she held herself erect. Who knew if her own negligence at this or at any other instant would not be paid for by Verenka. Her heart thumping with fear, she stretched her body upright. Now she knew she was a slave.

Claudia strolled round the naked bodies, her high-heeled boots gleaming; she exuded an odour of musk, sex liquids and leather.

"The gaping mouth of the fair-haired slave seems ready, my love," Claudia murmured. "Why not try it for size? It has sucked the other slut's cunt plentifully enough and is probably ripe for your magnificent cock. How would you wish us to start, dearest Master, if not with that?"

Mikhail also walked slowly round the kneeling nudes, tapping the buttock meat with the tip of his crop. Finally he said: "My own desire would be to have you, my love, flagellate our dark slave, as only you know how, stretched out between the columns and allow the fair-haired female to suck her off while you deal with her. After you have lashed her big rump well, I shall gladly take her in the anus and I suggest you use the other, for her mouth will be only too ready, lubricated and hot after servicing her sister."

Claudia stroked Marina's breasts, lifting them to cradle them in her firm grasp. "My own inclination, dear whipmaster," she said quietly, touching her own clit, "is to believe that these fine breasts require the quirt—at least a dozen lashes. The slave is new and needs some sort of welcome. She should not be allowed to become idle and jealous."

"I entirely agree. But later, my sweet flagellatrix. She should be permitted to grow accustomed to our rituals first. Then her breasts can bounce under your quirt as often as may be desirable. But I agree she requires strict treatment."

Suddenly, and as if to compensate for her disappointment, Claudia lashed Verenka's rump with her three-thonged whip. "Get to the columns and stretch your gorgeous flesh for the whip. And you," she turned to the trembling Marina, "kneel and suck her while she is thrashed. That, at least, you know how to do, you slave slut."

In a moment Verenka was spread aloft between the library pillars, presenting her rich, oiled buttocks to the scourge and her sex to her lover. She hung in a perfect cross of nude flesh.

"Kneel and tongue her!" The man ordered Marina abruptly. She moved and grasped the labia, opened them wide and sank in, keeping her hands well away from the lash.

Standing to the side and measuring her swing, Claudia struck. Methodically, she worked across the flaccid globes, which rebounded with every stroke, laid on with pauses, to allow the effect to penetrate well into the nerves of the epidermis. After ten lashes, the rhythm accelerated. The slave twisted and thrust forwards with each slash, slapping her sex against Marina's face. The flagellation grew in intensity until the rump meat was marked from the summit of the bulges below the coccyx to the thigh crease. Crimson turned to purple as the welts rose on the surface with minute knots where the blood was gathering. Claudia, sweating and panting, wondered if not to slit her open for once.

After twenty lashes, Verenka, biting her lip cruelly to prevent her screams, was leaping bodily in her thongs, and yet she managed to thrust out her pelvis to Marina.

Claudia was astonished at the slave's resistance and her resignation as she absorbed the force of each stroke. A dominant's dream. This slut hardly needed a gag. She refused to cry out, probably, Claudia judged, not to disgrace herself before her lover. She was far from suffering trauma; she was irreproachable. True flogging flesh, Claudia gasped.

Almost simultaneously with Claudia's final stroke, Verenka shrieked hysterically and came in her lover's mouth, shuddering as her orgasm destroyed her.

For good measure, the man released his genitals, throwing the thong across the library floor, and grasped the whipped body by the pelvis bones. Claudia guided the cock directly to the puckered sphincter; the pulsating head slid in deep, Mikhail's loins slapping against the welted rump as he enjoyed the girl's generously enlarged, half-slackened orifice.

It was then that Claudia decided to test Marina. She beckoned her to the great table and laid herself out upon it, her buttocks crushed against the edge. Dutifully, Marina went to her knees again. "Suck and frig better than you've ever done on that slut of yours."

The slave did not need to splay the labia, already retracted by the cunt straps. Claudia propped her body up on her elbows to witness and judge the performance.

The new slave exercised every talent she had learnt. The sex was beautiful, drooling with viscid, clammy but translucent juices; among the matted curls, the clitoris reared bared and stiff as Marina, with a sort of solicitude for the woman's frantic need, let the jerking nubble slither in between her lips. Seizing it between the teeth, daringly she bit into its base and extended the organ with her suction. Then she used her fingers, rolling the thing that was more like gristle or cartilage than the ductile clits she had kissed and urged to orgasm in the past. While she tongued into the silken, glutted vagina, she experienced in herself a harrowing trepidation; uncontrollably, whirling eddies of lust ruffled through her womb as the mucous sludge commenced its surge down and out of her own sex.

Oh, heavens! Let her come! Let her come before I do, she screamed silently, fighting to stem the inevitable tide throbbing down her inner membranes. She worked hard, caressing the woman's belly and thrusting her fingers beneath the straps over the ribs, tearing at the white skin, reaching for the erect nipples above. She tried to sublimate her own sexual desires, cursing herself, execrating her sensuality. But it was of no avail. She wrenched her face from the pungently perfumed crotch and cried aloud. She orgasmed impenitently and heedlessly, still mauling the woman's clitoris with her fingers. Claudia rose upon the table to thrust the slave aside. Marina slumped before the shining boots that suddenly stabbed viciously into her breasts.

"You will pay for this, slut! And dearly. A slave performs. She does not enjoy herself at her Mistress's expense." Claudia drove her heel deep into the crushed breast. "That piece of uninspired, unmitigated selfishness is sheer disobedience. You will receive three dozen lashes of the quirt over the breasts roped to that column over there." The woman indicated the far left pillar with her scourge. "But I'm too tired to thrash you now."

She turned to look into the shadows beyond the candles. "Gemma, take this whore of a slave back to her quarters and tie her to the end of her bed for the night, head between the thighs, arms reversed and wrists joined to the uprights."

As Marina left the library, she heard her Master groan, still plunged within Verenka's buttocks and gutting the anus, as he filled the loose rectum with his spunk.

On her return, the maid detached the exhausted girl from the columns and led her in turn out of the presence of her owners. Even to Gemma, the performance was worthless.

The session had lasted well over an hour. The man and woman refreshed themselves with an excellent Chateau Lafitte 1985. The slaves' conduct, despite Verenka's efforts to satisfy her owners, had been far from adequate. They required intensive training; that was quite clear—to Claudia, at least.

"Marina is only just embarking on her long voyage into pain and pleasure," Mikhail gently pacified his mistress. "But it is certain that further measures are definitely called for if they are to be up to demonstration standards. And like you, darling, I want to be able to put them on show, as Marcus and Juliette do with their Tansu."

Claudia was far from convinced, as she stripped off her straps and had Gemma pull off her boots. When the woman had left, he added for Claudia's benefit. "And as for you, darling, you are in need of cock."

Consolation was, for Claudia, indeed there, between his thighs. She had herself used back and front for a long moment and finally, after several inevitably postponed spasms, she fellated her lover smoothly and drank down the semen, as if famished for nutrition.

Before they dissolved into sleep, Claudia had one more thing to say. "Mishka, I need these girls of ours, you understand? I need them terribly but I realize they are far from ready. You know, once in the Touraine at the Chateau de Bressac, I think it was, I saw the teats of a deliciously tough Russian girl nailed through the holes, where her rings had been a moment before, and hammered on to a crucifix and her ringed cunt lips torn open, while two masked men whipped her back and buttocks to the blood. She orgasmed, Mishka, she orgasmed like a wild animal…"

"Claudia darling, be patient," her lover murmured. The man was already fully aware of his mistress's languishing desires as well as her ambitions. He was in full agreement but preoccupied by her unjustifiable eagerness.

"Step by step, Claudia, my avenging angel."

Unpredictably, his gorgeous mistress promptly fell asleep in his arms. As he held her and cherished her lithe body close beside him, he meditated whether he should not have kept Juliette as his main mistress—Marcus never raised the slightest objection to that—and enjoyed her lascivious evenings and the sessions she organized so elegantly with the sexual help of her fabulous, exquisite Tansu. He would see how Claudia and the two girls acted.

CHAPTER 6

It was a week before Claudia could reach Juliette, absent in Rome. Meanwhile, Marina had seemed to be far more obedient when called upon to service her, ensuring that her Mistress, prostrated naked either on the black silk sheets or on the library table, regaled herself fully and at ease beneath her agile tongue that flicked and curled dutifully. Further, her duties towards her Master developed, with hints from Verenka, even more conclusively. Her fellatio became increasingly proficient; she had learnt a host of wiles and techniques that rendered her performances with previous cocks mere travesties of what adroit fellatio should bring about on a rampant prick. In the past, she had equivocated too often with men's needs, neglecting the anal ring, disregarding the vas deferens gorging and pulsating along the enigmatic but exciting perineum between the anus and the balls, waiting to spurt. And frequently she omitted to stimulate out the necessary supply of lubrication, using her saliva in its place. But she was learning. With Verenka's knowledge prompting her, she never failed to strip the foreskin back promptly to ensure that the hard ridge of the cock received full friction. The results on Mikhail's shaft, standing swollen with blue veins, were promising; she could urge him on or restrain him, maintaining him in a limbo of tension until the man could bear the ripple of her lips, tongue and teeth no longer. As the clots of semen surged into her gullet, she drank it down with relish, just as she slurped up Claudia's and Verenka's discharges.

Handling the demands of the clitoris was less of a problem for Marina as an experienced lesbian but with Claudia, she discovered numerous new tricks, including her Mistress's insistence on the Grafenberg point hidden in the inner roof of her sex. The girl derived unmitigated delight when the pungent, astringent discharge flooded her mouth, bringing her own sex to readiness. She looked forward to servicing the beautiful, tender cleft.

Marina's sole problem lay in the initial lashes of the whip over her flesh but, there too, she began gradually, in the successive whippings she endured in that first week, to sense the pain changing into sexual pleasure as her delicate epidermis grew used to the strokes. Towards the end of the week she received her sentence of three dozen lashes to the breasts. Claudia laid them on hard and as she leaped and twisted in her bonds while the fleshy lumps rebounded and bounced under the flagellation and Verenka sucked hungrily at her cunt, Marina at last fully transcended the pain and found her first true slave's orgasm.

Above all, she became conscious of how her superb nudity invigorated her flagellators. This in turn exhilarated her and generated the orgasms she sought. Claudia seemed tolerably pleased with the progress and particularly with the girl's docility. Marina would do anything to stay with her sister slave—and that Claudia knew. Slavery closed around her.

Nevertheless, her Mistress envisaged far more challenging and arduous activities for her, for both the slaves. And increased pleasure for all concerned. Indeed, she badly needed Juliette to advise her. And at last, the anticipated meeting was arranged.

Claudia had Antoine leave her in the rue de Rivoli so that she could walk a little before entering the Hotel de Crillon where Juliette had fixed the rendezvous. As she strolled along in the soft autumn sunshine, she rehearsed the questions to which she needed answers. And she decided to share her sentiments openly with Juliette as one dominant to another. Be frank, she told herself.

Juliette was at her best, groomed and dressed by Ungaro in a fawn costume that clung to her slender form, an outfit obviously made for her. The two women kissed in the hushed luxury of the lounge of the Crillon which Juliette frequented so regularly and where sometimes she took Tansu whom she made to sit naked, except for stiletto-heeled shoes and a cloak.

Claudia listened with rapt attention to the woman's account

of the long Roman weekend and to the description of the Renaissance hall where Tansu and several other slaves had been exposed to ceremonial whippings and long sessions of servicing distinguished guests. Finally, Claudia's turn to speak came as the white-gloved waiter brought the tea. Squeezing the lemon in her delicate fingers, Claudia sipped and announced the news.

"They are making progress, Juliette dearest, yes, but I'm afraid they are novices. But you mentioned once some place where I could get them properly trained."

"Ah, you mean Beaucastel, darling. Yes, Beaucastel. I've used their services both for Veronique whom Marcus and I sold to that Dutch diplomat and for darling Tansu last year. The place is highly exclusive and rather expensive, but that's no dilemma for you two! It's situated in a magnificent chateau in the rather austere countryside of the Rouergue, not far from Rodez, if I recall. But, Claudia, you can't just send them down there at the drop of a hat. There must be spaces available and the Master of Beaucastel—an extraordinary individual, to say the least—has to accept them."

Claudia nodded. "Perhaps you and Marcus could recommend us, Juliette. It sounds promising."

"With the utmost pleasure. And I assure you that neither you nor your slaves will regret going there. If you like, I'll call them to see how they're placed for new inductions. But you'll have to have them ringed first."

"But can't the people do that down there?"

"Absolutely not, darling, if you and Mishka are really serious about Beaucastel, I would advise you to get your girls pierced and ringed forthwith. It takes some time for them to become accustomed to the hardware. I can recommend a man near the Place Victor-Hugo who pierces admirably, all seven points for the female."

Claudia marshalled her courage. "And what are the seven, Juliette?"

Unhesitatingly, the woman touched her friend's bosom

lightly, letting her hand drift to the crotch. It was only a second's gesture, but it excited Claudia with an unaccountable thrill.

"Both nipples, deep near the base, all four labia, both inner and outer, and the clitoris hood. That's the statutory minimum but several of the slaves I saw on my visit there were wearing rings in the navel and septum."

The Comtesse poured out the tea while her neighbour listened.

"A course at the castle lasts normally two weeks. As to the actual training, it's severe but covers everything you could wish for, my dear. A slave never looks back after a naked fortnight in those cellars."

"Juliette, where can I get equipment made? I mean trestles, a crucifix and breast-whipping bars and so on?" Claudia was determined to extract what she could from her friend while the climate was favourable.

The woman delved into her Gucci bag to draw out a gold pencil and visiting cards.

"Go to these people, out at Montreuil. They make everything. Whatever you require from huge oak flogging benches, completely fitted with bondage rings, to torture slabs covered with nails that teach an excellent lesson once in a while. They have harnesses, hoods, dildos, gags, what have you. You already possess slave helmets to mask and stifle your girls, I suspect?"

Unable to resist the temptation, Claudia told her of Mikhail's latest acquisition. For once she could be a trifle arrogant, for it was a precious and rare object. On a trip to Venice he had come across an ancient hood of crimson calf-leather, it had ear and eye pads and a wooden gag sewn into the lining. The gag was scored with the marks of countless gritted teeth.

"We used it on Verenka and it fitted and worked perfectly but the older girl put up a bit of a fight at first…"

"Scourge her, darling, scourge her until she implores you to use it on her." The Comtesse's approach was direct and to the point, as usual. "Sorry, go on."

"Do you think your man out at Montreuil could make me another hood like that one?"

"Of course, darling. Meanwhile, you'll have to use a normal one, won't you? Just as effective and the gag's of nice tough rubber. Tansu adores its girth."

The conversation seemed to Claudia to have lasted long enough. She had her briefing.

And she realized that she had to leave quickly; her crotch was worrying her. It was flowing liberally into her slip. Her clit was excruciatingly rigid. The thing was demanding, compelling attention.

Urgently…

The women kissed warmly as the cars were summoned. The older woman felt attracted to Claudia and said as much.

"You are very beautiful and I want to get to know you better." The remark, charged with salaciousness, was not lost on the blonde dominant.

When the Comtesse arrived at her hugeapartment, Tansu was there, lying on the bed, open and naked. And properly ringed as a slave should be. Juliette wondered whether Claudia would really go ahead with her plans. Beaucastel certainly awaited clients like her… And Juliette had undertaken to enquire for her. Which she did that same night. The answer was mid-November. That would give Claudia time.

Driving home in the opposite direction, Claudia was desperate as the traffic slowed up Antoine and the Mercedes. Then she was home, viscous with an uncontrollable trickle sliding down the hot inner reaches of her thighs.

She promptly opened the girls' door. "Marina, I need you for a moment. Come." She clasped the girl's thin wrist, drawing her towards the black sheets beyond the passage, separating the rooms. Rapidly Claudia stripped herself to her garter belt; she could not wait for Mikhail's cock. Where on earth was the man every time she needed fucking during the day? She bent Marina's head down, making her kneel,

66

elongating her own tense body, casting her arms out above her head, her thighs sprawled wide.

"Suck me off. Quickly. Get into me with your tongue…"

On her knees before the dripping sex, Marina took the pale stub of jerking flesh into her mouth, still astringent with the tang of Verenka's spicy come. The orgasm had heaped up within her Mistress and broke abruptly; it matched the proportion of the woman's need and the distracted cry rang through the apartment, frightening the slobbering girl. My God, she's going to die, Marina thought in a sudden rush of panic.

Both remained inert for a long moment until Claudia roused herself. Hoarsely, she told Marina the good news.

"I'm going to have you both, well… pierced and ringed next week. And sent to a place where you will both learn to become adequate slaves. Which is not the case at present. Go to your room and share this with your sister in sin, you slut. You'll both dine with us tonight." She felt extenuated for once, as she caressed the girl's tangled, flaxen strands of hair. The slave had worked admirably—that she had to admit.

Marina was lost in the maze of her Mistress's utterances. She thought it best simply to bow in silence. She's quite demented, was the sole conclusion she could summon up. Surreptitiously, she wiped the cloying liquid from her face, after tasting it again hungrily with the tip of her tongue. Then she left very quietly, her duty done. It had been far more gratifying than she had foreseen and yet each act of this nature was, she knew, drawing her inexorably into a web of collusion with her new owners. She felt she was voyaging out into uncharted seas, both alarming and thrilling to her docile temperament. One inference she drew from the situation was that strict conformity must prevail over resistance and even questioning. Above all, obedience, however humiliating, would safeguard her relationship with Verenka. Be obsequious and you keep her, Marina reminded herself; act obstreperously and you'll lose her. Moreover, these imposed sexual duties stimulated her own libido; at the same time, the prospect of piercing—quite apart from the further flagellations certainly to come perturbed her to an extent she had not expected.

"What does the woman mean, for heaven's sakes?" she queried Verenka who listened quietly while showering and having Marina smear a balm lotion over her buttocks. The younger girl took the threat with surprising sang-froid, recalling to mind some of the illustrations she had studied in the library, magnificently naked slave women, bearing flesh rings in various parts of their bodies, were loaded with weights that distended the flesh while they were prepared for torture.

As Marina dried and perfumed her body, chafing her teats into the required erection, the younger girl smiled encouragement.

"Don't be scared, darling. You'll look stupendous with rings in you. How stimulating darling! Just think of it!"

"You can't mean that, Verenka!" But she knew her lover meant it in all seriousness. Perhaps she was right, but still Marina worried.

Promptly at eight, Gemma entered to inspect them, glancing at the welts on Verenka's rear cheeks, and then ordered them to table.

For once, however, their naked dinner was devoid of the usual joy. Mikhail, fresh from the squash courts, was puzzled; his attempts to add gaiety failed and he could only look questioningly, first at Marina's glum countenance and then at his mistress.

"What's been going on here, may I ask?"

"I'll tell you later, Mishka. Would you care to have our little slaves make love together in our bed tonight while you enjoy me?"

"If you wish, darling. But tell me what's afoot."

"I saw Juliette," was Claudia's only reply. "She gave me some ideas, Mishka."

Chapter 7

The following five days and nights were replete with entertainment. Marina was most often beaten and Verenka loved watching her graceful body twisting and jerking under the lash. The girls were allowed to spend two afternoons in the Jardin du Luxembourg in short dresses and sandals, accompanied by the inevitable Gemma, with Antoine waiting in the car. The cool air caressing Marina's flogged buttocks made her cunt clench under the scant covering.

The piercing took place without difficulty. The staff were efficacious with the sterilization and anaesthetizing of the relevant portions of flesh to be dealt with and the business was carried out deftly on a white operating table in silence, Claudia checking the rings were disinfected; saw them threaded through and immovably affixed with the clamping tool. All arrangements had been agreed upon beforehand and the only remark made during the time the girls spent there, came from the nurse who noticed the buttocks when it was Marina's turn to strip for piercing. "Oh, good grief!" she commented, "They have whipped you well, haven't they?" Marina blushed crimson like her nates.

It took time for the slaves to grow accustomed to the presence and the strange, if unexacting, weight of the metal in their sensitive extremities. They felt no real discomfort when the anaesthesia wore off except occasionally in the nipples and clitoris hood but soon they were manipulating the rings with pride. The erotic effect the steel had on both girls provided them with a new source of excitement. They played with the shining, circles like youngsters with toys; the regular suckings they lavished on each other assumed a new dimension by enabling them to splay the vaginal labia wide open and even to tie back the lips with silk cords passed round the buttock crease. This lent itself to new sexual exploration and orgasms more delirious than ever before. They were proud to be ringed slaves. And Verenka, while she masturbated her yearning lover, invented hallucinating fantasies, in which white-skinned, naked prostitutes, were hooked by their flesh-rings to flogging posts in the depths of Venetian prisons... Her tales brought forth staggeringly powerful orgasms and screams more akin to sessions in a torture cellar than in a Parisian bedroom.

Claudia seemed more content than even they. She admired them continuously, snaring each girl in turn with her crooked finger to haul the body towards her or towards the library pillars around which she could now secure the nude by the rings elongating the pierced flesh. Mikhail agreed her initiative had been worthwhile. He began to derive pleasure by reducing the girls' bondage to a single thong through the clit ring, watching them teetering on tiptoe, striving to safeguard the delicate hood. The rings embellished the slaves and heightened the erotic effect and cruelty of the regular flagellations.

When the phone buzzed by her side, Claudia was sitting on the balcony, dappled with autumn sunlight flickering off the Seine. It was Juliette to enquire how the piercing had gone.

Claudia was thrilled. That slightly hoarse voice always excited her. "Splendidly, Juliette. Thank you so much for the address."

"Listen, darling, talking of slaves, would you care to come down to our place in the Sologne this weekend? You remember I invited you that night when we met on the lakeside? Come to the Avenue Kleber for lunch on Saturday and I'll show you my little town set-up. And you can meet my Tansu. Then we'll all drive down and have some fun. I'm taking Tansu and my two slave handlers. There'll be a couple of male slaves too who are 'en pension chez moi' for a spell while their owners are abroad. It'll be fun."

The prospect of meeting at last the famous Tansu in itself made the occasion well worthwhile. And the chance of seeing Juliette's set-up, as she termed it, was not to be missed.

Claudia agreed at once. Mishka would take the exclusion in his stride; a weekend at home alone with Verenka and Marina would please him.

"So, Saturday around one, angel," Juliette confirmed. "I'll send the car for you. Ciao!"

Juliette's compelling personality seemed to linger on long after the phone went dead.

After lunch and coffee the hostess invited her beautiful blonde guest to 'peep' at her cellar.

"We'll just take a glance, treasure. My Pipilotti and Johannes are busy packing Tansu and the males up for the journey but at least you'll see my little dungeon at last."

Little? The confinement cellar was extensive. After a descent in the lift that, as so often in Paris, seemed to date back to Haussmann, Juliette opened a door at the end of a long passage. She used her own passkey. The place consisted of two chambers, the first room being a comfortable lounge, harmoniously furnished with high backed Henri IV chairs on magnificent carpets—Turkish like Tansu? Claudia wondered—and couches. The saffron-draped walls displayed elegantly framed scenes of slave torture: naked saints with suffering countenances turned heavenwards in ecstasy as the nipples or penises were wrenched with pincers; nubile maidens contorted in erotic writhings as they were flagellated in medieval surroundings by handsome youths with knotted scourges. Claudia readily identified the celebrated illustration from de Sade's Justine (or was it, like her hostess, in Juliette?), depicting the deserted torture chamber with its pillars sporting razor-edged falchions, ropes, hooks…

Juliette tinkled a silver bell, as if celebrating Mass. Instantly two silken-masked figures, practically naked, appeared from the archway leading from the adjoining room. Claudia caught her breath at the sleek build of the couple. They were like young athletes, the female somewhat older than the man.

"Ah, there you are, you two," Juliette said, kissing each lightly on the lace-covered cheek. "I trust we're all set for departure. This is my friend Claudia, also a slave owner. Is Tansu ready? And the males?"

The female, a tall, sinuous figure in latex tights, her thorax bridled in a latticework of straps, bowed gracefully and nodded, as her mistress introduced her.

"This gorgeous creature, Claudia, is my Pipilotti."

The woman must be in her early thirties, alarmingly attractive but intimidating, almost frosty. A sheaf of thongs drooped from the belt, its corrugated, studded haft fashioned in the form of an erect penis. Claudia stared at the female's well-combed flourish of pubic thatch, dyed bright turquoise; similarly tinted, the areoles allowed the swollen teats to emerge from silver cones armed with slender barbs like straightened fish hooks. Claudia made a note carefully to avoid having to embrace the slave mistress.

The youth appeared somewhat less spine-chilling in his billowing silk blouse and jabot but most of his neat figure was also sheathed in clinging nylon, a triangular gash leaving his ponderous cock to hang loose, awaiting orders. A pad of sharp spikes strapped over the pubic mound promised scant pleasure for any slave he fucked. There too Claudia made point of steering clear of his sexual attentions. Below the lace mask, the lips were thin, almost a line that seemed to have forgotten how to smile.

"And that's Johannes," the hostess added. "Now come and see my Tansu. I trust you've whipped her arse, Pipilotti dear, so that she has a really uncomfortable journey down."

"Yes, Madame la Comtesse, thirty lashes. An hour ago."

Juliette led the way into the next room, which was dark, overheated and L-shaped. Candles flickered over the stone walls and flagstones to reveal several pieces of apparatus of torture. In the centre, suspended by the wrists from a massive chain reaching down from a pulley in the arched ceiling, hung Juliette's mythical piece of Turkish delight.

Frankly, Claudia felt at first a trifle disillusioned. True, the body displayed a wealth of brown flesh of a certain elegance but Tansu was solidly built, big-boned and muscular, her assets however became clearer, as Juliette ran her hands over the flesh. The ringed breasts stood out like the howitzer shells one sees on war memorials and were matched by the bulging, depilated sex with its jangling cluster of more rings than Claudia imagined the female genitals could hold; they dragged down the labia a couple of fingers' breadth below the vulva. But what intrigued the visitor was the mauve and crimson tattoo representing barbed wire encircling the impressive hips; the design issued out of the sex slit, followed the groins up to and round the pelvis to disappear down the buttock crease into the rectum.

The dark head of hair had been sheared short. The slave was indeed very special.

"Goodness me, that's something, Juliette." Claudia had to concede finally as she strolled round the wealth of nude flesh. In profile the body indeed yielded its full attraction: the huge buttocks, not unlike Verenka's, Claudia saw, had been well flogged into scarlet welts; the powerful thighs, concave belly and erect contours of the breasts—it all added up to what Juliette evidently fancied: ample meat available for use, a stamina capable of holding out under whatever Juliette did to the girl. Claudia tried to picture the torrid sessions inflicted on Tansu by her proprietor or by the slave handlers in front of Juliette watching from a throne…

"Does she scream a great deal?" she asked for something plausible to say and admiring the marks of the recent flagellation

"Scream? Never, darling. Just moans delightfully. She hankers after punishment and the fiercer the better. She's been trained and conditioned by her former owners in Istanbul to a degree you can't imagine. The more ingenious the torture, the more incredibly responsive her feedback."

Juliette slapped the girl's udders hard. "Right, Tansu?"

The shorn head nodded.

"You see, she doesn't speak much, first because she doesn't understand a thing and secondly because she has an impediment. Stick your whore's tongue out, Tansu, to show my friend."

73

Again Juliette slapped the breasts hard and made them roll and ripple.

Claudia gasped as the mouth opened and the tongue came out; through it was pierced a circle of stainless steel. It clinked once on the teeth and was withdrawn.

"I'll you her story on the drive down," Juliette said. "But now, we've got to get a move on. Release her, Pipilotti, and cloak them all up. You five will travel in the van, and see she and the others are tied tight,"

The journey to the Sologne residence, driven by an obsequious chauffeur, proved more delightful than Claudia had expected. The car took the two elegant women along pleasant secondary roads under the shade of the plane trees as evening began to close in. Some respectable way behind, the grey van with its pair of cloaked servants and triad of slaves, bound and gagged, followed with Pipilotti at the wheel.

"Now, about Tansu," Claudia's hostess said, remembering her promise. "Well, I grew tired of Veronique. We both needed a change. So I sold her off. Then I heard of a slave auction taking place in Turkey, so off Marcus and I went in his new yacht and stayed at the best hotel in Istanbul, the one looking out over the Bosphorus.

"We contacted the sellers and they drove us out into the country to a rather shabby, run-down place. But the harem quarters were stiff with slaves for sale or leasing, females and males of all sorts. They were arranged on their knees, heavily chained, round a steaming pool where we were invited to bathe. Delightful, darling. The slaves were kept alert by servants in baggy, harem pants and turbans, armed with bamboos and malacca canes. I saw this Tansu girl straightaway among the others, her thighs splayed wide to show her mass of sex rings—she has ten of them, by the way. I knew the size of the breasts and buttocks was just right and I pointed to her from the pool. A turnkey whipped her to her feet and we saw the whole of her stupendous body, barbed wire tattoo and all. Of course Marcus wanted to see all the other pieces but I'd

74

decided. So we bid and got her. Expensive but worth every dollar or whatever my sweet Marcus paid."

"And how does one ship a naked slave back to Paris from the banks of the Bosphorus? Air freight, fragile, this side up?"

"But, darling, we had Marcus's big yacht. I used to tie Tansu to the mast and whip her solidly before having her service us down in the lounge. She slept in the hold, tied up like a mainsail. Great voyage, and was she beautiful, staked naked out on the deck, all suntanned! And here she is."

The car had turned down a sandy drive, overhung with oaks. Far more than the simple weekend shooting lodge Claudia had expected, the gabled house stood between lawns, kennels and outhouses, sheltered amid firs. Here and there sounded the croak of the pheasants Marcus raised for shoots in season.

Several servants welcomed their august employer: maids in starched aprons and valets with striped waistcoats. Claudia was conducted to her room where she unpacked her lone toothbrush. Then she looked out over the purple heather and the dense Solognat woods and below she caught sight of the tethered slaves being hustled into a side door.

The dinner served rustically in the beam-ceilinged salle a manger, surrounded with boars' heads on shields of wood, proved a delight. The fare of fricassee de poulet was a treat, the Loire wine nicely chambre and Juliette in corduroy breeches, riding boots and a silk shirt that showed much of her bosom. The three slaves ate in the gunroom, chained to the bench by their cocks and Tansu by her clit ring.

Juliette summoned Joel, the gamekeeper and told him to have the slaves presented at nine, refreshments to be served at ten.

"Now, down to business, sweet one." her hostess announced after the cognac. "I don't know how you want to appear but there's my private wardrobe on the first landing, full of body straps, tights, cloaks, boots, what have you. Select what you want. Some of my colleagues prefer to be nude. Do as you usually do. Wear a mask if you want to look medieval and very cruel!"

Claudia chose a sleeveless leather waistcoat, long, pale purple gloves and a hip belt of black leather. To it, she clipped a thin whip of several thongs, after fingering through the vast array of alternatives. She decided to keep her high-heeled shoes but the idea of stockings appalled her.

"Claudia darling, you look simple divine," came the compliment from her hostess, superb in thigh-high boots. Abruptly, the blonde visitor realized she had, of course, never stood as she was, cunt bare, before Juliette. She admitted to herself that even that stimulated her.

"Now, I'm going to give you Tansu to whip, hung by the breasts and I want to watch. Then you can work on the males, if you wish. I'm a great one for a stiff, circumcised cock and a dangling sack of balls throttled at the root with a steel clasp. I can bring a male off with a quirt, you know, before you can say Torquemada!"

Claudia knew she was out of her depth. "Well, I'd love to whip your Tansu, if that's all right, Juliette," she murmured. "I rather go for females as a matter of fact."

The prospect of slave whipping in this house hidden in the woods sent loads of sap oozing out of Claudia; the vaginal gutter under the flaxen triangle of hair was responding fully. She knew she was very beautiful under her leather waistcoat and needed to show her body in action.

Under the vacuous gaze of the antlered deer and a chamois Marcus had shot on the Jalouve in the Haute-Savoie, they entered the chamber.

As Pipilotti bowed ceremoniously, Claudia gazed round the room. Several whipping stakes rose to the rafters and beyond, the trestles, on two of which were bound the male slaves. Prostrated backward, chained by the wrists and ankles, the nude bodies exposed their tensed cocks, throbbing vertically from the curved loins; the stem of the flaccid scrotum was crammed into a broad circle of steel, and that had been screwed very tight.

Then Claudia saw Tansu. Her wrists bound behind to a throat strap, she hung by the roots of her breasts, swaying from the chain supporting her superb body and the ropes encircling the mammaries. A steel spreader bar parted the legs to the extent the hip joints would permit without dislocation and the mass of cunt rings dangled like iron fruit on a tree. The body shimmered with oil, Pipilotti still holding the jar from which she had anointed the slave. A silence seemed to freeze the room like an old photograph.

"She's all yours, Claudia, love. She's waiting for her daily punishment…" Juliette spread herself out on a chair to watch.

Disconcerted, Claudia felt the handle of her whip slither in her grasp and wiped it in a fold of her waistcoat. Then she let fly across the lower belly. It welted easily but Tansu barely moved. She delivered a couple of dozen lashes, back and front, watching the nude sway under the thuds, but failing to get even a groan from the girl. A dozen more hard strokes and still the slave swung in silence.

"She's quite something," she repeated her initial compliment, sensing she was in the eye of a storm she could not fully control.

"She certainly is," Juliette assented. "But she warrants more than that. What about her huge arse, Claudia? Lay into it, that's if you want to… If you can make her scream, I'll give her to you for the night and that'll really wear your clit and nipples out."

"But she's been welted already there, Juliette," the blonde murmured, thoroughly intimidated by the slave's stoicism

"All right, darling. Just leave her to me. And you give those cocks a load of the quirt. And when you're done, let Pipilotti bring them off. They deserve it, I suppose."

As Juliette rose and approached her slave, Claudia accepted the leather quirt from Pipilotti's hand, the slave handler giving her a look of disdain.

No expert in whipping cock, Claudia hesitated. Then she struck into the rigid shaft, watching it slap back on to the belly and revert to its tumescent erection. She lashed backwards and forwards until the rod was crimson, bulging with pulsing veins. The victim groaned but took it admirably, Claudia thought. Then, after a score of cuts, Pipilotti stepped forward and grabbed the engorged cock in her leather and— Claudia guessed—studded grasp. Only a dozen fist-tight caresses up and down the bloated shaft sufficed; the slit spewed out its spunk high in the air, the cum slapping into and covering the youth's chest and belly. Claudia watched the huge organ subside between the thighs and shrink.

Meanwhile, Juliette had ferociously whipped her favourite into frenzy, helped by Johannes who twisted the girl's nipples, swollen under the throttling and tension, with a pair of breast pincers. Then a touch of the same steel on the clit sent the slave into violent orgasm. Jerking maniacally on her breast bondage, she came with the roar of a wild animal.

No one seemed to pay particular attention to the massive climax nor to the breasts beginning to turn dark purple under their garrotting.

"Relieve that slave over there," Juliette ordered hoarsely, ignoring Tansu and pointing with her whip to the other male slave. "He's ready to come. Let him spurt."

Johannes obeyed immediately by seizing the huge prick in a pair of cock tongs and elongating the shaft with violent jerks. The spunk gushed out of the bloated glans like an Icelandic geyser, arching over almost to where Juliette stood watching the performance.

"Now for some refreshments, darlings," announced the mistress of ceremonies.

Marguerite trotted in, oblivious of the scenario and the sperm anointing her floor, to place the food and drinks on the table. The chilled Chablis revived Claudia who was feeling sorely taxed by the need of orgasm after the excitement. As she tried to relax and enjoy the wine, she saw Juliette signal to Johannes to shift a chair so she could be close to her. The older woman ran her hand through the blonde hair that had lost its velvet bow.

'Well, there you are, Claudia. You saw Tansu—no inhibitions. Unconditional. Pure sex. That's why I love her. But now, you, darling, you need your orgasm. I give you a choice, as you're a guest. You can either have Johannes to fuck you right now—he'll have Pipilotti all night anyway—or you can come to bed with me and Tansu when we retire. I really don't know you well enough sexually yet, you see.'

The hand smoothing her thigh, the nails grazing the engorged clit, tempted Claudia; but the prospect of bed with the whipped Tansu and her mistress together suffocated her. And Juliette sensed it. Brusquely, she called over the handsome Johannes.

'Fuck this gorgeous woman and make it good,' she ordered. 'On the mattress over there,' she pointed to one of the many beddings on the floor which Claudia had guessed were for precisely that function.

The young man kissed Claudia's hand and led her to the far side of the room.

Rarely, even with Mishka or her former lovers, had she had such sex. It was not entirely to the credit of the young man's cock; the session had involved her in such a maelstrom of excitement that any cock would have sufficed Claudia simply let go and died the death.

No sooner was her third orgasm complete than Juliette came over to where she was lying exhausted on the mat. The dark eyes looked into the blue.

'Ready for more?'

The party eventually wound down slowly after all the actors had had their fill. Even Claudia had had a moment—she could not remember at what point—with Pipilotti and the older of the male slaves who, unchained from the trestle, had taken Claudia while she leaned against it. Juliette continued with her Tansu to the very end; she seemed incapable of separating herself from the Turk. At last released from the breast ropes, she leant over her mistress's crotch and did her service.

Finally, all passion spent, the group broke up. Physically and emotionally exhausted, she climbed the stairs and, too tired even to sponge away the residues of the evening, slumped into the huge bed and fell asleep.

The hand that later curled round her breast woke her not suddenly but gradually. The spicy, pungent smell of the body sliding into the bed immediately identified Tansu. Claudia felt the girl's lap close up against her bottom, the sex rings cold and strange on her. Then, half awake, she turned towards the slave girl and let her hands rove hazily over the strong body, her fingertips feeling the rope furrows at the root of the breasts and the whip welts ridging the rump and much more of the slave besides.

The odour from the girl's flesh and crotch cusp filled the bed, exciting Claudia anew. Softly she kissed the wet lips and suddenly felt the ringed tongue flick into her mouth; she closed her teeth, imprisoning it. Then she pressed the shorn head down into the bed and opened her thighs...

Next day, Tansu was gone. Only the musky smell of cinnamon and sex remained. And Claudia's sore clitoris.

The household let the visitor sleep and dream until noon. Then she showered and went down to the brunch laid out in the dining room. On the way, she stole into the room where she had spent so many hours. There was no evidence of the night's enjoyments. All was spruce and trim; the whipping posts seemed to have been moved back to dovetail into the walls.

As she listened to the far off cuckoo in somebody else's nest, Claudia felt she was trespassing too... She wanted to get back to reality, to Verenka and Marina and to Mishka. All the same, one learnt a lot chez Juliette de Frejaviole, mainly about oneself. Claudia was not sure if she wanted to accept a second invitation to the Sologne. She had her own project in hand and needed to work on it. Some day she would do the inviting.

It was Claudia, quite naturally, who ordered her girls to

prepare themselves for the journey to Beaucastel, two days later. They would travel by night express in a reserved sleeper with Gemma next door; they were, she instructed Gemma, to wear not their silk cloaks but, now Autumn was upon them, rough, woollen smocks, heavy velvet riding cloaks with copes, and sandals. No underclothes. They should, she added, be attached together by the wrist, at least until they were in the train. At Rodez, they would be met by car from Beaucastel where Gemma was to sign them in, returning the same day.

On the appointed Thursday, the girls were ready, excited and, at the same time, alarmed. "Won't Gemma stay with us, Mistress?" Marina was apprehensive. Claudia kissed them and advised them to be co-operative, proud and obedient. Antoine drove the trio to the Austerlitz station in good time to install them in the luxury of the first-class sleeper. Gemma had the corridor door locked by the controlleur and handed in the tickets.

"Where the hell are we going, Verenka darling?" Marina was nervous, as she took off her velvet cloak in the train and was nude, both being unmanacled for the journey.

"Hell's probably right. I haven't a clue, darling. Relax. Did you see the people staring at us as we walked along the platform? If they only knew!" She smiled. "Now darling. Come over here and do your duty."

They made unabashed love in the limited space the SNCF bed allowed, each thrilled by the chink of metal clustered around their sexes. A quivering solace invaded each as the steel rings ground together. The cries of orgasm superimposed themselves over the rush of the train heading south to Beaucastel. Next door, Gemma shook her grey head and slept.

At Rodez, under a dark drizzle of rain, a Rolls awaited them with a faceless driver, complete with cap and an air of collusion with Gemma. They set off into the dawn.

They arrived before the enormous walls and gate of Beaucastel at seven, quite chilled.

CHAPTER 8

The little group waited rather pathetically under the rain, while the chauffeur tugged several times on a bell chain to earn a distant peal of a bell somewhere in the entrails of the castle. For a long moment nothing happened apart from the frantic barking and baying of several terrifying Neapolitan mastiffs, padding and slobbering on the battlements above. The man rang again. Abruptly, the rain transformed into metal wires in the beam of floodlights, blinding the shivering girls. The judas in the colossal gate finally opened to allow a study of the intruders.

"Two slaves to be delivered, sir, according to orders." The chauffeur was evidently anxious to be rid of his charges. "And their servant."

The eyes in the square of light blinked and a voice said: "We have no knowledge of arrivals. But let them enter, though I have no instructions either from the Master or from the overseers. But get them in, while I check. Morning arrivals are a real pain."

There ensued a prolonged drawing of bolts and grating of keys as the postern was cautiously opened. In the entry stood a hooded figure, holding the creaking door. The girls entered, Verenka towing Marina after her by the chain that wedded them. They found themselves in a small courtyard surrounded with thick rhododendron bushes; an ornate, melancholy well stood in the centre under the frigid downpour.

"Straight up the pathway, over the drawbridge and wait under the portcullis until you are sent for." The man's gruff instructions were at least clear. The girls ascended the slope, looking back at Gemma who had rejoined the chauffeur. Gemma—the last palpable contact with reality—was being severed from them. There were no goodbyes.

Crouching together under the shelter of the huge archway, the girls waited, terrified.

"Well, that was quite a welcome," Marina muttered. "But I

suppose slaves don't warrant more. What an awful place!"
Scared, she grasped her lover's clammy hand. Long minutes
passed, the rain continuing to fall on the black hounds growling
above.

Suddenly the man reappeared, his head uncovered, giving
the girls ample opportunity to take stock of him. He was of
middle height, slender, wearing a cloak not unlike their own,
handsome with rough-cut features and grey eyes that seemed
to have had insufficient sleep. As he approached them, the
girls were startled at the sight of his ponderous genitals hanging
bare beneath a mass of black hair on the lower belly. Buckled
above the loins was a belt of worn leather, slanting sideways
towards a heavy tawse—a single thong of horsehide, split at
the end. His thorax was bound in narrow straps of leather. He
wore riding boots and small spurs that glinted in the pale light
of the dawn.

Huddling against the stone wall of the archway, the girls
watched the gloved hands wind up the portcullis gateway of
what seemed to be the castle keep. He beckoned to them, his
genitals swaying indolently, threateningly.

"I apologise for the welcome to Beaucastel, Mesdames,"
he said with what the girls took to be Beaucastel irony, "but
please enter. You need warmth and comfort after your journey,
all the way from Amsterdam." The voice was colourless and
flat. Neither girl sought to correct him as to their origin,
dismayed that they were so anonymous. "My name is Restif.
I am your custodian here with the rank of senior valet. You
will address me as 'Sir', just as you will address my superiors,
the overseers, as 'Mistress' and 'Master'. You will never
address a servant, male or female, in any way whatsoever. I
mention these items to avoid you running into serious trouble
in your first moments here. The complete rules of Beaucastel
will be read to you after your induction and following the
marking of your flesh with our house numbers for
identification during training. Your induction will take place
at midday." He paused, looking carefully at the nude slaves.

"You will not speak here unless you are given permission, even during sex. Follow me."

He led them into a small chamber in the gatehouse. It was grossly overheated, so much so that tiny beads of sweat broke out amid the down and faint freckles on Marina's cheeks. Coming out of the cold, the prisoners were taken aback but welcomed the warmth.

"Kindly strip stark naked and place your belongings in the lockers marked '106' and '107' over there." He indicated a long row of square cupboards. "Those are the numbers by which you will be known during your stay at Beaucastel. You will wait here until the overseers summon you for identification. Breakfast will be served in a moment." To the girls' astonishment he asked: "Do you prefer coffee or tea or something else? English, continental or oriental. We cater for all tastes."

As the girls drew off and folded their coverings, adding their sopping sandals, the man approached to check their flesh rings and nodded. "Appropriately ringed, I see. Well and good."

Satisfied, the man left them, nude and solitary in the small, windowless chamber which boasted several chairs, a table and, in full evidence on the wall, a short whip of three tough tongues of bull's hide, far more frightening than anything Claudia and Mikhail had yet contemplated using on them. In the ceiling a heavy ring hung from a hook, which the slaves noted with trepidation. All the objects threw grotesque shadows in the light of a single bulb above the door. But one more item drew their attention: from the far corner, the eye of a video camera stared down at them. Verenka gestured at it with her chin and Marina saw it and grimaced.

Neither dared even whisper in the eerie silence enshrouding them. They merely held hands, standing mute in the chamber, waiting in servile obedience. Then, unexpectedly, their breakfast was brought in and placed on the table. The servant was a dark-haired, lovely woman of about thirty, wearing white stockings and high-heeled shoes, leather manacles around the wrists, ankles and throat but nothing else. Her buttocks had evidently been severely and very recently flogged to judge from the welts. She was not ringed and carried herself with grace. She offered a momentary smile to the two newcomers. "Bon appetit," she wished them softly in broken French. Marina guessed she was from Croatia or perhaps from Slovenia. She was extremely sexual, the sultry sort Marina liked.

The meal was sheer delight; the fresh croissants were hot and soft, the honey trickling viscously. As they ate, Verenka risked a word.

"There's obviously a strict hierarchy here. That female must be a servant, at the foot of the pyramid, and the overseers somewhere near the top, I suppose. This Restif character must be in between, don't you think, darling?"

Marina found it difficult and hazardous to chat. And she was right.

When, sometime later, Restif returned to lead them to their induction, he mentioned the fact. "It is forbidden to speak other than in the slave quarters or, I repeat, when spoken to by senior castle staff. This could earn you thirty lashes on the service trestles in solitary confinement, chained and hooded. In future," he added, "the rules are there to be obeyed. Follow me."

The man deftly released their wrists, placing the chain Claudia had supplied for the journey in one of the cupboards; then he snapped two long chains to the girls' nipple rings and tugged smartly. The procession began.

They walked down what seemed to be endless passages, turning corners, mounting steps and then descending again through labyrinths dimly lit with violet bulbs. At one point on their itinerary, the group passed a naked female outspread wide against the stone wall of the corridor, a huge dildo plunged into her sex, her breasts elongated with heavy spiked weights dangling from chains hooked to the teat rings; she seemed oblivious of her colleagues passing a step from her. Her head lolled downwards as she moaned. The sight unnerved the girls, around the body there roamed a distinct acrid odour of stale semen and obviously she had been there for hours. Restif sensed his charges' hesitation as they stumbled.

"Disobedience," he remarked, wrenching on the chains, "to be fucked, flogged and tortured tonight in the Master's personal cellar. Whore trash!" The girls hurried forward.

Finally, they arrived before a stout studded door. Restif knocked with the shaft of his whip, inclining his head to catch the word of permission to enter.

The room was a surprise. Strewn richly with carpets, mirrors round the stone walls, the place was luxuriously furnished and at a long table sat a woman with a man slightly to the rear. Again, video lenses kept track of the proceedings.

On the wall hung several instruments of flagellation, more, Marina sensed, as decoration than for use, but who could tell? To the right of the couple several gilt-framed notices leaned from the stone; in Gothic script the first read very simply: 'The degree to which flogged slaves surrender themselves to their owners is the sole measure of their worth.' Beyond it, Marina read the second: 'Submission and pain are the harbingers of ecstasy'. Other encouraging messages were beyond her view. Matters were becoming serious.

Behind the desk with its grey computer, the woman was austere. Her eyes were narrowed and dark under the long lashes; her arms, extending from her strap-harnessed chest and superb bare breasts, were enclosed in thin kid gloves from her armpits. Her hair was pageboy style, carefully brushed. Peering at her screen, she did not look up when the group entered.

"Kneel! Thighs open, breasts out, arms across the rump," the valet ordered and now Marina was certain he was probably a chief valet with broad powers. Then the man stood aside, holding his service whip ready for any eventuality, with the right to lash a slave on any pretext and with total impunity.

The woman finally looked up and scrutinized the two superb naked bodies.

"My name is Vasa, principal overseer at Beaucastel. This is Lalanière," she turned her head a fraction, "my colleague. We, together with the other overseers, are charged with your training here. Your owners have paid for this and we shall try to meet their requirements, delivering totally trained flesh in return for their confidence. Your fortnight with us here will be well spent, that I assure you. All laxity, slovenly behaviour or hesitation will be severely punished. You will be taught every conceivable aspect of carnal slavery, some of it will be hard but all will benefit you. You will never be the same after Beaucastel. You will issue forth from here as exquisite sex slaves, worth a great deal on the international market."

She leaned back calmly in her high-back throne. "The simple fact that, as sex slaves, you have graduated through Beaucastel will ensure you of austere, powerful and grateful owners, if ever you are put up for sale or rental."

Beads of perspiration began to gather on both girls' brows; it was not the heat but sheer fear that afflicted them. They dared not regard the woman in the eyes; they kept their heads bowed, as Claudia had taught them. The terrifying Vasa rose and walked round the desk. The girls saw that she was attired in clinging black vinyl that left her bush and crotch bare; the high, glittering boots were in themselves sufficient to scare any slave. Claudia was child's play compared with this threat, Marina thought, beginning to waver. The straps that gripped the Gorgon's firm breasts, like parcels from hell, frightened Verenka too. God help us! And I'll wager, she supposed, the scarlet band round her throat indicates her high rank.

The woman jerked Verenka's right breast up viciously by the teat ring. "Why hasn't this slut been marked?"

She flashed a glance at the valet.

"Neither, Mistress, has been marked yet. They've just arrived."

"Well, see to it immediately afterwards. This slave is 106

and this blonde beauty," she slapped Marina's bosom, is 107. Get it done, man!"

"Yes, Mistress." The man agreed with alacrity. The hierarchical patterns were plain.

While the woman circled round the two kneeling figures, Marina glanced at the man sitting beyond the desk. He was strikingly handsome, a little akin to Mikhail in build and by reason of the pointed beard. He was muscular, well shaped and immensely compelling; she could imagine the man's penis without seeing it—heavy and overpowering, capable of long staying, durable erections and massive ejaculations of opaque, compact semen. She rather liked the long hair brushed back from the brow and the dark eyes.

The overseer Vasa returned to her desk and scrolled down on the computer screen. "I see they are recommended by the Comtesse de Frejaviole—a discriminating sponsor. All seven rings in place, used to the whip and, more or less, to triple orifice usage... I see that a certain amount of sex is recorded here and some degree of flagellation but little or no sex torture. Restif, see to it they are manacled forthwith. The owners, I see, desire the best, permanent fixtures we provide." Then she halted, peering at the screen. "Oh, I see from the curriculum they are lesbians. Well, now..." She paused and leaned over the desk. "I want to make our rules clear, 106 and107. In the slave quarters you can do what you like, sleep together, suck each other off, frig each other stupid but never in session, unless expressly ordered. Moreover, you will be frequently trained separately and put to male slaves for fucking, to assess your competence and adaptability. You are both accustomed, I trust, to the male cock?" There was a silence. "Speak!"

Verenka managed a nod and Marina a sibilant 'yes'.

Vasa acknowledged their bisexual competence by switching off her computer. "Right. That is all. You will have your first course this afternoon at four in Cellar I: naked deportment, overt masturbation and oral sex servicing of other female and male slaves. Elementary, maybe, but essential. Your first

88

flagellation and anal use will be tomorrow at five in Cellar III. Meanwhile you, 106," she gestured at Verenka, "you will service me tonight in my chambers and Lalanière, my friend, you may wish to exercise your prerogatives with the blonde one, 107, exchanging with me tomorrow."

The male overseer did not seem to mind with which flesh he passed the night, as long as the body was attractive enough. He nodded and rose, displaying his superb genitals to the girls for the first time. Marina was right but she caught her breath all the same while Verenka gazed with awe. The cock was at half-erection and superb. A pure monster, a true female's dream—even if Marina and Verenka were inclined towards vulvas. The cock was, of course, the girls deduced, one of the justifications of the man's rank at Beaucastel, apart probably from his qualities as an elegant, experienced flagellator. They wondered how long it would be before they, too, would be transpierced by and impaled on the thing that swayed before them. Only too soon, if they had understood the proposed programme laid out for them.

"I must be getting back, Vasa," he said, kissing her gloved hand. "I have to work on the Swedish bitch also, you know." He uttered a sigh of the overworked.

"What you mean is that you're about to fuck the beautiful English slave! Well, I don't criticize or blame you. We've not had a slave of that quality here for months. As to the Swedish slut, you're becoming infatuated also with that big, obdurate whore of a slave! She needs the crop not the cock. But go ahead."

As he left for either his 'English bitch' or his 'Swedish slut', or both, Vasa issued her final orders to the valet.

"Take them to the Slave Hall, explain the rules, introduce them to the others and allot them bed space."

Both girls rose from their knees at a jerk on their chains from the valet and bowed as Vasa walked majestically out of the induction chamber.

Their first ordeal was over and had proceeded tolerably

well—at least as far as the girls could assess. They were free to meet the other inmates. And perhaps make love.

As they were led back along interminable corridors, some hewn out of the living rock, Verenka strove to lessen the tension on the chain wrenching uncharitably at the rings in her already raw nipples, a traction that, strangely, did not displease her. It excited her and she was aware how the teats connected to her sex.

As they passed the iron rings where they thought they had glimpsed on their way down the nude female hanging, they saw she had disappeared; in her place stood a good-looking, naked youth, heavily chained and almost suspended by a thong round his bunched genitals. He was the first male slave they had seen.

Finally, they entered a wide, pleasantly lighted chamber that stretched a long way to the right. The whole of one side of the room was occupied by a row of beds, each joined to the next; above each bed hung a ring and chain from the wall. Further aloft were a series of barred windows through which the girls saw the morning clouds scudding above the rain. Two huge chandeliers, the bulbs still glowing, threw a mellow light on the scene, which was completed by a long table and benches in the centre of the room. They were in the Slave Hall. And there were a number of females in it.

As Restif detached the nipple chains and designated two mattresses side by side, covered with fresh linen sheets, the slaves looked at the occupants of the hall. All were indeed female, some still in bed, reading or talking, others sitting at the table among the remains of breakfast. A couple of girls were lying enlaced together on the far end of the bedding, obviously making love which Verenka felt was the best augury of the day so far. The man then took a board from the wall and read out the rules in a toneless voice.

While slaves were free to amuse themselves in the Hall, where they ate and slept, they were obliged to obey summons at any time, day or night, to training sessions or to special assignments. Inmates' numbers would be called and immediate attendance was required at the far end of the Hall where the doorway led to the Preparation Chamber and the cellars below, as well as to the Hall of Ceremony. Before attendance at sessions, all slaves would sluice themselves out and present their bodies in total cleanliness.

Clauses followed governing oral contraception and reporting menstruation, after which a long list of punishments was appended, citing errors of conduct, such as lack of hygiene and personal beauty; disobedience; insubordination; attempts to bribe servants with sexual favours—something the girls had not imagined possible. Each item carried with it its specific punishment, so many lashes, so many hours on the cross, so many sessions in Cellar IV—whatever that implied. The final paragraph merely stated that all slaves were at the entire sexual disposal of (1) the Master and guests; (2) the overseers; and (3) the senior valets and maids, at the express discretion of the overseers. Naturally, all sex would be performed stark naked.

Restif rehearsed the list so rapidly that neither girl grasped the half. Then he hung the board on the wall and left, after designating the beds reserved for the newcomers and stating that they would be fitted with their riveted bondage straps that evening.

CHAPTER 9

"Don't worry about the rules. They don't mean a thing." It was a superbly handsome, dark-skinned woman with raven black, cropped hair, who addressed them from the table. She seemed older than the other inmates, sitting around her. "My name's Nastasia, better known as 71, which won't mean much to you except that I've been here quite some time. I've seen slaves come and go. What are your names? Are you here to be sold or just for mere training?" Then she added: "Does either of you play chess or bridge?"

The girls coyly went to their beds and sat on the edge, looking at the inmates. Some were very beautiful, some less so, but all were fascinated at the arrival of the two new slaves.

The dark-skinned woman introduced the others promptly, after asking the girls their names. "This is Krystyna, an old-timer too." She pointed to a completely shaven female, playing cards with another inmate. "She's a Polak and very good fun, you'll see. She's waiting for a buyer too, poor darling. She can take a lot of whipping but just can't find the right owner who likes her body." Then she asked: "I suppose you are owned, no?"

Verenka nodded, looking at the strong, lascivious Polish body at the table. "We're together," she said lamely.

"Oh, you mean you're lesies?" Nastasia smiled. "Well, over there, you have our blonde, freckled Sylvie and her delicious Renée, a bit timid but a nice girl if you can get her to talk. They make love most of the time but you may be able to get a word in sideways. They're owned by a German countess of some sort who wants them toughened up, if we understand the idea. They're rather special, Verenka," she addressed the younger girl as Marina was holding back in embarrassment, "because they have gold rings. Their bitch of an owner is filthily wealthy and flogs them before guests once a week, crucified."

The bald Krystyna laughed. "You're just jealous, darling. Admit it! Leave them alone, Renée's about to come. Can't you hear her groans? Don't distract them."

Nastasia grinned. "Well, over there," she threw out her arm, "is our special companion and someone we really love. Come here, Marie-Laure, and say hello to our new flesh."

A gorgeous redhead, with superb ringed breasts, rose from the table and came across to kiss the new arrivals. "I've been here a week and I'm managing to put up with it. They tease me because I'm allowed to wear high heels but that's what my master requires. It's not my fault!" The woman was extraordinarily sexual to look at. Both girls stared at her perfect body; it was lacerated with whip marks.

It was Krystyna who then continued with the introductions. "Katia, over there, doing crosswords, is our Russian…"

"For the last time, Krystyna, I'm not Russian, I'm Ukrainian!" the well-fleshed woman replied with a smile. "I was an emigrant, you see, and got bought up. The only way I could survive in West Germany. I didn't want to become a simple whore. And anyway, I'm in good hands."

"What she means," put in Nastasia, "is that she has found a master who says he loves her. Isn't that right, Katia? And he beats her into kingdom come."

"So what?" the lovely Katia replied. "That's what I want. And to be looked after as a proper slave should be. He spoils me terribly."

The girls noticed that Katia carried a ring in her septum, hanging to her upper lip. They were learning a great deal very rapidly. And learned even more when Nastasia introduced the lovely Marja.

Pale-skinned, thin, with a boy's slender body, Marja had been the slave of an important industrialist who, said Nastasia, adored her but flogged her mercilessly and offered her to guests night after night, weighted with chains, hooded and pierced with scores of needles. "She's here, aren't you, darling, to be sold as your master's fed up with you! And to learn how torture is inflicted on lovely tits? As if a competent slave hadn't already enjoyed that mundane entertainment! Marja's really only half trained, aren't you, sweetheart?"

"Maybe," the sallow-fleshed girl admitted, "but I can take the quirt over my breasts now, which is probably more than you can, Nastasia."

"Oh, for goodness sake, Marja, my darling. I've had that and cunt flogging, which is more than you've had. But you've only another week and then, who knows? Back to Dusseldorf or wherever, if ever you get purchased!"

The girls listened in trepidation. "Then, there's our Birgit. She's our oldest," Nastasia went on. She seemed obviously to be the head girl in rank in the Slave Hall, even if, apparently, she too was for sale. "Well, Birgit's not here for the moment. She's undergoing sex torture down below. She's the slave of a very important couple of Swedes who want her to be relegated to total subjugation and, for some reason, quite beyond us docile darlings, she refuses to give in, I mean to fellate and do normal sex service. She thinks she is adequate as she is. Which obviously is not her owners' conception of her role. Our Birgit, flogged and tortured, but refusing any other cock or clit but those of her owners! And she has still four days to go, if not longer."

Krystyna added her view of things. "Birgit is trying to outplay Beaucastel, the poor whore. Here one gives in and learns, as Ashley, our princess, would tell you, were she here. She's been down in the cellars a long time—probably with Lalanière, poor thing."

Almost at the same moment as this was said, the girls saw a woman enter the Hall from the far end. She was so beautiful, so exquisitely modelled and moulded that the girls held their breath. It was obvious she had just been flagellated—and certainly used sexually—to judge by her condition. Restif led her to her bed, released her nipple chains, and left her lying on the sheets, breathing heavily with pain. She was extraordinarily lovely.

"Well, talk of the devil!" the high-heeled Marie-Laure exclaimed. "There she is, our princess, well beaten, as usual, but at least not on the cross, for a change."

She indicated a monstrous crucifix in the penumbra at the end of the hall. "This girl can take more than any of us. That's

94

Ashley. English and tough!"

The two girls looked at the reclining body. It was true that she had been severely whipped but the woman did not seem extenuated. She even lifted her head to glance at the newcomers.

"It's senseless, all this flogging," Nastasia remarked. "We are trained already but the overseers, and particularly those bitches Gerda and Gabrielle, take delight in reducing us to flagellated flesh. There's no reason for such beatings, except to pleasure them."

Suddenly, the beautiful English girl rose from her bunk to walk unsteadily towards the group. She was more than superb. Her body was unadulterated sexual beauty; immaculate except for the lash marks across most of her flesh, utterly lovely in all its respects: the breasts were flawless with full nipples reaching outwards, the belly withdrawn over the swell of the thickly haired pubis. The thighs were magnificent. Neither girl had seen a body to rival the splendour of Ashley's. The face was serene, framed in chestnut hair, which although matted and dishevelled after her ordeal, curled round her neck. The eyes were still wide and tearful from the effect of the treatment she had just endured.

"What are you telling these new girls?" she said softly. "You have all become whip happy and miss the point."

Exhausted, she leaned carefully with one thigh against the edge of the table before the two girls. "Don't ever listen to slaves who seek a master or a mistress! My name's Ashley. What are yours?"

The newcomers introduced themselves, gazing at the spectacular body. They noticed that her sex was carrying at least ten rings pierced through the inner and outer lips, the mass of metal gathered to a point and linked firmly with a padlock, enclosing the entry to the vagina. The clitoris ring was dragged down to espouse the same imprisonment.

"I don't know what they have been telling you two," Ashley said, "but let me just say that you are here to learn. To give your bodies to the whip and to cocks and clits until you are competent slaves. If that is what your proud owners demand of you, then you must obey and surrender your flesh to what these people here are paid to do. Only with training," she said earnestly, "can you become properly submissive slaves. The pain is immaterial—the pleasure, for yourselves and for your owners, is the criterion. That is what this place is here for. To make sexual slaves of us. If that is what you want to be, well and good. If not, then you protest like Birgit or Nastasia here."

"I don't protest!" Nastasia frowned. "I just think these overseers and valets take sexual advantage of us, whipping and fucking us whenever they feel like it."

"Nastasia, darling, that's not true! They have a duty to perform. You're just a body slave like me. Accept your calling and become a true, dedicated sex slave and accept. That's what we're made for as sexual submissives. Be proud of your humiliation."

The girls listened with awe to Ashley. Indeed, they too were sex slaves, even if they were novices, and basically their deepest wish, apart from staying together, was to serve their owners. Ashley was right. Sex slaves served their masters and mistresses sexually and erotically. That was all there was to it. Otherwise, one retracted and became a housewife, a pathetic bourgeoisie going to market. A nothing.

"It's all very well, Ashley darling," Krystyna objected, "for you to preach subservience and obedience. You endure the whip better than any of us and have special sessions with all the overseers because of your wonderful body but you're safe and sound in the hands of loving owners, powerful people who adore you. Some of us are just saleable flesh."

"Maybe, but it's up to you to relinquish yourselves totally to sex and flagellation and sex torture, if that's what you aspire to. Otherwise you'll be on sale for a long while."

Nastasia and the others knew she was right. They held back too often.

Co-operate docilely, surrender to their whips and irons and

bodkins, and try to enjoy the endless nights in the cellars, stretched naked and hooded, awaiting the inevitable lash across the breasts and belly. That was Beaucastel

Ashley became less formal and sat down at the table, though her buttocks pained her. The group then told the newcomers what awaited them: the summons to the cellars, the unpredictable subterfuges of the maids and valets when they wanted sex and, above all, the horrendous week-end sessions in the Hall of Ceremony in the presence of the Master, buyers and owners who were anxious to see the progress made on their slaves.

Then they mentioned Alana. "Quite apart from the warder Gabrielle, be very careful of Alana," Krystyna warned the girls. Alana was neither slave nor servant; she was below the level of both but attended all sequences of preparation, training and whippings. She seemed doomed to act as a house slave; being used for any task the servants, maids or menials found distasteful or demeaning. She was always naked, carrying a pair of chains linking her neck, wrists and ankles. The inmates feared her since she seemed to ferret herself everywhere, listening in to conversations and reporting all to the valet, Restif, who used the slut unashamedly and openly. Alana's rump was consistently welted with crimson and purple bruises; she was scourged daily, it appeared, which merely sharpened her gifts of espionage. Moreover, Marie-Laure informed the newcomers, it was Alana whom the overseers charged with organizing one of the games popular among the valets and maids as entertainment and a pastime to while away the time between formal sessions.

"It's called 'Dodging the Candle'," the lovely redhead told them.

"Candle?" Verenka's queried.

"Not for what you think a girl uses a candle, Verenka! No, a nasty bit of spiteful fun they have at our expense. Tell them, Katia. You had it the other night in the valets' quarters."

In her exotic Russian accent, the golden-haired woman

explained that a slave was bound to a trestle with her torso bent forward horizontal with the ground and held there by binding the arms to an overhead chain behind the back. The breasts thus hung over a low table or stool advanced beneath them; on this Alana placed a couple of lighted candles just below the slave's nipples. To avoid being burnt, the girl was obliged, to the delight of the onlookers, to rotate the torso to keep her breasts swinging over and across the flames. The valets would keep the slave swivelling frantically from side to side for long periods until she sagged exhausted and the metal of the rings began heating in the flames. Then, guffawing, the company would order Alana to snuff out the candles, allowing the enfeebled slave to slump forwards with relief, only to receive a lashing across the buttocks for good measure. The beating was almost a welcome respite, for the extremities of the breasts could suffer badly over the candles. "If you don't dodge them," Katia concluded.

The girls heard many stories of the same type but above all they paid particular attention to Nastasia's description of the overseers, valets and service maids. As to the Master of Beaucastel, no one present had ever really seen him, even in the Hall of Ceremony where he appeared during the end-of-week formal sessions with guests; the light in the Hall was too dim to allow the slaves to discern his features. If ever, Krystyna added, a slave was taken up to the Master's luxurious apartments for his amusement which was rarely pleasant— she was usually hooded, gagged and chained, seeing and hearing nothing but feeling a great deal. Depending on the number of slaves in residence at any given time, Beaucastel functioned on a two-shift system: the overseers Vasa and Lalanière were assisted by the valet Restif; the overseers Roscoff and the dreaded Gerda having the equally feared Gabrielle as assistant. Overseers had total rights over slaves' bodies and could delegate these to the valet or service maid, empowering them to scourge. Natasia pointed out that such rules were rarely observed—a slave could be seized at any time of day or night by Restif or Gabrielle, flogged, tortured or used sexually with absolute impunity. There was little an inmate could do about the situation since, to report such licence and laxity to the overseers, would merely result in a rough night, spread naked with chains weighting the flesh rings, in one of the torture cells below the cellars, with Restif or Gabrielle—or often both—in very active attendance. Therefore, bear it and try to smile, was the motto, and emerge from Beaucastel as little damaged as possible.

When lunch came, it was delicious, served in expensive Gien crockery, silverware and crystal by nude waitresses— the term 'maid' (femme de salle) Marina discovered was reserved for the female version of the valet. The inmates sat on the long velvet-covered benches—a trifle stained with sex juices here and there—and chatted gaily, telling their individual stories, which fascinated the new arrivals. They also described the underworld of Beaucastel and some of the arcane procedures, essential knowledge for survival. They described the various cellars: Cell One where deportment and sexual servicing was taught, frequently with the help of male slaves, brought over in erection from the masculine prisons; Cell Two where worn-out, jaded slaves were recycled with the encouragement of the breast quirt; Cell Three that dealt exclusively with triple orifice penetrations and the manner in which females should react to stringent, dutiful servicing.

Nastasia then depicted the performances that took place in Cell Four, a place to be avoided at all costs—and she knew its uses—for there sex torture with tongs, ropes and bodkins was applied to the slave bodies, principally on the breasts and sex.

"Then, there's Cell Five where they deal with male slaves and where probably, as you're new, you'll have to participate. But that's rather fun if, like me, you relish a stout cock bound up in leathers and loads of hot spunk. Plenty of spunk there."

There was a silence before Ashley spoke. "Cell Six is rather special and I must say I've never been in there, thank goodness."

Verenka wanted the whole picture. "Well, Ashley, what goes on there?"

"The last slave we saw go into that cell was Mirta. She's gone now, back to her boat on the Adriatic or somewhere, branded with her owners' initials on both buttocks and over the shaved pubis. It marked her terribly but she was so proud. Yes, they brand very neatly with white-hot irons—but that's the owners' requirement." She paused before enquiring: "Do you think your people have ordered branding for you? It's very popular these days."

Marina frowned. "God forbid!" she exclaimed, seating herself on the bench next to Katia, the Ukrainian girl with the septum ring in her nose. "I don't think our proprietors would go that far. I wouldn't stand for it."

Katia smiled and stroked the girl's pubis. "You never know, dearest. You never know. The point is that, once you're branded, there's little likelihood of your owners discarding you. A branded slave is not worth much on the market, you see. You're theirs for good, in a way. It only takes a minute but it's there for eternity."

It was Ashley, the gorgeous English femme fatale, who again took up the listing of cellars; she knew most of them well after her fortnight of refresher training. "Cell Seven is a particularly unpleasant place," she wrinkled her lovely nose as she spoke, "but I guess you'll have to get to know it sooner or later. A lot of whipping goes on there and sex torture to bring you to the level they want. Impalement, too. But once you've been through that, your price goes up fantastically…"

"But we're not for sale!" Marina choked as she said it. "Ashley, we're not for sale!"

"Well, they're lucky, aren't they?" Ashley shook her chestnut hair back and fingered her sex rings, looking round at her colleagues. "But you won't escape whipping, especially with Gerda. The others, and particularly Lalanière, are fairly tolerable. But not Gerda."

When lunch was over and the coffee offered by the nude

serving girls, Verenka and Marina were shown around. First, they were conducted by the shaved Renée, content with two orgasms with her freckled Sylvie before lunch, to the cleansing rooms. The bathroom was magnificent, equipped with deep floor-level baths of black marble and faucets in the shape of swans' beaks. Beyond were two saunas, a large Turkish bath, in which the slender form of Marja was sweating naked on the porcelain tiles. To the side yawned a sort of boudoir lined with shelves, ladened with flasks and phials of perfumed oils; a slab of stone reared in the centre. It was evidently there, Marina guessed, that the slave bodies were flushed out and scented for their descent into the cellars. Strangely, the scene excited and frightened her and she told Verenka so.

"You smell good as you are, darling." And Verenka kissed the girl's teats in rapture. She was beginning to enjoy the place.

That evening, Restif handed over the two newcomers to Gabrielle. The woman was booted with black stockings appearing above, over the thighs; her sex was shaved and alluringly plump, split by a raw length of leather that cut into the slit, to disappear between the cheeks of the strong buttocks. The belt she wore was broad, adorned with a golden buckle above the pubis, and from it, next to a bunch of keys, hung a classical quirt, the lashes punctured along their short length with holes pierced into the five digits of tough hide. Her ash-blonde hair, drawn strictly back, glistened on either side of a handsome face with sensuous lips and unusual eyes; there was an almost imperceptible strabismus in them, which lent her a look of immense, mean cruelty.

Her fine breasts swinging heavily above the nudes, Gabrielle affixed the bondage straps to the girls' limbs, laying the bodies over the slab in the bathroom area. It was done in silence, the rivets being flattened with the bondage, clamping tool. Each manacle, lined with felt, fitted perfectly, boasting a ring at each ankle and wrist and four equally spaced rings in the throat strap; the steel rings matched the girls' flesh rings in size and weight. Stoically, Verenka and Marina accepted the bondage, exalted at last to be like their colleagues. Gabrielle then marked the underside of each girl's left breast with the requisite slave number, using special indelible ink. They were ready.

The girls rose, sensing the grip of the leathers of slavery, and knelt before their female warder.

"You are free for the evening—except for your routine sex service, naturally, later with the overseers. Tomorrow, you will both be summoned and dealt with in Cell I. I hope you enjoy it. It's fairly mild." Then she added: "To begin with."

With that, the half-naked warder allowed the girls to return to the Slave Hall.

As they rejoined the group, they experienced a bizarre sensation; both sexes were flooded, leaking with lust occasioned by the bondaging. Without a word of greeting to the others, Verenka drew her lover to the bed.

"Suck me off, darling. I can't wait."

As the group prepared for dinner, no one paid the least attention to the festivity of predatory cunnilingus, even when Verenka screamed obscenely, juddering under Marina's tongue, mucilage discharging viscously over the girl's face. Four closed-circuit TV cameras in the Slave Hall recorded the orgasms faithfully—no doubt, Katia added, for the benefit of the Master monitoring somewhere in the far reaches of the castle.

The deportment session in Cell I the next day was lenient. At least, both girls were allowed to carry out together their posturing, walking and naked exhibitioning, which delighted them. Lalanière seemed content, as did Vasa who watched with professional concern. The girls' performance the night before in the overseers' quarters had been proficient, despite their apprehension; Lalanière had hammered Marina with energy, surging into her sex and throat but fortunately sparing her anus. Vasa had discovered in Verenka a new delight; the slave sucked with avid competence. The girls regained confidence but were glad to return to their beds.

Profound enjoyment was the hallmark of the next day. Each

inmate recounted her experience in the outside world. Nastasia and Krystyna had been left high and dry by owners, who had selected younger and more voracious body slaves; neither knew what awaited them if and when, in a week-end ceremony, they might be purchased or at least rented. The lesbians, Sylvie and Renée, who rarely left each other's arms, declared themselves deliriously happy with their wealthy proprietor; true, they were beaten, put on show hung together by the ankles, made to perform on each other's crotch and given to guests without discrimination but they adored it all.

Her red hair cut short, forever striding around on her high heels, Marie-Laure seemed to constitute the most highly-sexed of the inmates; she yearned for sex, in whatever form, ceaselessly but her owner required she be trained for more serious flogging than she was used to. She longed to return to her beloved master who, she confided nervously, owned a second whipping slave whose performances in bed and on the trestles were a manifest threat to her. But Beaucastel had done her a world of good. As to Katia and Marja they were apparently both treated atrociously; secretly they hoped their dissatisfied owners would agree to arrange an exchange between them, now they had learnt to withstand the power of the overseers' cocks and whips.

As to Ashley, the resplendent Ashley, Verenka found her immensely attractive, never failing to smile at her when they were at table together.

The girls felt comforted and exceptionally fortunate. Claudia and Mishka—and even Gemma—were worth Beaucastel.

The drama took place the following evening.

The two girls were separated for the first time, Marina being summoned to the Preparation Chamber at nine, alone. After being sluiced out, greased and perfumed, she was hooded up cruelly, depriving her of all her senses except that which allowed her to feel; her seven flesh rings were weighted with gross iron spheres that hauled her fragile extremities to lengths she did not believe possible. She screamed mutely within the

103

grappling clasp of the leather hood, the gag suffocating her. Led down, stumbling, dragged on the end of a tight chain, she felt herself being thrust into a sweltering, confined space. Cell I was not like this, she panicked. That tame place had carpets, she recalled. Oh, no, could it be Cell Three, perhaps? Surely not Cell Four! After just two days! Surely not that place! Her mind reeled with progressive waves of utter fear. Her womb clenched within her. Instead of lush carpets, the ground under her bare feet seemed to be strewn with straw and gravel. She felt the presence of human beings around her nudity; gloved hands armed with trenchant barbs caressed her sweating ribs as she was tugged forwards blind, deaf and speechless. She was too paralysed to react to her terror.

Then she was spread, the wrist rings clinking as they were hooked to chains, to be lifted abruptly off her feet. The thigh joints cracked as the limbs were parted to their utmost reach and tied; she sensed her labial folds gape, despite the lugging weights dragging them down, wrenching the clitoris hood from the cusp of her sex. Her moans were lost in the taut leather as she thrashed her masked head madly, champing on the enormous gag. Voiceless, she shrieked for Verenka, for Claudia, for Mikhail, even for Vasa—anyone to help her. In her striving innocence, she could not know that Vasa stood one step from the gorgeous hollowed thorax, running a plaited scourge through her gloved fingers, waiting until Lalanière had, with Gabrielle's eager pull on the limbs, satisfactorily secured the writhing slave flesh that had to be educated.

She received the scourging over the buttocks, thighs and belly in raving pain, trying to heave her body away from the lashes, the iron spheres rebounding against her nude abdomen and between the tensed thigh muscles. The body was honoured with the whips of both overseers, laid on viciously and precisely. The white flesh welted readily, perfectly.

Suddenly it was over and she was penetrated where she hung, the voluptuous cock thrusting past the dangling clit chain to thud and ream the innermost reaches of her dripping, clenching vagina. Clawing with her fingers on the bonds that tore her arms upwards, Marina felt the inexorable, inexplicable response seething deep within her. Then she orgasmed in a lightning flash of sensual craving, responding without restraint, frantic with lust. The whipping had brought her to a height she had never known—not even with Mikhail inside her. The floggers appreciated the muffled shrieks; they were supremely aware that pain had duly led into pleasure. That was their objective.

It was close on four in the morning, the rain beating against the barred windows of the Hall, when the slave was led back to the dormitory, relieved of her chains and hood, slick with sweat, flushed full with acrid semen.

She was thrown on her bed without even being linked to the statutory wall hook. A flogged slave rarely presented the need for even token bondage. In any event and to take account of their physical needs during the night, the girls were only cursorily hooked by their collars to the rings cemented in above their beds, predominantly to remind them, even in sleep, of their servitude.

Sobbing and shaken by the flagellation and her orgasm, she sought compassion. Marina groped instinctively for her lover. The bed was empty. Raising herself on her elbow in alarm, the girl peered into the penumbra of the Hall. Her heart missed a beat, her eyes widening in disbelief.

Verenka was in Ashley's arms seven beds further down.

CHAPTER 10

The rain had cleared outside, as far as the inmates could tell, but storms were threatening, the principal one being Marina's fury. The other girls, even when they were summoned to the training cellars, had to smile at the local problem that had arisen. After all, they were all sex slaves and sex was their stock in trade. The mere fact that one girl slept with another was of no importance; a body was a body with breasts and a ready sex; only vicious beating and unmitigated torture would deter them from enjoying whatever was at hand. No one could understand Marina's anger. She kept herself apart and even had her place on the row of beds changed. She refused to address a word to Verenka who offered no sympathy for the session Marina had undergone below the previous night. Nastasia attempted to mend the rift but was curtly spurned by Marina.

"Leave me alone," she muttered, "and get yourself an owner." The insult not only hurt Nastasia but also shocked the others.

The training sessions proceeded regularly, the girls being used and abused as usual. The conversation diminished, the females taking up the pornographic literature to read, playing chess and maintaining a healthy distance between the two lovers and themselves. Marina was not called below throughout the following days and nights, although she was taken by Gabrielle twice to her rooms and returned exhausted, severely whipped for no reason.

As the weekend approached, the group began to preen their appearances, particularly those who anxiously awaited buyers. The initial three days and nights of education had, contrary to Verenka, appalled Marina. Verenka seemed to accept the strictly imposed exigencies with equanimity and even a curious excitement; she was well accustomed to being handled naked and used in all orifices. Above all, she was ready for the whip, displaying the magnificence of her nude body, fully aware of its effect on the overseers carrying out their duties with spontaneous lust. She participated willingly with whatever the fornicating floggers did to her. Marina deplored the ceremonial antics of the grim, leather-clad torturers, and suffered increasingly from the stringency of bondage and scourging. She exerted her sexual powers to the best of her diminishing ability; the co-operation demanded of her began to take its toll.

The callous, flagrant treachery and venality of her lover infuriated her. Even when Verenka attempted to reason with her—"it's only sex, darling, just unvarnished sex, nothing more"—and tried to cajole her into bed again, Marina fulminated, crazy with resentment. The other inmates exercised discretion, leaving the pair to settle their dispute alone. Curiously, it was Birgit who consoled Marina. With touching compassion, she claimed that, for different reasons, they were, both of them, wronged and humiliated.

Sitting on Birgit's bunk the next day during the lazy, after-lunch period of rest, Marina confided in her, looking into the handsome Swedish eyes that reflected the azure of her Scandinavian lakes and also the blue whip marks over her rump and breasts.

"Birgit," her voice was no more than a whisper, "I'm going to escape."

An old-timer, Birgit was not overly disturbed but she warned her of the dangers.

"Just think what they would do to you if you were caught. And your owners! Imagine their embarrassment after all the trust they put in you and in this stupid place. I would never do that, darling, but then I love my wonderful owners and don't condescend to bow before these so-called educators. They're just vicious professionals without elegance."

Yet Birgit was understanding. Acquainted intimately with Beaucastel, she offered her counsel with genuine, candid affection.

"Listen, darling. There's a guy who cleans out the ablution

rooms adjacent to the Preparation Chamber, a squat, ugly fellow but amenable. You see, he's not permitted access to our bodies. He's a menial."

Marina listened carefully with the serious expression of a decided woman.

Birgit suggested that, for a small price, the man could be tempted to arrange for a slave to abscond—at least, that was the rumour. It appeared that a ravishing Lithuanian slave whose spirit had been broken in Cell Seven some two months before, had concluded a sort of contract involving her flesh and money, and had escaped. Birgit admitted she did not know the result; it was before her first visit but the attempt had been made. One had to trust people, which at Beaucastel was perilous but nevertheless feasible.

With a courage that startled even herself, Marina made the decision and, at the moment when the man was scouring out the ablution room, discussed rapidly with him.

The precise timing was fixed, with instructions how to elude the vigilant video cameras by crawling to the door leading to the small garden surrounded by the castle walls; how to scuttle across the opening and enter the gardeners' shed in the yard where the man would await the slave. While striking the bargain, the loutish under-valet stared at the exquisite, sophisticated nude before him whose body, by reason of his subordinate rank, was beyond his jurisdiction.

In return for an agreed sum to be paid indirectly to him once the slave was safely home and for the full use of her body during the night, the individual undertook to provide money for the journey by the 0715 hours express from Rodez to Paris, as well as a cloak and shoes. She would, after being fucked in the shed, leave by the wicket-gate in the nearby wall, used for deliveries to the castle. Despite the hour, he agreed to arrange by phone for a taxi to convey Marina to the station; it would be waiting at the last oak on the descending pathway.

She would have only an hour or two to wait for the train.

Beaucastel, he assured her, would be still dormant.

He would await her at 2 a.m. in the shack.

With a racing heart and a last piece of advice from her Swedish confidante, she went to bed and read, waiting for the moment, within earshot of Verenka's perfidious groaning beneath Ashley's sweating body. Except for Nastasia, whose tender, heavily ringed labia were being attended to by Roscoff and Gerda in Cell VII, the other inmates were all asleep. The Slave Hall lights had long since dimmed to a glimmer.

Close on two o'clock, Marina nervously slipped off her neck chain; with one last glance at Verenka writhing under Ashley, she crawled out of the Slave Hall on hands and knees, her flesh rings hanging loose. She avoided the cameras and the faint lights.

Sleet was falling in chilling curtains over the deserted courtyard as she ran, slithering, towards the hut where her flunkey was waiting. The door creaked open to reveal a bare interior with a bed, table and rickety chairs; despite the small fire burning in a grate, the place was rife with the mephitic smell of earth and potted plants.

In the centre of the room, lit by a single candle, stood the ally, his breeches open, revealing a sizeable cock in total erection. Marina admitted to herself that she had seen less attractive shafts.

She was used with disgusting haste, after being thrown face down across the table. The man took her savagely, without a word, among the flowerpots and gardening tools, first penetrating her behind cruelly; then it was the throat and finally, after restraining himself over the half hour of brutal viciousness, in the sex that was dry and sapless with tension. Never had Marina been taken with such force. Tugging on the nipple rings, the man grunted once and came; she felt the successive jets of thick cream jerk into her vagina. Her own orgasm was as far away as the train at Rodez; she grasped the sides of the table, longing for the nightmare to be over. She felt dispossessed of her sexuality—a mere object with holes.

The nauseating figure threw the cloak and shoes at her feet as she rose, hurt and humiliated to a degree she found loathsome. But it would be worth it...

"Get out of here, whore!" the creature muttered, buttoning up his crotch. "The wicket gate's open. Over there." He pointed across the sleeting cold of the yard beyond the filthy window. Marina shuffled into the shoes, twice too big for her, and gathered the rough cloak around her. She made for the gate, gratefully grasping four 100-franc notes offered.

Hesitatingly, she fumbled with the latch, her fingers frigid again after the man's warmth and the heat of the shack. She eased the wicket-gate ajar. A floodlight suddenly shattered the streaks of sleet; she stood face to face with Restif leaning nonchalantly against the doorjamb, a braided horsewhip in hand. At his side three mastiffs slobbered.

"Let's go back to the warm Hall, slave, shall we?" His voice was calm. "It's far too cold to be walking around the countryside almost naked at this time of night."

He ripped off the girl's cloak to deliver a blow of the doubled whip across the buttocks. The stroke left a fierce, purple laceration from the hipbone to the lower thigh as Marina crumpled in agony.

"We don't want a sick slave in the house, do we? Get back, you brainless whore, into your cosy bunk before I flay the goose-fleshed hide off you!"

In Marina's head dumb phrases formed: Let me go, you bastard. I've had enough of this place. Don't you touch me again. But her throat was clogged with fear.

Restif threaded the lash of his whip through the girl's clitoris ring, doubling it back again into his grasp and hauling her towards the castle. Marina seized the leather with both her hands to protect her distending flesh below. She was soaked with sleet, quivering.

"What would your lesbian slave friend say to leaving her all alone?" the man asked sardonically. "And your owners? And the Master? Ungrateful slut! You'll be whipped to the blood for this."

While Restif threw her on to her bed, heads bobbed up round the Hall at the commotion. Such interruptions were common whenever slaves were abruptly dragged out from their repose or brought back, flagellated and running with semen. The inmates turned over and went back to sleep.

Marina burst into tears, quaking from the shock of the treason and the shock of her abortive escape. I should have known better, she sobbed. The bastards, the black bastards, she moaned, running her fingers along the welt of the whip's lash that by then had flared up in a gruesome ridge over her buttock meat. It was the token of what her stupidity deserved. Somehow she managed to drift into a fitful sleep, as the dawn slowly coloured the barred windows high in the Hall masonry with the sickly hue of an early winter morning. At first, Marina's flesh rings lay like circles of ice on her loins and on the taut, frozen teats of her resplendent breasts; then they warmed and, singularly, she was content to be back in her bed, anguished and perhaps disparaged, but among her sister slaves again. One cannot elude one's destiny. If only Verenka would come to her with her incandescent body.

It was Birgit who sidled up to her bed, long after breakfast had been served by the naked servants.

"Try to sleep, darling," she soothed and kissed the girl on the lips with a furtive gentleness. "Well, you tried. You have guts, I must say," she murmured. "Now you'll have to pay for your recklessness. I warned you but, darling Marina, don't blame me."

"I'm not blaming anyone, Birgit. Really. Not even Verenka."

At that moment, her lover passed by. "What a scatty thing to do!" Verenka remarked, holding one of Ashley's buttock cheeks in her hand. "You don't own me, Marina!"

The terse remark only made her lover burst into tears again.

Behind the sinister walls of Beaucastel, Restif's punctilious report of the attempted escape traced its inevitable way up through the overseers to the Master of Beaucastel. In the course of the day, the Master duly admonished the servant implicated in the event, adding a word of appreciation for his reliability in informing higher authority of the slave's intentions. The journey money offered to Marina was promptly restored to him with the Master's thanks; the man's conduct would certainly weigh in his favour when it came to future promotions to the rank of senior valets.

As to sex slave 107 herself, there would have to be consultation regarding her impending punishment; this involved not only the overseers but also her owners in Paris. The Master of Beaucastel decreed that the weekend in the Hall of Ceremony would be devoted to that punishment. He desired it to be just, ferocious and unforgettable.

The reputation of Beaucastel had been blemished by a misguided female and this naturally had to be suitably redressed in public session with the whip. And later in the dreaded Black Cellar that only Birgit had experienced.

Claudia happened to be in at the Quai d'Anjou when the call came through.

She was mortified. The little bitch had done this to her! What would Juliette think? It was shocking. A sex slave in whom she had confidence kicking over the traces! The irresponsible slut needed an impressive correction.

On the phone the Master proposed a special session that weekend at which he desired Mikhail and Claudia to be present. He asked if he could be given a free hand. Without seeking the endorsement of Mikhail, who was in New York on business, Claudia assented.

"Master," she responded immediately, "please apply your most strenuous and most austere rules to the woman. We shall be present. Of that I can assure you!"

She instantly put in a call to her lover and Mikhail flew back for the Friday in order to travel down with Claudia to Beaucastel.

Meanwhile, Marina had been summoned into the august presence of the Master. Led by Vasa, who had now taken over possession from the valet, the slave was towed by a chain, snapped into her nipple rings into the fabulously furnished apartments of the owner of Beaucastel with its mixture of odours, of exotic perfumes, of rich leather and cigar smoke but also of flesh and the acrid scent of sex. Marina trembled as she was drawn through the great door, marked with crossed whips, the crest being headed with an erect penis. Beneath the heraldic regalia, a scroll read: 'The tawse cures all ambition'. It seemed tragically appropriate.

What Marina saw of the enormous room was superficial but she sensed the luxury: richly silenced with thick Iranian carpets and surrounded with antiques. Glancing furtively at the inlaid cabinet, she caught sight of the display of priceless Lalique vases, jade curios, aged opium pipes and snuff boxes. On the velvet-draped wall to the left hung a series of preciously worked whipping quirts, fashioned from Turkish leather embossed with flowers, the five tongues pierced with holes which Marina knew by now were there to blister the victim's flesh. Dozens of other whips of different sorts were suspended there, hideous but erotic thongs from silver hooks, resembling trophies. On the oak desk stood a grey computer and above leaned a row of flickering screens monitoring the chambers of the castle; on one Marina glimpsed Gerda suspending Marja's boyish body by the wrists from a meat hook in one of the more frightening cells, probably, Marina thought, Cell Four.

To the right reared an exquisitely carved trestle bristling with barbed studs, crimson silken cords lying fastidiously curled at the feet of the uprights. Marina experienced a contraction in her gut as she recognized the pyramid to be a ceremonial flogging frame that she had heard about in the Slave Hall. Something to be avoided at all costs…

Before Vasa could order her to lower her head and kneel, Marina saw the figure reposing on the huge bed. The man's ascetic face was sallow, the cheeks hollow below cold, grey eyes, the thinning hair brushed back from a high forehead.

113

He wore a strange kimono of woven silk, open over his body. To his right knelt a thin, immensely attractive female with cropped hair, rather like Marina's own, the colour of rye ripe for harvest. She was gently but firmly masturbating the man's glistening erection that reared up from a completely shaven groin; she massaged the cock with one hand, kneading the base of the scrotum with the other. Her tongue protruded, ready to lap over the bulbous, meaty head when the gathering semen finally spurted…

The man calmly scrutinized his papers, casting page after page to the floor when read. He did not look up as the couple entered. Then, with lethargy, he raised his head

"Report!" The tone alone sent a tremor through Marina's entrails as she knelt in fear.

Vasa brought Marina forward with a wrench on her nipples. She now lay prostrate.

"The lesbian whore slave, Master, who attempted escape. Brought before your Honour for judgement."

The Master regarded the extended body, its face against the carpet.

"An extremely sexual, succulent body," the remark was almost clinical. "Has she been routinely flogged?"

"Yes, Master, every day," Vasa replied, "twenty-one lashes. She takes it well."

The man stared down at Marina and again complimented her. "The body is worth the lash. The slave is admirable and succulent. But attempted escape is inexcusable." The man bent the masturbating woman's head forward towards his groin.

"Suck, slave," he ordered. The naked woman leaned forward and swallowed the cock into her throat, down to the base, still grasping the sack of heavy balls. Almost unconscious of the expert fellatio, the man looked at Marina, who slightly envied the sanctioned slave's mouth gluttonising the huge shaft of veined meat. If only she were to be given the chance to suck that magnificent stake of manhood, she might be able to mitigate the terrible punishment that awaited her; her own body was as majestic as that of the slave now servicing her Master. The bitch was not even ringed; she was just a common flesh whore, of which there were many in the castle; but she had the Master's cock in her mouth.

"Let her be prepared, fully weighted on all rings, for the week-end ceremony. She will suffer alone. You know the ritual. Hung by the four limbs, belly down, and scourged by all four of you. Then the Black Dungeon—hung by the legs and crotch-flogged. Hung by the breasts and the body whipped to the blood. Maximum force, if I make myself clear?"

Stupefied, Marina drew her breath with a hiss through her teeth, her head laid sideways on the rich carpet, the rump high in the air. So, patently, what Birgit had recounted a day or two before was true: blood could be drawn, very rarely in the training cells but irrevocably in the Hall of Ceremony for gross infractions and, above all, in the Black Cellar or Dungeon, without the least solicitude for the victim's body.

Marina clenched her teeth. Ask for pardon? Appeal to her owners? Her mind reeled. But she shrewdly brought her thoughts together as best she could. At least she could attempt to seek a modicum of compassion. She prepared her words inwardly as the man continued to watch the whore-slave descend and mount his erection.

Suddenly the Master looked down at Marina. "Do you have anything to say, slave?"

Marina saw her chance. She lifted her blonde head and tense neck, the throat collar crushing her arteries.

"No, Master," she murmured, her cheek off the carpet; her wrists, bound behind her neck, were also in intense pain. "I should like permission to suck your cock, sir, and draw sperm. It would be an honour for a guilty slave."

"Then since you make no appeal for clemency, I see no reason why you should not enjoy your last moments of freedom. Suck and receive my discharge. It may give you some courage for what is to going to be done to your body.

Rise and fellate."

Vasa was astonished at Marina's audacity, yet she admired her for it. She helped the girl to struggle to her feet but declined to release the wrists, despite Marina's pleading look, for her hands had, with Mikhail, become highly adroit on the male genitals. The Master kicked his fellating slave aside and held his cock towards Marina.

"Since you have the insolence to propose it, suck me out slave. The better you fellate, the less will be your future pain." Marina bowed her head low as the man went on. The man's hairless genitals intrigued her. "Whatever prowess you display on my cock that you have the pluck to say you desire, will be taken into account in your sentence. You may be a docile sex slave—when you are not attempting evasion—but you are also a brave, intrepid woman and the sort that appeals to me. The type I like to have around me here as staff in Beaucastel."

The Master shifted on his pillows, holding his erection firmly. "Get to work and suck the life-giving semen out of my shaft. I permit you to swallow rather than to hold the semen and inject it into this whore's mouth or sex—which is our usual practice with two females at work on me. This sex slave of mine here," he jerked his chin again towards the girl he had thrust aside, "will, however, lick me clean afterwards." He dragged Marina forwards by the nipple rings. "Put your whore mouth to me," he ordered, "and pleasure me."

Marina took the place of the privileged domestic fellatrice and sank down on the throbbing erection. To her own amazement, she was sucking the Master of Beaucastel himself! Not just a lascivious Lalanière or a Roscoff or even the insatiable Restif. She knew the Master was playing with her but also offering a measure of leniency; she could not afford to make a mistake. She performed with energy and finesse, her cheeks hollowing with the suction down the stiff rod, knotted with violet veins. The Master had been well prepared for over a quarter of an hour and came smoothly under the girl's virtuosity; as the rush exploded in her gullet, she

116

swallowed the rich load of semen voluptuously, showing her pleasure. She really relished the refreshing discharge with its delicious taste of salt and acrid seaweed she had been starved of all day.

"If she takes the scourge as well as she takes a cock," the Master gasped, "she can come to no harm. Take her away, Vasa, and prepare her for flogging and sex in ceremonial session. Her owners are present and she's sure to behave as well as she has done here."

He looked straight at Vasa. "Maybe a potential candidate for a post at Beaucastel?"

The overseer lifted an eyebrow but saw that her Master meant what he said. And Vasa could not disagree.

The beautiful creature had guts. There was no doubt about it.

CHAPTER 11

In accepting an invitation to a weekend at Beaucastel, guests—whether they were slave owners or prospective purchasers—knew they would be entertained royally in the presence of the Master himself. Not only were the comparing of notes and the conversations rewarding but also they provided ample opportunity for exchanges of slaves. Claudia was fascinated by the requirements of some of the proprietors; she and Mikhail listened with avid interest to the exigencies—the degrees of flagellation imposed, the resilience of their slaves and the sexual duties they were called upon to perform. Above all, there were the discussions with the probable buyers and these intrigued Claudia even more. She had never had, so far, to purchase a sex slave as Juliette had. But here were men and women from different countries discussing prices and the qualities of human flesh. The market was rich with girls and youths seeking owners. All candidates were of age and conveniently provided with papers of some sort to permit transfer from one country to another.

The inmates at Beaucastel were equal to its reputation. Although prices were high, the merchandise was of consummate quality and the welcome that owners and buyers received was conducive to rapid transactions. Every slave was admirably trained according to the criteria established by the Master. In addition, specific courses were available at a cost, laying the accent, quite apart from s/m activities, on particular sexual stipulations, such as urine, intimate styles of attire and, naturally, all types of branding. The major success, however, for which Beaucastel was renowned, resided in meeting routine s/m exigencies, such as those defined by Mikhail and Claudia. Beaucastel slaves became expensive on the market but were of reliable, first-class standard.

The weekends at Beaucastel were renowned for three things: an admirable reception, good food and the finest wines stocked in the cave—one of the few cellars not utilised for whipping and torturing slaves. Secondly, Beaucastel provided exquisite accommodation for visitors, each suite possessing its private bathroom, flagellation posts conveniently erected before the beds, chains and every conceivable appurtenance for slave disciplining.

Finally, the whole geography of cells, cellars and torture chambers was at the guests' full disposal.

Prior to the exhibition of the slaves, full printed curricula were distributed to guests, depicting the characteristics of those for sale. It was no secret to some that the Master was especially anxious to divest himself of saleable merchandise as soon as possible: the slaves occupied training space of future candidates.

Shocked by Marina's offence, Claudia for a moment envisaged putting her up for sale there and then and discussed the possibility with Mikhail who had no objection as long as Verenka remained with them. The prices for young, blonde slaves such as Marina were attractive but Marina's contract and the recent scandal were drawbacks. Perhaps later, Mikhail suggested, for during the weekend the guests quickly learned that a slave was to be corrected in full session and that the recalcitrant girl belonged to Claudia and Mikhail. This put a stop to Claudia's intentions. At least for the time being.

The guests at lunch on the Saturday, when all had arrived, numbered a dozen, Claudia and Mikhail being, thus far, the only owners present. Ashley was about to be returned to her adored Venetian proprietors and Sylvie and Renée also in a few days time to their Countess. Katia was not sure as to her fate and whether her German master would retrieve her but it was common knowledge that her man doted on her, yet kept her in anxiety. En pension, Birgit awaited the call from her Swedish couple, currently travelling in China where a blonde sex slave was hardly the thing to be seen around with. Marie-Laure lived with a married, middle-aged s/m couple near St Tropez and was extremely happy but would be happier when she was out of Beaucastel. Apart from Verenka and Marina, the other three slaves out of the eleven—Maria, Krystyna and Nastasia—were for sale. It was a sort of requiem for Nastasia; she had been turned down four times.

Four of the five male slaves were owned by women in various parts of Europe and only one—a handsome, well-membered Romanian youth—was for purchase. And not cheap.

Among the three female slaves on sale, the shaved, pale-skinned Marja found a buyer after an hour or two with an elderly Spaniard in his room; nevertheless, he wanted her to be whipped and used by a male slave in one of the cellars before signing. The performance went off well and the price was reasonable, the Master collecting his percentage.

Nastasia did her utmost to render herself erotic. Ashley had given her hints but the girl presented herself laboriously. An exotic, over made-up Austrian woman took a fancy to her but, after a spell in bed together, finally discarded her in favour of Krystyna whose bald head and shaven vulva gave her more excitement. Thus, only Nastasia aroused no special interest.

The dinner on the Saturday night was a grand affair. All the serving maids were present, stark naked and wearing special makeup, particularly the woman who had brought the girls' breakfast several days before; she was painted silver from head to foot and wore glittering chains. Beneath the sheen of chrome, the flesh was ridged with fearful welts.

Several guests requested service under the long table during the meal, in reply to which Vasa ordered the male slaves to offer their tongues to the women diners, while designating Marie-Laure, Katia and Sylvie to go to work on the male shafts. Ashley escaped this duty by squatting next to the Master, laying her fabulous breasts on the table next to him and surreptitiously caressing his cock into rigidity. At the same time she could not keep her hazel eyes off Verenka, who, even while sucking Mikhail, returned her delicious smile quite openly. Being the most beautiful of the slaves present, Ashley spread a sexual contagion among the guests, some mesmerized by her smile and hoping to benefit from her mouth or sex; but the latter was firmly obstructed with the bunched rings locked together. She seemed a rank above the other slaves who were from various social strata. Her poor French with an upper-class English accent rendered her attractive to all present; but it was also that same load of rings inserted into her labia and clitoris that excited the men. The fact that the rings were padlocked did not seem to deter them. Yet it was contemplation only, for Ashley's prestigious owners from Venice were about to arrive to take their ward home; the Master wanted her in pristine condition, unflogged and unused.

Mikhail was delighted to feel Verenka's lips and teeth skinning his cock again, as he had taught her, while Claudia succeeded, with some difficulty and discussion with a smartly half-dressed American woman, to reserve Sylvie's mouth for herself, the Californian dominant contenting herself with the terrified Renée.

Claudia, on the other hand, was delighted to feel Sylvie's experienced tongue lapping and slicking over her clit. She orgasmed massively, discharging smoothly over Sylvie's face the cum that had congested in her entrails for hours. The girl sucked a lot better than either Verenka or Marina. That she had to admit.

Encouraged, the American took her own slave in hand, thrusting Renée's head deeper between her strong, tennis-trained thighs. Renée did what she could but appeared to fall short of what was required of her, to judge from the slaps she received while hard at work. Finally, almost in tears, Renée succeeded...

Several other orgasms accompanied the meal until the Master ordered Gerda to recall and line up the slaves on the stage while the next course was served. The male and female bodies stood motionless; their beauty was extraordinary against the purple curtains while a silence fell over the dinner table as the flesh was exhibited anew.

Then the comments began. One guest complimenting

Sylvie's freckled nudity, another opining that Marie-Laure looked as if she could do with a good flogging at the stake. The Master was able to report that her owners had sanctioned any use of her, up to and including hanging by the legs in Cell Three or Four, provided she needed no more than a day's recuperation. Mikhail looked with curiosity at the Master. He was clad in sable, the heavy cloak enshrouding his slim body; the eyes were masked beneath a strip of mauve organdie. About his neck hung a gold chain and emblem consisting of curiously fashioned intersecting whips—insignia of the old Inquisition. Like Mikhail, the Master was a learned historical student of female—and male—flagellation. Beaucastel was, in many aspects, not unlike the old dungeons of that institution.

The Master made it clear that, apart from the adequately equipped bedrooms, the entire range of cellars below was at the disposal of the guests, together with the assistance, as might be needed, of all four overseers and the valets. However, this would be subsequent to the ceremony involving Slave 107, the exquisite, blonde Marina.

"That whore-flesh of a slave!" Claudia castigated herself. "That bitch!"

She had been aware during the evening of the curious glances she had been receiving from some of the guests: an owner who could not flog her slaves into obedience. Others seemed to sympathize. In any event, her own slave was to be the star in this terrifying night at Beaucastel. Before the major part of the evening commenced, the best Pomerol chateau vintages were decanted by the female maids down below in the cellars where they could hear the hisses and thuds of Restif's plaited scourge and the stifled groans nearby in a cell as Birgit was dealt with by him and Gabrielle, the nude Swede spread-eagled on a revolving cartwheel, a lesson she had by then learnt by heart.

Above, the ceremonial parading of the slaves continued, and the Master graciously allowed Marie-Laure to frig a youth with a most impressively straining erection. He addressed his overseer in a languorous voice.

"Give that slave's erection a few lashes to excite it fully and get the slut to frig it."

"And have it ejaculate over her face," a bearded guest added.

The overseer seized the red-haired Marie-Laure by a nipple ring to drag her, stumbling in her transparent mules, before the male slave's erection. She watched him lash the straining cock across its blue-veined length with the quirt he held; she watched the rigid flesh rebound at each blow, the youth standing immobile, thrusting out his hips, as he had been taught, to allow the whip full purchase on his penis. Lalanière laid on six strokes; the pole seemed to swell up as the head turned deep violet, the steel ring below the glans leaping. The clump of clustered genitals jutted out almost arrogantly as the youth gave himself to the leathers, revelling in the attention he was receiving. He was for sale and he knew it. He was far from cheap being hardened by the whip, being bisexual and equipped with an exceptional cock. In fact the Master had already accepted an offer for him from a Swiss woman.

Lalanière then sliced his whip savagely into Marie-Laure's rump. "Get to the thing, bitch 96, and frig it out," he ordered. "See to it the spunk arches well out… No mouthing, just frig, slave." He gave her a further tremendous lash across the rotund hunks of buttock meat. Marie-Laure cringed, the breath smitten suddenly out of her lungs. Lalanière was a clean and accurate flogger, one of the finest in the profession. And Marie-Laure was delicate.

The girl crawled to the cock stem and, as ordered, masturbated with all her force and skill, holding the man's body with her left arm—a body she had often serviced in Cell Five. She knew the penis well and the potency of its ejaculation. The group at table watched with complaisant interest, Claudia studying the girl's technique that concentrated first on the rim of the globe before attending to the whole length of the shaft. It took only about a couple of dozen long strokes of the hand to release the jets of seething spume across the stage.

The youth grunted and lunged as the clotted load shot from the slit, spasm after spasm, the cream splattering over the flagstones. Claudia found it sensational, but she would rather have had the youth bound to a stake or cross, limbs wrenched backwards to emphasize the hard penis.

"Empty the cock!" the overseer ordered. "And lick it up."

Marie-Laure squeezed the last glob from the still throbbing spout and instantly went to her hands and knees. In a minute the floor was lapped clean of the discharge.

There was spellbound silence during which the new owner hooked an eager finger into her slave's prepuce ring and made him kneel before her thighs.

At a nod from the throne, Restif and Gabrielle entered and crossed the spot lit stage to whisper to the Master who again nodded. The couple, dressed in leather and booted, then brought in the scourges and the rods that had been steeping in brine. These they placed carefully on a nearby table, already arrayed with other trouncing whips, hoods, flesh weights of globed iron and a heap of restraining thongs. Torture trestles, already equipped with chains, were hauled into place on either side of the dais; at a further sign from the Master, it was the overseers who drew aside the purple curtains at the rear of the stage. Apart from the whipping stake already revealed, chains were attached to overhead rings, dangling over the empty stage; to the sides of the area, large drums and ratchets were bolted to the wall. The scenario, the threatening objects and the overpowering heat of the Hall combined to increase the slaves' apprehensions, at the same time stimulating deep in the brain and entrails that sexual thrill all submissives experienced at the prospect of what was about to be enacted. The slaves were whipped again off the stage down into the broad area where the guests now lounged on thrones or couches; side tables bore wines, cognacs and triangles of caviar on rye. The guests needed nourishment—the night would be long.

Mikhail had to admire the scene. Each body slave exhibited his or her superb thorax and ringed nipples as the wrists were detached to allow them to service the company. The male slaves were magnificent when they stepped down towards the waiting visitors; each youth was, apart from the nipples and scrotum, pierced and ringed through the underside of his erect cock, some with their shaft braided with leather thongs, protruding rivets holding the ligatures where they intersected. Mikhail was amazed that girls could make love with youths so encumbered with impedimenta. A pellucid thread of sex liquid trailed to the knees of each male and each female was already wet with anticipation as they immediately went to work on fellating the male guests or titillating the female clits.

Instinctively, Verenka stepped towards Mikhail and knelt before him with a smile on her lips. Mikhail rammed into the mouth as it were an orifice in an object while Claudia was serviced by a handsome Norwegian youth with an agile tongue. For a long period the sole sounds in the Hall of Ceremony were those of suction, lapping and groans of pleasure. Several orgasms were brought about fairly rapidly, while other slaves sat upon the guests' laps for penetration and protracted servicing. Strangely, although someone as ravishing as Ashley was available, it was the slut Alana, still loaded with her chains, who officiated on the Master's hairless upsurge of tumescence. After some minutes, the man kicked her aside and, facing the gathering, addressed his guests.

"This evening, dear friends of Beaucastel, is somewhat special. Quite apart from the enjoyment you will derive from the slaves, who are at your disposal here and elsewhere afterwards, I have the duty to bring before you a female slave I have condemned, with her owners' full consent, to exceptional treatment for attempted escape. What is about to be inflicted on the slut is entirely justified by the rules of Beaucastel. After the formal portion of punishment here, the guilty body will be taken to the Black Cellar to continue the ordeal through the night. All who are not otherwise engaged

125

are cordially invited to see what we have in store…"

He turned slowly to Vasa standing, whip in hand, half-naked to the side of the stage.

"Bring in the condemned slave!"

CHAPTER 12

Marina had been prepared with meticulous attention and stood waiting to be led out for punishment. During her sauna where she had sweated out copiously to tone up her body for what was to come, she had a moment of tranquillity in which to reflect. To her knowledge none of her companions had ever repudiated her role of a sex slave; on the contrary, all in their own way seemed to delight in utter subordination. It had become a natural mission, answering a deep instinctive need to be dominated and hurt but not unduly harmed. At the same time Marina wondered what it was like to dominate instead of being humiliated. The bitch Verenka who had jilted her so cruelly was the one who needed flogging. In some way or other Marina would make Verenka pay for her low perfidiousness. But first there was the suffering to come, something Marina would have gladly accepted as long as Verenka remained her lover. Now the foolish attempt at escape had to be requited alone. She would make the girl pay somehow. Somehow...

Gabrielle had prepared her. She had been laid on a grooming slab, her sex and skull shaved, her body perfumed and her entrails sluiced out. The overseer's strong hands had aroused her and as she had worked she had told Marina what a fool she was to try and deny her slavery. She had talent, she said, she herself wouldn't mind a night's flogging and sex with her and Lalanière himself had expressed an attraction to her. That had startled her; the man had flogged her as hard as any and had never even kissed her before subsequent penetrations.

As a finale, Gabrielle had clipped heavy, spiked steel balls to her seven rings and these now tugged with erotic discomfort at her labia and teats and swung viciously into her flesh at the slightest movement. She had left her standing against the whipping stake and it was here that Marina now stood, trying not to move, pressing her back and rump against the rough wood.

In the dense heat and unnerving silence of the Preparation Chamber, Marina continued to stand obediently and motionless, fighting the loaded weight of the flesh chains, conscious that her superb body was on display on screens far away above, men and women appraising her oiled nudity. While waiting frustrated and nervous, she tried to gather her confused thoughts together.

Already she knew she was to be whipped in public, before a select gathering of s/m devotees like Claudia and Mikhail who would be present. The prospect of being the principal attraction both scared and thrilled her. In the brief time prior to her ludicrous attempt to escape, she had sensed during the routine sessions in the training cells, the presence of shadowy figures, often masked and quaintly dressed; they too, she had deduced, were guests, either prospective buyers or simply onlookers, spending a brief, lascivious stay at the castle. To Marina it was immaterial who wielded the scourge; the pain was what she had to contend with. She had begun to endure these anonymous onslaughts with a resignation where pain and a curiously overpowering pleasure seemed to coalesce. The whippings were totally impersonal; both the flogger and she, the flogged slave, were deprived of personality. Conscious of her beauty, Marina had become impervious to her humiliation; she well knew that her superb body and its physical writhing under the scourge gave untold delight to her flagellator and provided a mysterious surge of sexual pleasure in every fibre of her own being.

She fully understood why men and women wanted to whip and torture her, leave alone use her orifices. She had seen other girls writhing, panting, groaning with pain and gasping, shrieking with pleasure; and, yes, they were so utterly beautiful. And again Marina wondered what it was like to hold the whip and flog. She would not demur if offered the shaft of a whip and a naked girl stretched taut before her. Particularly if that girl had number 106 stencilled in under her fat breast and happened to be called Verenka Lucia Aurelia de Courton. Revenge was proverbially sweet; the whip substantially sweeter.

How she would relish an hour, not even an hour—whatever the Master would accord her—to deal with that empty-headed slut, that bitch, crucified before her on the cross in the Slave Hall before all the inmates and she, Marina Sylvia Messery, potential overseer, swinging the scourge... Ah, what perfect delight... And Verenka had such voluminous buttocks. Oh, God, yes, it would be sweet to whip them to the blood...

She closed her eyes to rid herself of the vengeful thought and as she did so, the iron-braced door of the chamber was flung open as Lalanière entered. He was equipped for the session in customary flagellator's garb, a medium-length horsewhip suspended from his belt. A swift glance at the handsome overseer showed Marina that he was admiring her with a hardly perceptible smile, a smile not of the usual sardonic, predatory cruelty but a subtle look of affection. Marina was frightened; she knew not to trust the expressions of these ghastly, unpredictable dominants; but it was the first time she had seen him look at her thus. He ran his studded palms over her oiled and taut nakedness and finally he drew his forefinger up the sex slit behind the clitoris chain, he glanced at the residue.

"Wet already, I see," he muttered. "Why are you seeping so disgustingly, slave? All this curd is disgraceful. Have you no shame?"

"It's because... because, Master..." Marina's mouth was as parched as her vagina was awash with fresh discharge. "Because... I'm to be whipped in public, I suppose."

"You suppose correctly, you slut. And this excites you?"

"Yes Master," she murmured.

"Well, you have a tremendous night before you and the Master expects you to honour Beaucastel and our distinguished guests to the best of your sexual ability. We expect orgasms, slave."

The man smiled again and squeezed the girl's elongated

nipples as if pressing pips out of a lemon. Marina winced with a gasp, throwing back her shaved head. As she did so, she saw Gabrielle slide into the chamber.

"You've prepared her well, Gaby. She's been fully sluiced out, I assume?"

Touched by her superior's compliment the warder bowed. "Yes, the anus is clean, ready to be entered."

"Then we can commence." Lalanière turned to the trembling slave. "We do not want to keep the company waiting, particularly as your owners are present. Attach the chains!"

The warder clipped a long length of links to the throat strap and a shorter span between the ankles. Marina was dragged forward, hobbling, through the iron-studded door, Lalanière leading and hauling with jerks on the neck. The spiked globes swung murderously.

The group traversed several dimly lit passages. At one point, Marina caught sight of a stark naked body, chained by the four parted limbs against the wall and glistening in the wavering glimmer of a nearby lantern. The girl was unknown to her—probably a delinquent servant, for she was devoid of flesh rings—but obviously a member of the staff; she had been atrociously whipped across the throttled breasts and flat belly.

As the cortege passed, Lalanière delivered a vicious stroke of his whip across the thighs, leaving a vivid stripe that flared up in the gloom. The chained nude leapt once and subsided in her manacles, moaning. She was very beautiful in Marina's eyes.

Trammelled by her chains, she did what she could to keep up with the group, feeling the inner surface of her thighs slithering together with the warm viscous fluid flushing down slowly beyond constraint from her slit. The sight of the naked scullion had affected and excited her; soon she too would be in the same condition, whipped and shuddering. The adrenaline and endorphins raced through her... Claudia would be there. Mikhail would be there, watching her penance. And that unbridled, promiscuous bitch, Verenka, too, cuddling with Ashley, both staring…

The entry into the Hall of Ceremony, with its overpowering heat, the candles, spotlights and odour of sex, made Marina's heart miss a beat and then race uncontrollably. The yawning vault in the very centre of the Beaucastel edifice loomed before her; she found herself on a stage and below, beyond the blinding lights, a mist of obscurity. Vaguely she glimpsed the throng of guests being serviced by her colleagues—male and female, all naked—and others. Instinctively she tried to pick out Verenka and Ashley but in vain; the penumbra shrouded the company, which spontaneously fell silent as Marina was forced to her knees, the pain of her chains mercifully assuaged for a moment. In the centre of the dais, as if in some long-forgotten mystery play or slow-moving ballet, the slave presented her nudity to the lusting eyes…

As the overseers retired to the side, she glanced around at the ominous stake with docile chains and straps drooping from its summit; the motionless chains hanging from the ceiling, the trestles. Marina's spirit wavered, her bowels clenched in pure fear. And her panic increased when, like abstruse, occult sounds from another universe, two voices rang out. The first was Vasa's.

"The naked slave victim, gracious Master, awaits your pronouncement."

In turn, the Master responded. "Proceed! Let the slave be suspended according to the rites of Beaucastel!"

While the lights were being lowered, leaving a single spot and candles, Mikhail eased Marie-Laure's ginger head aside from his cock to move over to sit by Claudia who seized his erection with joy. As she bent to take the rigid, throbbing shaft into her mouth, she caught sight of Verenka flicking and sucking the nipples of a handsome, lissom beauty with chestnut hair. Ashley was responding with her thumb on the girl's clitoris, her hand plunged deep into the vulva. Claudia was taken aback at the girls' assurance.

"So that's the girl Verenka's fallen for!" she whispered to Mikhail, jerking her chin towards the sweating couple. "She's playing a dangerous game!"

"Forget it, darling. In any event, the other girl's owners have apparently just arrived to take her home. They live in Venice and that's far enough to prevent Verenka playing around." Mikhail had correctly surmised that the handsome, greying couple who had just arrived had come only to retrieve their English slave. He had noticed them enter at the rear of the Hall. The man had handed his cloak to a naked serving girl and looked out of place in his neat tuxedo; his companion was tall, in evening dress, her quiet, dark eyes slowly surveying the scene with a signal grace that seemed to set her apart from the other women present. They had the look of the very wealthy and seemed to fit the role of owners of the most lovely of the Beaucastel slaves. Ashley merely smiled at them and continued to masturbate Verenka openly. The Venetian couple returned her smile, the woman throwing her a kiss.

"Watch the stage, Claudia," Mikhail urged his mistress. He felt a certain anxiety for Marina, completely sheared and shaved; after all, she was his responsibility, bound to him by a frail contract. But he knew the slender lycee teacher's resilience, as long as the punishment remained within reasonable limits. Certainly she should be taught a lesson but not damaged. He needed her back in the Quai d'Anjou where he would in turn make her writhe, begging for mercy...

Suddenly the Master's hoarse voice grated in the silence.

"Slave 107, you have offended the canons of Beaucastel to whose walls you were consigned for training. You have affronted me, your Master. You have offended your owners here present and disgraced your colleagues. You will now be punished. After the established ceremony, your body will be taken down to the Black Dungeon for further treatment and be at the entire disposal and pleasure of any of my guests who may care to enjoy or participate in your ordeal." The man paused in the tingling silence.

"Before I order you to be hooded up and put to the whips, have you anything to say?" The meaningless privilege was offered only as part of the ritual.

From her tight gullet, the words that Gabrielle had drilled into her during her preparation issued forth as if from the bottom of the well in the courtyard where Marina had sinned.

"Master of Beaucastel," Claudia could hardly hear the thin voice, "your slave has trespassed in attempting to abscond from the delights of your castle, in committing fornication with a menial and in accepting money like a whore. She is..." the voice trailed off into sobs. "She is ready... naked and shaved... to be punished..."

The Master coughed. He detested tears. "On account of your recent performance in my chambers, I have exceptionally decided to spare you the customary whipping of your open crotch and also suspension by the breasts." He marked a short pause. "I cannot exempt you further nor spare you from whatever may be inflicted on you in the Black Dungeon. You will now discharge your debt of slavery. Let the session commence."

He rang the silver bell he held delicately in his gloved fingers.

Vasa seized the girl, drawing the slack hood of leather over the skull, forcing the huge gag into the mouth and buckling the straps tight.

The experience of Claudia's Inquisitor's mask at the Quai d'Anjou fell far short of the smothering cowl; it blocked the ears, pressing into the eye sockets and gouging into the mouth. Deprived of her other senses, all that remained in her dumb, deaf blindness was the smell of sweated leather and the enhanced sense of feeling, a sense the slave was now to exercise to the full.

Gerda and Roscoff let down the chains as Vasa forced the body, face downwards, on the flagstones of the stage. The four chains, clipped to the legs and wrists, rattled over the pulleys, the far extremities descending down the side walls to the ratchets and drums. With slow turns, the warder and valet cranked up the beautiful nakedness until it extended, spread and curved, in full tension. Marina was wrenched apart to the uttermost reach of her limbs, the flesh weights tugging on the tender nipples and sex. At the walls, the suspension chains were smartly cleated off.

Below the superb arch of nudity the iron spheres swayed; blue veins stood out over the stretched breasts; the holes pierced through the labia and nipples became clearly visible and the stress began.

Gerda then stepped between the splayed legs to bore into the anus with a ridged plug; the dildo sank in deep to ensure the orifice would be satisfactorily dilated to receive the male erections later. Content with the dildo's hold in the sphincter, Gerda dragged her spiked palm over the length of the sweating curves to stimulate the victim to the apex of readiness; she left fine scarlet lines from shoulders to calves. Marina lurched, thrashing her head; then she relaxed, saving her strength.

The silver bell chimed again for the four flagellators to take their stand, two on each side of the body.

The bell rang out again and the scourging began.

Claudia watched as Lalanière, his great cock swinging, lashed the back, using a thin six-thonged whip, from the armpits to the coccyx. She watched as Roscoff slashed the left thigh and Gerda dealt with the right from the buttock crease to the knee, ensuring the tip of her thong bit into the soft underside of the perineum and distended labia. As was her habit—and privilege—Vasa reserved the white buttock meat for herself, beating the quivering mounds that clenched under each descent of what she always referred to as her 'hot whore-humbler'. Vasa scourged with her usual truculent vigour, each shock of the curtailed sjambok summoning up mauve bruises over the twin cheeks.

Claudia had admired Mikhail—and her own lithe body reflected in the wall mirrors—as thrashings were administered in Paris but here professionals were at work. The lunges of the overseers' bodies and the thud of the whips exhilarated her; it was of unearthly beauty and it was her own slave jerking in frenzy. Claudia leaned voluptuously back in her chair, sensing her viscous secretions pouring from her vagina. The flagellation was beyond her wildest fantasies. Rising to straddle her lover, she closed her eyes and let Mikhail in.

The silver bell rang only when Marina's haunches and rump were running with blood. The slave hung motionless. The sight made Claudia come twice in succession and then she held herself back. She wondered if Marina had fainted and what would happen next.

The sequence that followed entailed first the two male overseers after Gerda had peeled off the lower portion of the hood and extracted the gag. Marina's mouth was agape as if locked open. But she was ready. Roscoff lifted the head and thrust into the throat.

Gerda withdrew the anal plug with a wrench, making the slave heave and again Claudia saw that the body was ready. Lalanière stepped over the chained leg and plunged in. With weird, revitalized energy, the flogged girl rode the double entry. After several minutes, Marina began to tighten her muscles. She came with a shudder, delivering to her torturers a fantastic orgasm without end. Then she took what was offered to her, swallowing as best she could Roscoff's sperm and jerking as Lalanière moved to the anus to release his load of boiling cream into the entrails that had been scoured out to receive just that.

It was then Vasa's turn to demand the attention of the mouth. To Claudia's astonishment, her blonde submissive used her tongue with fury on the female genitals that crushed against her face. Finally Gerda, the junior, had her moment of pleasure on the same weary lips, grunting with lust as her orgasm filled the Hall.

Only then did the bell ring again. Claudia, refreshed, noticed that a reckless orgy was in progress among the guests, each using a male or female slave. To her bewilderment she saw that Verenka had managed to remain glued to Ashley throughout the session, possibly on account of the presence of Ashley's owners.

While the overseers wiped off their scourges and cleaned up their bodies, the valet Restif helped Gabrielle to lower the victim. She slumped to the flagstones and lay still, thoroughly beaten. The Master was satisfied with two hundred lashes.

Food was served by the naked girl attendants and the conversation resumed as before the session. Restif ripped off Marina's hood and, to Claudia's surprise, also unhooked the spiked spheres from the body, laying them carefully, almost with devotion, on the instrument table. Gerda did her duty also—again to Claudia's startled eyes—by rubbing ointment into the girl's teats that had become extended to twice their normal length, and into the sex. Marina lay sprawled on the ground as she was treated, licking her lips caked with discharge.

What she had endured was a long voyage between the depths of Beaucastel's hell and the incredible reaches of its heaven. The torture had lasted an hour.

Salmon, soufflés, fruit and two Bordeaux were brought in and few noticed Gabrielle and Restif lifting Marina by the armpits to carry her out.

They helped her to stagger to the doorway and then escorted her down an interminable flight of stone steps.

The Black Dungeon was already fully prepared to receive its guest. But she was not to be alone. Marina would have company, unexpected company.

CHAPTER 13

During the intermission Vasa strode over to Claudia and Mikhail. She was freshly showered, perfumed and sensually arrayed in a tight, night-blue vinyl sheath from head to foot, slit only over the combed pubis and allowing the sharp breasts to rear out bare from the encircling grasp of the stretch. Her sjambok, newly cleaned and greased, swung menacingly from the slope of her hip belt. She addressed Mikhail imperiously, conscious of the effect her figure was causing.

"The Master would be obliged, Monsieur, if you would spare a moment to meet with him in his chambers for matter of some importance." The woman turned to Claudia who sat calmly euphoric, her loins open and wet. "It will not be for long, Madame. Do not hesitate to call on a warder or valet should you care to amuse yourself here or in your room or in a cell below with a male or female slave." She gestured towards a well-proportioned youth against the wall, the only slave not in use but ready, his vast, thonged erection in hand, and then towards the trembling Renée, cringing against a table leg.

"Frankly, I'd rather chat to one of your colleagues, if possible. The blonde one with the ponytail," Claudia proposed, the workings of the castle interested her more.

"Certainly. I'll send you Gerda, our little intellectual."

While Mikhail was following Vasa out, Claudia watched Gerda approach; she was radiant, slick in vinyl like Vasa but displaying far more flesh, the corset reaching to the waist where black suspender thongs descended to the scarlet stockings. Below was the sleek length of the riding boots. She was perfectly made up in shades of mauve—eyelids and cheekbones, lips, nipples and areoles, navel and the bulging fig of the sex. The handsome pageboy cut framed the face and gave her added neatness. And authority.

She greeted Claudia with an enigmatic smile and having ordered champagne from a naked serving wench told her how she came to be at Beaucastel, in answer to Claudia's question.

137

Crossing her legs before Claudia's admiring glance she recounted how she had worked at a German institution catering for a select clientele and with its own stock of slaves. Her beauty and dedication had attracted the attention of the Master when he had visited once, and after using her and testing her for hours had engaged her. She had rapidly proved her worth, she said proudly, when employing the whips.

Claudia started to enjoy the sight of the sleek female next to her. The latex sheath was like a second skin, Gerda's curves clasped as it were by a thousand hands or rather sucked by a thousand mouths over the entire body except the breasts, lower belly, buttocks and sex. Claudia caught the sensuous squelching of the sheath on the sweating flesh beneath as the woman's body slithered with each movement she made. She felt intensely attracted to the overseer.

Encouraged by the overseer's expansiveness, Claudia asked to be told more about Beaucastel, and she obliged, explaining how the throat straps of various colours which the slaves wore denoted their various stages of competence.

Gerda sipped her drink with relaxed self-composure; she liked briefing visitors on procedures. Claudia was fascinated. She stared at the full, taut breasts, tipped with fine, elongated teats set in smooth areoles like her own, devoid of imperfections. She wondered what the woman was like in bed. Incredibly sensual and voracious, no doubt.

She smiled and had the naked attendant fill the flutes again before concluding "As you can imagine, we overseers are absolutely not prepared to tongue mere slaves! To spare us that, we organize cunnilingus and fellatio training between the slaves themselves. They graduate upwards highly competent, like your two."

Some of the pleasure in listening to Gerda tarnished when the overseer referred directly to Marina.

"It's such a shame your beautiful blonde girl, Number 107, who was so promising, had to go and make a fool of herself. But she is extremely gifted. We'll see how she co-operates

138

during the sequel in the Dungeon later. She'll probably enjoy it thoroughly. That female has intelligence as well as enormous reserves of lascivious strength. She'll go a long way along the s/m turnpike."

"Tell me about all the cells, Gerda." Claudia asked to change the subject.

Gerda uncrossed her muscular thighs. Claudia saw the luscious labia part slightly; like her own, they were humid with a wealth of mucilage as the flesh peeled open, and above stood the rampant clit, throbbing. She would have willingly knelt to take the prong between her lips. She would have given much to sense the overseer orgasm over her face. But, desperate to learn, she checked her desire. Gerda told her that the best way to learn was to attend a few sessions.

"We have a massively resilient Swedish whore of a slave here just now, Number 102. You should watch her under the whip. Fantastic! Her owners are in China or somewhere, travelling. We whip her to the blood regularly. That is what her proprietors demand. A tough cookie. And she adores it to the full. She's very proud of her body."

"And you beat slaves across the sex?" Claudia wanted the full account.

"Certainly, just like the males have their cocks whipped. But the best, as far as I'm concerned, is to have a female bound to the breast gallows. The breasts bounce like swollen balloons. We use a riding crop to ensure they are well marked. You should spend a moment, Claudia darling, in Cell Seven and observe."

Claudia wished for nothing better. She was on the point of orgasm. Then she risked it.

"Gerda, my dear, would you be offended if I frigged off? I'm thoroughly turned on."

"Of course not, Claudia. Go ahead. Would you like me to pitch you off the mountaintop with the handle of my whip? Just say so. I'd like it."

Craning back in her chair, Claudia hooked her thighs over

the armrests and let her head drop backwards, holding her labia open with her fingers. Gerda smiled, leaning forwards, to help by inserting the leather haft into the glutted oval of flesh that was pulsating strenuously with need. The thick handle reamed into the trench for a moment before rasping the engorged clitoris, dragging it downwards and inwards, grinding the woman with a slow, remorseless friction. Claudia gripped the sides of her chair, moaning helplessly. And suddenly she convulsed and came with a long, piercing shriek of satisfaction that echoed through the Hall. Gerda let the blonde body collapse like a corpse and then revive.

"Feel better now?" She signalled to the naked serving wench, standing to the side watching the orgasm unfurl.

"Wipe the lady clean, slut!"

The girl's fabulous breasts swung over Claudia's crotch as the servant mopped up the discharge with a silken, embroidered napkin.

"God, that was unearthly, Gerda! Unbelievable! Thank you, darling!"

"Don't thank me, thank your big clit. It's very responsive." Then, as if to revert to the realities of the moment, she pointed her humid whip towards the scullion. "This flesh of ours, by the way, is due to be corded by the breast roots in Passage Seven tomorrow and whipped raw by Vasa before being offered to the warders and valets as compensation for their work tonight. Isn't that right, Leonora, you drab of a whore?" She smacked the girl's trim buttocks that had obviously not been scourged for some time.

The wench bowed obsequiously, clenching the damp rag in her trembling hands. "Yes, Mistress. Fifty lashes, hung by the breasts, as ordered. It's my turn."

Gerda thrust the girl aside and took up the trend of the conversation again.

"Talking of sex torture, Claudia—now you feel relieved— I believe you're having trouble with your girls, as we all have from time to time. Well, I just hope that your slaves escape the black throat strap. We have a special chamber below, not unlike the Black Dungeon you're about to see, where jaded and what we term 'trash flesh' or recalcitrants are reconditioned. We use gorgeous, long needles like the ones your Slave 107 is about to become acquainted with, until the slave is ready to enjoy life and sex again. The girls rather like it."

"Oh, Gerda, I've always wanted to use needles!"

"And so you should, Claudia! I'm sure you would become an expert." She paused, looking at the beautiful dominant blonde before her with an intuitive shrewdness. "You know, there are always openings here for true, dedicated dominants, of a certain class, of course…"

Claudia listened carefully. The idea of her being part of Beaucastel like this nimble, intelligent woman attracted her; to be given her head with countless naked slaves, male and female, in the entrails of Beaucastel was tempting. But there was Mikhail and her own slaves—something she had yearned for and now had. Yet, her sensual curiosity wondered if she herself could not spend a week or two as a wealthy dominant at Beaucastel. Or else—and here her imagination moved rapidly ahead maybe Gerda and she could form an exquisite team, exchanging roles of top and bottom and sharing the same victims. Claudia imagined the Quai d'Anjou with Gerda present, dressed as she was now, sublime and half-naked, sauntering across the library floor in front of Mishka who would be taken aback at her perfection, his great cock swaying as he observed the tight buttocks shifting above the high boots…

Yes, the Quai d'Anjou would be ideal, once it was appropriately equipped—and here Gerda could be of immense assistance.

Claudia described her place to her colleague. The place she had planned.

The great bookcases could be adapted to swing round, each panel revealing its reverse, hidden half. On one there would be the black, velvet-covered crucifix with its golden chains, chromium manacles and honed barbs to punish the elongated slave body as it slapped against the surface, the sleek leathers slitting the rump…

Yes, the slave would thrust her fabulous arse outwards, exhausting herself in avoiding the points piercing her arms, belly and thighs.

Then the real flagellation would commence, Gerda to one side and Claudia on the other, beating the wealth of buttock meat, making the girl count the lashes as the tongues welted the globed masses deserving all the strength the floggers could muster.

A second bookcase opposite would revolve also, to display the solid phalluses Claudia would have had bolted to the crimson silk facing, so that the victim could be bound tight and penetrated either by the mouth and sex or up the anus before scourging…

Then there would be the bookcase at the end of the library, which, once reversed, would provide a vertical cartwheel on a central axle… She closed her eyes.

Reluctantly, Claudia forced herself back to Beaucastel. Gerda had listened with interest to the beautiful, vicious woman's account or rather what the overseer construed as her imaginings. But certainly the place in Paris had promise. And to Gerda's mind, Claudia also; she began to admire her determination. And she liked her narrow thighs and neat sex. And the smooth, golden hair down there and along her forearms. Gerda would not have said no to a night with the sparkling blonde. Perhaps roped down and gorgeously crucified on the bed…

"Maybe you should have a word with the Master, Claudia. He's very accommodating. You might like to spend a spell here in Beaucastel. You know, we have unbelievable privileges as overseers. And the pay! I've almost made enough already after a year to start up my own place somewhere, maybe in Hamburg or Zurich. I've learnt all the tricks of the trade and…"

"Why not in Paris?" Claudia interjected quickly. "Perhaps we could put our ideas together, Gerda dear. As I say, I've a huge apartment on the banks of the Seine. Maybe not fully equipped but you could help me to arrange it. Here's my address card, call me when the iron's hot and let's talk."

"Tell me more about your set-up."

Claudia told her everything, concluding that the beatings would do Marina good.

"And I hope it hurts," she added

"Oh, it's hurting all right," Gerda confirmed. "What she got in the Hall, hung like a side of meat, was pretty drastic, even by Beaucastel standards, but what's to come will really test her guts. As I told you, they're going to pierce her. But don't worry, the bodkins heads transpierce easily and almost painlessly—at least after the flesh has been well whipped. And no real harm's done. You know, Claudia, although it's psychologically harrowing to be probed, spiked and transfixed, every slave is excited by it. And your 107 is particularly resilient." Gerda paused as if wondering whether to risk it. "That's why the Master has his eye on her as a potential employee here."

Claudia felt a little shock run like a ferret through her loins. She had to talk to Mikhail. Where the hell was the man, leaving her alone like this?

Worried and trying to think, Claudia tried politely to ignore her companion's chat which had reverted to the training cells, the licking up of spilt semen from the flagstones and the accompanying flagellation. Then Gerda let slip the dogs, if not of war, at least of agonizing doubt.

"You know, Claudia, one should not become too attached to one's flesh slaves, however servile, responsive and attractive they may seem. If relationships are uneasy," Gerda went on seriously, "and uncongenial, it's far best to get rid of your females. Sell them off and get yourself something new, preferably something that has been trained and toughened to take plenty of wholesome sex torture without making a song

143

and dance. Look ahead, Claudia, especially if your Verenka female is bought tonight by the Contessa."

"By the Contessa? What on earth do you mean?" Claudia paled and frowned, glancing towards where Verenka, stretched back over a dining table, was being sucked voraciously by Ashley, whose lovely nose and chin were lost in the matted hair of the crotch. "Verenka being sold? You must be joking, Gerda."

"No, it's true, my sweet darling. At least from what I've heard. She's being sold to the Conte and Contessa Consenzia della Potenza. Apparently they want your girl for their whipping harem at their palazzo in Venice."

Suddenly the reason for Mikhail being convened to the Master's presence dawned on Claudia. These Italians were purchasing Verenka. Buying her body. Over Claudia's head.

Events were taking a course of their own beyond Claudia's control. She had to react.

Before she could stand up to leave. Vasa entered, striding across the stage superbly booted and haltered, her breasts freshly powdered and firmly strapped to display their full volume. The customary sjambok, the terror of Beaucastel, swung demoralizingly from her belt.

A sudden quiet fell upon the Hall, the sweating, coupling groups pausing, rigid penises taken by surprise as Vasa's usual hoarse voice filled the silence—that voice both slaves and servants present knew too well, when it issued atrocious orders and yelled abuse at copulating or flagellated bodies.

"Distinguished guests, we cordially invite you to attend the next session of the night. This will take place in the Black Dungeon, which enjoys a certain renown among the more specialized connoisseurs among you. You will be entertained by three stark naked slaves, among them, of course, the guilty blonde whom you have just seen flagellated. All three are condemned to undergo different disciplinings."

Claudia frowned again towards Gerda. Three slaves? Who were the two others? Claudia somehow grudged the fact that

Marina was not to be the sole star. Gerda did not reply as Vasa gave her no chance. The voice grated on

"If you prefer to retire, please feel free to do so and take with you to your appointed chambers any male or female inmate you fancy. All the Cells below are free and staffed. On the other hand, should any guest wish to indulge in severe flagellation or sex torture in strict privacy, my colleagues will make the arrangements so that you can work undisturbed."

Vasa walked slowly along the stage, conscious of the effect she was producing and indicated the six practically naked girls behind her, lined up in the half-light.

"These menials will escort you down to the lower regions."

Immediately the female guides stepped down into the Hall, threading their way between the bodies interlocked in sex or relaxing after satiety of both sex and food.

At a sign from Vasa, Gerda rose and clipped her whip to the belt sloping across her flat belly and hips that Claudia admired so intensely. What a sensuous sight the woman was as she straightened up, adjusting her harness and smoothing the wet pubic triangle, parting the hairs to either side so that the stiff clitoris could protrude in presumptuous vanity.

"I've got to go to work now, Claudia dear. It's been exciting talking to you. We'll see each other again before you leave. Enjoy yourself. And above all, don't worry about your slaves. Everything will work out for the best. Just be adaptable."

With that she marched off over to Vasa and reported for duty. Claudia followed the long-limbed, fluid figure with her eyes. Gerda was something else.

Together the two overseers crossed to where Ashley and Verenka were sprawled out, now no longer over the edge of the table but on the rich carpets. Verenka was working on the older woman with lascivious lust and energy, her fingers probing, as far she could insert them, into the cunt, her tongue flicking from nipple to lip, from lip to earlobe and thence down to the throb of the clitoris that had thrust back its hood and ring to present itself for the girl's suction.

Vasa lashed out twice to uncouple—or, as she expressed it, to 'deglutinate'—the viscous crotches that were gaily preparing further orgasms. They were awash with cum.

Ashley knew better than to protest and let Verenka go. Later she would frig herself off briskly and neatly, tugging on the labial rings. She heaved herself to her feet as Verenka was handed over to Gerda. Vasa addressed Ashley with a mixture of aggression and deference; she was well aware that the girl's owners were shareholders in Beaucastel.

"You go and stand there by the door, Number 90, until your proprietors come for you. As you leave tomorrow, you'll take orders from them henceforward. And clean yourself up, girl, you look a repulsive sight! Wipe all that saliva and cum off your belly and thighs, shameless whore that you are. And don't let me catch you frigging that hungry clit of yours while you're waiting." Then she turned to Verenka and lifted her right breast with the handle of her whip to glance at the indelibly printed number.

"Right, Slave 106. Special night tonight. Follow the overseer to the Preparation Chamber. Then down to the Black Dungeon with you."

Verenka's swarthy complexion, still flushed and humid from the swelter of Ashley's sex, turned pale like the grey stone of the Hall masonry behind her. Someone had obviously called for her to be taken down to that place of suffering. But who? And why her? And why to the dreaded Black Dungeon? Surely that was Marina's problem not hers.

Gerda smartly clipped the haft of her whip to the girl's clit ring, glistening bright with the mingled liquids of both lesbians. Then she tugged once, savagely enough to make Verenka gasp; her clit was perilously close to climax and extravagantly sensitive but she managed to control herself. They crossed the Hall, mounted the stage, where Verenka for a moment thought and hoped she might be flung across a trestle, roped and whipped. But she was beguiling herself; she knew full well she was doomed to the Dungeon where far worse was in

146

store. And indeed, the couple exited through the same door by which Verenka had, without a grain of pity, seen Marina dragged bodily, half conscious, to her fate below. A cold terror invaded Verenka's entrails; yet, at the same time, a strange, inexplicable excitement took hold of her—the wild, delirious, barbaric feeling of being a naked, defenceless and very beautiful sex slave in the hands of torturers determined to flay her, to break her, to reduce her to whimpering flesh... But why her?

Watching her pathetic girl disappear to be prepared, Claudia became conscious of the lethargic disengagement of the couples around her as they rose to refresh themselves. Some dispersed to the upper chambers and the warm sheets of the beds awaiting them and their slaves; others, including Claudia who would not have missed one second of the hours of voluptuousness offered, strolled towards the studded door that led through the labyrinth of passages and stairways to the Black Dungeon. To converge on the dungeon was to descend into another world like Dante. Unsteadily she followed the naked serving wench guiding her; she trod very carefully down the steep, worn steps, the candlelight wavering and meagre. Suddenly she sensed the heat issuing out of the Dungeon, overwhelming her, promptly bathing the flesh under her cape in sweat, as if informing those who entered that nakedness was more appropriate than apparel. Accordingly, Claudia flung off her cloak.

Six more paces brought her into the vaulted space of what in fact constituted the principal torture chamber of the Chateau de Beaucastel, reserved for high occasions.

CHAPTER 14

Far above the dungeon, in the Master's room arrangements had been completed for Verenka's sale. Ashley's distinguished owners, the Conte Giuliano and Contessa Marisa Consenzia della Potenza had expressed a desire to obtain her. Apparently Ashley had asked them to buy Verenka for her and as the Conte and Contessa encouraged sexual intimacy amongst their slaves they were quite willing.

The only thing that Mikhail found surprising was that they seemed to know that selling Verenka had crossed his and Claudia's minds. She must, he supposed have been talking out of turn. A handsome price was agreed with a minimum of fuss and Mikhail had had to work hard to suppress his astonishment at the string of noughts that followed the first digit of the figure agreed upon. But the amount easily assuaged any qualms he had about selling his ward.

The Master then rang for his secretary who placed the already prepared bill of sale before the three parties for signature. As the bespectacled girl blotted the pages, Mikhail noticed that she was completely naked under her minute apron and this, as was the case with other domestics serving in the Hall of Ceremony, was fastened to her nipples by pins stabbed through the umber tips, probably, Mikhail thought, through the holes left by earlier rings, now discarded. As the woman left with the papers, Mikhail also noticed that her fine, heavy rump had been prodigiously beaten and that very recently. Every employee at the castle—apart from the overseers and valets—was subject to the whip; thus discipline was part of the normal routine and the secretary was an interesting example. Mikhail wondered where it was done. Had he but known it, it had been done right there in the Master's study, the female slapped over the end of the desk, her cunt pressed against the mahogany, her head among the curricula vitae of slaves. And the Master had thrashed her round bales of flesh with his riding crop until the secretary had urinated in abandon down the side of the desk. For which, as she knew, her rump and thighs would receive thirty further slashes. She adored the humiliation before her august Master. The sole disadvantage was the inability to sit on her behind for a day or so. Hence she typed kneeling and relished being seen in that ignominious posture. The whipping was weekly, always on Thursday.

"Now that the matter of the sale has been satisfactorily settled," the Contessa Marisa said, leaving her chair to stride up and own the length of the Master's chamber. "I have one request to make, egregio Maestro. I understand that you have at the moment a special session in hand—or even under way already—for corrective work on one or more of your slaves. Is this correct? It was Ashley who informed us."

The Master confirmed that the second part of the official evening was about to commence in an exclusive part of the castle, to which, naturally, the Conte and his spouse were warmly invited.

What the Contessa had in mind was something far more radical than mere attendance.

"I should like to try out our new acquisition if it does not interfere with your programme."

The Master looked at the woman. There was no question but that he had to accede.

"Of course, Contessa. Your request can be easily met within the context of what is to take place in the Black Dungeon. We have a slave to be tortured and whipped and, as it happens and in response to a special request by one of our regular customers, another slave to be branded. What precisely would your request entail, Contessa, if I may ask? Merely to make adequate arrangements."

The Contessa Marisa halted before the desk. "I should like to flagellate the girl just purchased and ascertain how she reacts. As you are well equipped, I can think of no better place. For this, I require a fairly wide space in your Black Dungeon or whatever you call it—and just a couple of chains from the roof."

The debonair Conte then contributed a word. "As is the practice at the Palazzo in Venice, my wife would wish the slave to be hung by the roots of the breasts for her scourging. We have the necessary cords and hooks and the Contessa will use her own instrument of flagellation."

There was a strange silence when the grey-eyed woman and her dapper husband had made their wishes known. Mikhail was relieved that the branding mentioned was not destined, as he thought for an uneasy moment, for Marina but for some other slave who must just have arrived or had been kept prisoner incommunicado somewhere in the bowels of the castle until the time was ripe for her body to be scorched with irons.

The Master rose. "There will be no problem, dearest Contessa. You may rely on me. I shall inform my chief overseer immediately so that your new chattel can be prepared for flogging. The three victims can coexist very pleasantly and be dealt with in turn. A truly rich session." Smiling, the Master turned to Mikhail. "Let me congratulate you on your sale, Monsieur. Your cheque will be ready immediately unless you wish to discuss some special mode of payment—perhaps via Zurich or Geneva? And moreover, allow me to express our unexpected delight that both your slaves will be on display in the Black Dungeon! That's quite an achievement at Beaucastel."

Mikhail was excited enough to sense his cock rising at the thought of the coming festival of sexual torture; this was worth the journey south and the fact that his own two bitches were in the thick of it only doubled his delight. He ached to get back to Claudia.

The definite arrangements were made for the issue of the cheque while the Master sent for Vasa to issue instructions regarding Verenka. Mikhail tucked the 'to the Bearer' cheque and the bill of sale away in the folds of his cloak. What would he do if the cheque bounced? He laughed. No, they were the

150

type of people who never reneged and whose cheques passed swiftly and noiselessly through hushed banks in Basel or Berne...

"Would you wish to have your former slave's address in Venice perhaps," the Master was enquiring, while beckoning Vasa towards him, "to send her belongings forward after her?"

"She has no belongings," Mikhail replied bluntly, "only her body and a fabulous capacity to orgasm. Enjoy her and beat her hard."

The group shook hands. The suave Italians smiled indulgently as Mikhail left; he had complied decently and with a polish they had hardly expected. Now Verenka was theirs. And Ashley's.

While waiting for Mikhail to join her and for activities to commence, Claudia had ample opportunity to size up the dungeon. Patently and as she had gathered, in the Middle Ages the huge rectangular vault with its series of alcoves and barred cells leading off, had served as the torture chamber of the Chateau de Beaucastel; if its current purpose remained essentially the same, the equipment and layout had changed. The former hideous furnishings of ugly brutality had given way to an array of exquisitely refined and exciting accessories calculated to display naked slave flesh in unbelievably erotic postures, glistening, shimmering and writhing in the light of dozens of candles of scarlet wax. The repulsive horror of the old bodkins, the rack, strappado and thumbscrew had been replaced by elegant whipping posts encased in velvet, well-equipped crucifixes with silver chains, tubular cages for delicious suspensions, and erotic gallows for binding the breasts of a kneeling slave. Polished stone slabs with bondage chains and much more, several of the items puzzling even Claudia, despite her experience of such places. She looked around with delight and envy.

To the far right, rough hewn and sturdy, stood the flogging and torture trestles, designed to stretch the victim to the extreme limit of the sinews before being worked upon. Claudia then examined another breast bench, more ingenious than others she had seen; built on a square platform, the twin beams reached upwards, joined at their head by a horizontal bar; lower, another bar was moveable in order to fit the size of the victim. Thin buckled straps were bolted to the bar, their inner surfaces glinting with barbs to cradle and grip the breast meat, holding it firm for the slash of the crop.

With her finger Claudia tested the steel spurs bristling within the straps. A sharp thrill coursed through her womb as the vagina contracted and liquefied. She fully approved of these adjuncts and the tighter a female's breasts—or, for that matter, a male's genitals—were throttled, the better the whipping. Frequently, she had herself envisaged installing such an apparatus in the Quai d'Anjou, with precisely such straps to constrict and bloat Verenka's all too flaccid mammary hunks for regular caning. Mentally, she made a note of the dimensions of the device, deciding to convince Juliette too to invest in one. The thought of Juliette brought to mind the fantastic slave Tansu: Claudia imagined the sumptuous nude tugging and wrenching on her impossibly lovely breasts as she was whipped and, if the session went well, there would be minute trickles of blood seeping from the straps. That would be worth watching…

Claudia felt a quick gush down her cunt. She needed sex. Badly. She was overreacting to the potentials of the Black Dungeon and to her subconscious desire to inflict pain on some trembling nude. To control herself, she turned to examine the rest of the cellar.

Glancing to the left of where the guests, who had accepted the invitation to descend, had taken their seats on various divans, couches and thrones, suddenly Claudia gasped. Half hidden by a pair of whipping stakes, Marina lay stretched out horizontally, gleaming like a star of tender, white flesh and quivering tendons. She had been staked out with fastidious care for what was to follow. Claudia was surprised she had not noticed the girl before but she was chained towards the

152

end of the cellar, her four limbs attached to rings cemented in the adjacent walls. The elongated nudity in massive traction fascinated Claudia. The main weight of the slung body appeared to be resting on the summit of a stake of timber that Claudia first thought might be sharpened to penetrate the anus. Then she saw that it merely bore the small of the back aloft. In any event, she realized, the anus would be required, like the gaping cunt and the mouth in the dangling head, for use during the session to come, all orifices being at the requisite height to service whoever was to perform on Marina.

To approach her slave, Claudia had to move round a great battery of instruments aligned on a rack: whips, canes, pincers, tongs, hoods, gags and straps. The nearby walls were festooned with chains. Leaning against the stonework, as if weakened by the effect of the spectacle, was a tall, sparse woman. Her short cloak was open from the throat, revealing a thin, pleasantly moulded body with small, tight breasts and a well-thatched sex. Most of the frame was enlaced with straps and belts. The woman, obviously older than Claudia herself, wore high boots reaching to the upper thighs. Amused, she watched Claudia touching the plaited scourges hanging on the rack.

"They look innocent enough, don't they? I mean, whips at rest seems so modest and lethargic and a moment later voracious for human flesh. My name is Janet. Janet Flixton-Clyde."

They did not touch hands but Claudia bowed slightly and this over the taut body of Marina that lay between her and Janet; after telling the woman her name, Claudia laid her hand on Marina's hollow belly, gathering up a meagre fold of flesh between her nails.

"I believe this is your slave," the tall woman said, noticing the gesture. "She's a tough gal to have put up with such a flogging, as she did up there." She gestured to the world above the vaulting. "And now she's in for more! We'll see how she endures the frontal whipping. Far more strenuous on the nerves. You know, breasts, teats, clit and so on. But, I must

153

say, she's very good looking. Do you make her live shaved?"

"No, that's Beaucastel. But it suits her." Claudia let her finger delve into Marina's vulva. The gesture was not to assert ownership over the nude but to ascertain if Marina was wet, stimulated by the preparations and her posture for punishment as well as by the remarks being bandied over her naked body. Claudia found the cunt torrid and saturated, still spicy and pungent, clogged with semen from the ejaculations an hour before. As she withdrew her perfectly manicured fingers, Janet leaned over the distended loins.

"May I?" she solicited quite naturally, thrusting in deep, almost up to the wrist, revolving the fist and the rings on her long fingers slowly round within the vagina. Marina convulsed abruptly, straining as far as her bondage would permit, which was very little but sufficient to grip and retain the gratifying hand for a moment in the hope of a long awaited masturbation. Janet immediately withdrew; she was not there to pleasure slaves.

"She clenches hard, your whore," she commented with a touch of admiration. "I wonder how she reacts to the flesh needles. I hear she's to receive thirty—into the breasts, nipples, labia and what's really worth staying up for until this unearthly hour, through the clit. And the slut has a fair sized nubbin." She smoothed the stub upwards along its length, making Marina arch her body with a hiss.

"Entertaining, Claudia, flesh needles."

Claudia peered at the cruel lines surrounding Janet's mouth and eyes. She evidently was accustomed to threading glittering steel through the breasts and sex—a sentence totally unannounced, of which Claudia had had no warning. Maybe Mikhail had agreed but surely he would not have done so without consulting her. She wondered how Janet knew of what was to follow and who had told her. Instead of enquiring, Claudia asked: "Do you employ needles?" It was said nonchalantly, as though comparing recipes.

"Of course I do, Claudia. That's why I want to attend this

session. And I also want to watch the branding. I'm very interested in branding, you see."

Claudia was again taken aback. "Branding? What branding?"

"Oh, don't worry, not your chattel. Some other slave who arrived during last evening, especially for marking. I truly enjoy the hot iron."

Janet turned to the side table and played with something metallic.

"Personally, I use thicker needles than they do here but then my girl Zelda can take any amount of perforation. She's very proud of it, especially when we perform in select company. Zelda has far bigger tits than your whore and longer sex folds. But then, a needle's a needle, isn't it?" She pointed to a sparking set of needles with jewelled ends lying in shallow trays of stainless steel; the antiseptic liquid was faintly pink.

Janet took one of Marina's outer labia in her fingers and spread it out over the thigh.

"Yes, plenty of scope here. You're lucky to have a well-fleshed cunt to play with."

Claudia looked at the dark, narrowed eyes. "To be honest, Janet, I've never used needles. Why don't you do it tonight on my slave and show me. If I ask that you be allowed to torture her, I know the Master and overseers will agree."

Janet's features crinkled into a genuine smile. "Oh, that would be great! And you could stand by and watch closely. But the slave has to be whipped first to excite and ready the flesh for the insertions. At least that's how we proceed."

"Well, why not propose you do the whipping too. I'm sure they can't but agree."

"Oh, they'll agree all right. You see, I'm probably going to buy a slave from them, out of the next bunch coming in for training. It's really for you to agree, Claudia. I'm pretty good with the whip. I'd use my six-thonged rawhide on a nude of this toughness. After all, God knows how many lashes she got in the Hall. Yes, my six-thong. I've not had it long and I'd dearly like to try it out on someone other than my Zelda. So if it's O.K. with you, Claudia, I could do the whole thing, whipping and piercing."

Claudia felt her womb clench with a sudden, sharp contraction of sexual frisson. The idea of offering her guilty slave to this comparative, if not total, stranger excited her with pure lascivious lust. It was as if she were throwing Marina's body out like trash, like garbage. An uncontrollable surge of hot, clammy liquid flooded Claudia's aching vagina.

"Well, the slut has to be punished and as all this seems to be your thing, why don't you go ahead? I'd rather it that way and the overseers couldn't care less, as the main session's over. My lover would welcome it too. He's too worried I might hurt the slave beyond repair! And I assure you there's a real chance of that. The damn bitch!"

Claudia slapped Marina's belly with her open hand very hard, leaving a red mark. Janet smiled one of her conniving looks. "I'll give her a lot to remember, Claudia. And you must come to my place in London. I'll return the compliment and you can have a couple of delirious hours with Zelda in my torture chamber. You'll love it."

Claudia nodded. In a way, a night with Janet might be fun. Or a night with Janet and Gerda... Suddenly she realized Janet had left to seek the sanction she needed to work on Marina.

Claudia went round to Marina's dangling head, feeling a rancorous, diabolical compulsion to taunt the offender, to humiliate her still further until she was slime.

"I've just given your whorish body to someone I don't even know, my little sex slut. That's what you're worth—to be traded around. It's because I've had just about enough of you and your haughty manners that I'm passing you on to her. She doesn't care about you any more than I do. All she wants is to hurt you and enjoy the reactions of your stupid body. I just hope she really hurts you." Claudia gave the girl a savage blow over the breasts. "You think you look tempting like this, don't you, you sly vixen? Well, just wait until I get you back in the library in Paris. I'll lash you and lash you until Beaucastel seems like a kindergarten. I'll slit that epidermis of yours you're so proud of until you're raw!"

In her gathering fury, Claudia drew a finger up a welt over the girl's hip where Vasa's scourge had reached to carve into the skin.

Suddenly and without the least warning, Marina's whole body tensed. She lifted her shaved head as high as she was physically capable, her eyes burning with hatred under the pale line where her eyebrows had been.

"I'll never—do you hear?—never come back to you, you stale, primitive bitch, you provincial whore! You can't even dominate a slave properly. You don't know how to whip a body and share the pleasure. You're just brutal. Just common. You're not even worth my body, you cheap cunt of a street whore! You don't own me. You couldn't own a street walker!"

"We'll see about that, my dear, between the columns next week in Paris." Claudia dragged with rage on the girl's clit ring, twisting it cruelly. She was confounded by her slave's effrontery, moreover in the earshot of other guests. "You despicable whore," she cried, her adrenaline pumping.

Marina screamed out again, even louder. "It's you, the whore! That's what you were born to be." She was choking with fury, her breasts rising and falling rapidly, the sweat beginning to run from her armpits. Then the girl heaved herself up higher and spat.

Slowly the saliva slid, like semen, over Claudia's downy cheek. The slave had spat at her. At her, Claudia!

The reaction was as fierce and sudden as it was unpremeditated; it stilled the low hum of conversation among the onlookers and the sound of Marie-Laure dutifully fellating the rampant cock of a male guest spread out over the couch. In the hush, Claudia wrenched one of the tall red candles from its socket, tipped it over Marina's midriff until the flame licked and guttered and the grease began to splutter and drip ruby globs over the nude.

As the scalding wax hardened over the breasts, ribs and solar plexus, Marina moaned with pain, her limbs jerking as each fresh, thick dribble of grease cauterised her flesh. Soon her writhing trunk was sheathed in scarlet armour, stiff with coagulated wax. The shrill hisses and moans mounted when the wax seared into the pubis, Claudia ensuring it dripped on to the pouting labia, the denuded clitoris and into the oval of the sex itself. Marina wrenched against her bonds, thrashing her body against the stump beneath her coccyx; she was encased in a vermilion carapace of Claudia's execration.

Janet returned in time to witness what Claudia had done to the slave and continued to do until, as if by way of a climax to her fury, she suddenly stabbed the candle between the girl's legs, ramming it in for the flame to sizzle and extinguish. The slave yelled once then subsided and lay inert.

"Take the sex-pot and do what you like with her," Claudia snapped. "I'm pretty well through with her disgusting, nauseating..." she sought a further epithet but could only find hatred in herself. She settled for: "The dirty whore tried to escape."

As the unprogrammed sequence had been monitored in other parts of the castle, Vasa was not slow in coming to investigate. Contrary to what Marina expected as she revived, encased in the scales of cooling wax, Vasa was delighted at the sight, congratulating Claudia on the way the flesh had been so neatly encrusted.

Then she turned to Janet who was already flexing the evil six-thonged scourge.

"Flog the grease off the slave until she's naked again. Then whip and heat up the breasts and cunt for the transpiercing." She paused. "But first allow my colleagues and the warders to lead in the two other victims." She clapped her leather-gloved hands twice, this in lieu of the silver bell used above.

Claudia, panting but assuaged, then received her second shock.

CHAPTER 15

Sumptuously oiled and made up, her hair piled up and secured on her head, the arms tightly bound at the wrists behind her lush buttocks, Verenka was led in, totally naked and manifestly scared. The girl was not on her feet but constrained to advance on her knees, her labial rings chained by a brief length of links to the throat strap. The bondage forced the body forward, the head, shoulders and rich breasts lowered to lessen the traction on the delicate flanges of vaginal flesh. Slowly and awkwardly, the beautiful, dark-skinned slave shifted to the place Vasa had reserved for her. It was Gerda who guided the girl by a chain passed backwards up the anal cleft to her hand. Once in place, the slave was released and told to stand erect.

There she was left, nude.

Claudia was baffled. Not one but both her slaves were now present in the grim precincts of the Black Dungeon, both naked and bound, clearly ready for whatever Beaucastel in its wisdom had decreed for them. What did this presage? Where on earth was Mikhail? What was afoot? Where was the Master?

The entry of yet a second naked woman hardly interested her. The prisoner was no youngster but about forty, well preserved and proudly fleshed although it was clear the body had been extravagantly used and whipped over the years. She wore a ball-gag and was blindfolded. Swiftly she was spread-eagled against a colossal iron grating, similar to an outsize harrow, and crucified, face inwards, the waist and thighs, as well as the extremities of the limbs, viciously strapped to the bars to ensure total immobility. Claudia at least grasped one aspect of the bondage: the straps served to elevate and tighten the otherwise sagging buttock meat ready for the branding irons. This was the slave due to be marked with her owner's initials. Restif, evidently charged with heating the irons, attended to the brazier in the background. The smoke began to irritate Claudia's eyes.

At that juncture, the other overseers, led by Lalanière,

entered, accompanied by naked serving girls carrying refreshments and by the heavily chained, ever-present Alana, bearing the irons.

Then, behind the onlookers, the great door opened to let in the Contessa Marisa, the Conte Franco and their darling Ashley whose eyes instantly sought out Verenka.

At the same time, to Claudia's delight, Mikhail strode in, kissed her and took his seat at her side. She fumbled for his rock-hard cock while he caressed her raw clitoris amid the seeping discharges.

Then he told her he had sold Verenka.

Claudia hardly blinked and even before learning the figure paid, she felt obliged to introduce Janet Flixton-Clyde.

"Janet's going to flog and pierce Marina, Mishka, instead of the overseers and instead of me. She's rather a specialist."

Mikhail nodded again but nevertheless took note of the woman's slender hips and the fearful whip she kept running through her fingers.

"Janet's someone after my own heart, Mishka. You've no objection to her dealing with our slut Marina, have you?"

"None at all, darling, as long as the authorities agree." Claudia assured him they did. "Well," he went on, "I must say, we're very popular as owners. Two slaves in chains!"

"But Verenka's no longer ours, Mishka, if I understood you. I'm simply delighted. The sooner the bitch is gone the better. I'd have done the same at that price. I'm sure she'll enjoy Venice." There was a minute trace of sour grapes in the voice, notwithstanding. "But why is she standing there, as if about to be slaughtered, she's so white?"

Mikhail filled her in on the agreement. "They just want her tested. Hung by the breasts."

"My God! They don't do things by halves." Claudia was really surprised and yet to see Verenka whipped swinging by those famous mammary treasures excited her.

Mikhail peered into the gloom. "What's the merry fireside blaze for over there? Not for ours, I hope. And what in hell has happened to Marina? She's like a female Redcoat."

Claudia explained, adding, "I'm just not attuned to that slut Marina any longer, Mishka. Do you think there's chance of selling her off like Verenka?"

"But darling, you'll have no one left to play with if she goes too! And I'd miss the suction of her anus. And the way she endures the whip and the cane. And her orgasms."

"All right, Cossack. We'll keep her even if her contract looks pretty phoney now that Verenka's gone…"

They were interrupted by Vasa's guttural announcement. "By order of the Master of Beaucastel, the condemned slave 107 will be whipped and needled. Slave 41B, a Beaucastel familiar, will then, by special request of her owner and in accord with the Master, be branded on the buttock meat. Thirdly, by special request and with the Master's concurrence, Slave 106 will be hung by the breasts and flagellated by her new owner here present. The number of lashes is discretionary."

The Contessa inclined her head a fraction where she sat at the rear of the dungeon.

Claudia listened with burning lust. All three sequences excited her, especially as two of the three bodies ready to be put to sex torture for the delight of their masters or mistresses, were, or had been, her own property. Her mind reeled for a moment when she thought what was about to be done to the submissive flesh stretched before the company of witnesses

She leaned over to grasp Mikhail's pounding erection and stripped down the prepuce to frig the purple head gently by way of welcome. The shaft was ridged with straining veins as she went down on it with her lips, spreading spittle over the starved monster. Then she lifted her head to smile at her lover.

What she saw also was Verenka being prepared for the whip. Then she knew the girl was to be suspended by the breasts and left so while Marina was dealt with.

A pair of chains were tugged downwards from the barrel-vaulted ceiling, the extremity of each consisting of a long length of narrow thong. These Roscoff and. Gerda, now summoned into service, along with Vasa and Lalanière, wound tightly round the base of each of Verenka's capacious breasts until the masses were fully throttled; the loose end of the thong was threaded into the bands. The lumps of flesh bulged like bladders, the areoles swollen, the teats enormous. Claudia had often treated her slaves to pleasures of this kind but had never ventured to compress the flesh to this extent.

Necessarily the constriction and suspension would have to be limited in time, Claudia knew. Yet, as Verenka was hauled upwards until her toes cleared the dungeon flagstones and she was swinging free, Claudia also guessed there was ample time for a prolonged flagellation to be carried out on Marina before damage could be incurred by Verenka. The timing was precise, for the slaves were in the competent hands of professional torturers. The hoarse groans from Verenka's throat bore ample witness to the pain she was called upon to endure. Her power of resistance was concentrated wholly on fighting the appalling stricture round the roots; her mouth gaped wide, struggling for breath, but the body hung straight and erotic, despite the torture. She could see her bulging tits before her face. She was terrified but determined to exhibit herself bravely; her new owners were watching. And so was Ashley who, doubtless, underwent such things regularly in Venice. Verenka was being challenged to equal her lover and this she was resolved to achieve, whatever the cost. One small compensation resided in the fact that Marina was to be whipped first. But the pain was almost insupportable.

She gritted her teeth and hung.

The attention of the dungeon then reverted to Marina, encased in her scarlet wax, with Janet standing near, still caressing her fearsome scourge that only Zelda had tasted.

Vasa nodded to the Englishwoman and withdrew to where Marina's bald head dangled, waiting. Much of the torture procedures at Beaucastel consisted in waiting.

Janet raised her leathers, paused and brought them down

across the belly with a dull thud. Marina heaved upwards as the whip bit into the wax. Scales of solid grease flew from the body as the thongs fell time after time. Janet worked her way upwards to the breast, still peeling the crusts off the flesh. Some twenty stokes cleared the upper reaches of the slave's body, leaving reddened areas that received additional colouring from the whip's kiss. As the thongs flayed the bouncing volumes of breast meat, Marina's first cries filled the dungeon; they were weird, strangled yells that Claudia recognized only too well. She was pleased to hear her ungagged slave give voice at last. Let the bitch yell her head off. Let her suffer— and be deprived of sex. Let her be flayed, ripped, blooded… The whore.

The removal of the clinging chain mail of wax from the loins and thighs—Claudia had left plenty there—brought forth even more strident shouts from the thrashing head. Some fifty strokes were needed for Janet to clear the body, after which she descended again from the armpits to the jerking hips, welting the skin. This done, the dominatrix, sweating as copiously as her victim, crawled under the stretched legs and laid her six tongues of tough leather directly over the girl's sex, dragging them slowly down from the navel to the four glittering rings that quivered in the fully equipped slave labia.

Marina knew what was coming. Her loins stiffened, the inner thigh muscles tensing into rigid ropes. Mikhail could sense the slave holding her breath. He was enjoying the flagellation, dividing his attention between the flogged body and the slender figure of the flogger. Janet was the quintessence of what, in his view, an s/m flagellator should display; a semi-nude, lithe, muscular and imperious presence dedicated to inflicting pain—and possibly, he trusted, a modicum of pleasure. After all, he mused, Marina possessed the perverse intransigence and courage of a submissive sex slave, capable of holding out until her mental and physical strength was sapped; she knew the thrills of stark naked flagellation, appreciated and even relished a skilful whipping in the same way as she rode a fucking. Above all, he knew the girl associated the whip with orgasm.

But Marina was far from orgasm. She was suffering grotesquely. The whipping at the hand of the expert Englishwoman was almost worse than the multiple scourging in the Hall of Ceremony.

Claudia did not count the lashes that fell over the cunt. All she observed in her mounting excitement was the way Janet's thongs carved into the ringed flesh, splitting the labia, measuring their length along the splayed vulva and smiting the erect clitoris. Each stroke caused the bright rings to leap in the swollen, tumefied lips that fluttered and glittered with discharge. The sex received its ration of thrashing with long, drawn-out moans, not unlike, to Claudia's ears, the low keening the slave made when approaching her orgasms. But here and now, she hoped the bitch would be denied her climax.

Without pausing but after cleaning off her whip, Janet returned to the side of the body. And the piercing commenced.

One by one, the bright needles were brought to the welted breasts. Expertly, the woman distended the nipple by its ring, placed the point of the steel against the taut flesh and thrust it through the skin. The process was performed with unhurried art; the needles remained embedded deep in the gorgeous chunks of mammary meat, Janet dealt with each breast in turn until a dozen spikes had found their way into each of the soft, trembling, organs. She reserved the last two for the teats, transfixing them below the ring perforations. Then she let the mounds subside back on to the chest. A murmur of approbation rose from the onlookers at which Janet smiled. She was accustomed to praise. She knew her prowess.

The piercing of the cunt lasted longer and was carried out with more dexterity. She inserted at least ten in one manner or the other until the loose flesh was weighted down. Marina drew in her breath at each insertion; the flesh had been so thoroughly whipped that the slave barely sensed the piercing. The mere thought sufficed.

It was, however, the long, treacherous needle transpiercing the robust clitoris that seemed to transcend the pain Marina had endured thitherto. She hauled her flagellated body off the post beneath her, arching upwards from her four manacles. She screamed once—a long, unearthly shriek that stilled the sounds of fornication and fellatio in the chamber. Then she slumped back and lay quivering, sobbing uncontrollably.

"Thank you, Madame," Vasa said. "A proficient performance, I must say." Her remark harboured a trace of jaundiced envy and, as if to recompense herself, she glued her cunt to Marina's face. "Suck, slave!" was all she said as she grasped the hanging head. At the same moment, Lalanière approached the splayed thighs, his cock rampant, almost obscene in its stiffness. Meticulously, the overseer parted two parallel needles to achieve space for entry, and thrust inwards. Marina heaved again as she was violated, the huge shaft stretching the pierced lips aside, the needles rasping the man's erection. The slave responded unbelievably.

As if intoxicated by her tortures, Marina tensed, servicing Vasa with all her force, tongue and lips at work on the dripping vulva and sopping hairs. Her loins rose and fell to the extreme extent her bondage allowed, while Janet stood beside the sweating, tortured girl, playing perniciously with the quavering, transpierced breasts.

Vasa came first, she groaned and came massively, crushing her cunt into the face. Releasing the head, she slapped the girl's face; the blow seemed to drive Marina into her own orgasm. She lurched and rose in her chains, her whole body tetanised as the sexual spasm exploded with wild, lascivious cries.

"Fuck me! Fuck me! Ahh… Ahh… More! Deeper!" The shrieks were poison to Claudia's ears. What a whore! To come cleanly, totally, carnally after such treatment! Claudia could resist no longer. She mounted across Mikhail's thighs and fed the great cock into her. She needed cock more than she had ever dreamt of in her lecherous, salacious life. Sex torture of this degree rendered her helpless, lost in the tornado that roared through her loins. Mikhail fucked her gut with all the power that had built up in his balls…

Comparatively, Lalanière's release of boiling sperm into Marina was almost complaisant. The pressure and torsion of the bodkins traversing her cunt had brought his ejaculation on rapidly, too rapidly for his liking. He withdrew reluctantly. He relished the tight cunt grip.

Inwardly, the overseer knew he was in love with this fabulous slave.

It was Vasa, after wiping herself clean, who invited the Contessa Marisa to step forward. The pale woman did not require persuading. Throwing off her ermine cloak, and grasping her plaited leather scourge, she approached Verenka. By then, the naked slave had hung for an unconscionable time. Her teats protruded to twice their normal size, revealing the slots through which her rings were inserted. The superb body gyrated slowly, the surface of the inner thighs shimmering with discharge. She had been shattered by the treatment reserved for Marina, however little she cared for her, and yet she had been inordinately excited by the flogging off of the wax and the needle torture, quite apart from the fucking her erstwhile lover had enjoyed. Now it was her turn. Although she had been whipped on countless occasions both in Paris and now here at Beaucastel, she apprehended what her new mistress was about to do to her. She was fully aware that her breasts could take little more however sturdy she knew them to be; but the flagellation now being prepared for her would certainly take her breasts into monstrous pain, leave alone the flesh of her hanging body. Yet Ashley, the divine Ashley was there watching.

Verenka gritted her teeth. She would show them how a nude girl could endure the whip. She looked apprehensively at the half-dressed, middle-aged Italian dominatrix steadying her revolving nakedness. She had been bought and therefore had to be put to the test. And then Venice. And Ashley!

"I shall give you, Verenka dearest, fifty lashes from neck to knees." The Contessa's soft accent in French scared her more than even Vasa's commands in Cell Three. "I want you to enjoy it. Sex will come later."

The noble lady, having divested herself of most of her clothing, revealing a pleasantly harmonious body but fairly desiccated breasts, was in no hurry to lay on her short plaited whip, fashioned from bulls' penises, an old favourite among experienced floggers.

The woman studied the nude figure, turning Verenka round with the handle of her fearsome scourge. She seemed to approve, particularly when the silver haft separated the girl's rich labia, seeping with the conviction of a highly-sexed whipping slave.

"I see you are dripping, Verenka. Well, that is admirable, my dear. As I say, you must enjoy everything we are going to do to you in future, just as Ashley enjoys her nights in chains." she corrected herself, "You will be whipped regularly and severely, naked, by myself, by Franco and by our servants. Solely during your periods will you be excused." She paused, caressing the straining breast flesh.

"You have magnificent breasts, which naturally you know." The jewelled hand followed the generous curve of the rump. "And a sublime bottom made for the whip and cane. Now, you may utter cries here but never at home. I hope this is clear, particularly as I flog hard."

Verenka nodded as best she could. "Si, carissima Contessa Claro."

And the lash fell.

She was flogged slowly but formidably hard, the woman ensuring the stiff lash curled round the body to punish every area of tender flesh. Claudia had never heard Verenka grind her teeth the way she did during the initial twenty strokes from the Contessa's tiny but vicious hand; but neither had Claudia ever heard shrieks such as those Verenka uttered throughout the second half of the flagellation. It seemed the more demented the cry from the beaten, the greater the verve the beater dedicated to her swing and cut across the nude. Rapidly, the flesh turned to crimson, the welts rising relentlessly. The slave heaved and jerked grotesquely for a time and then subsided into the torpor Mikhail and Claudia knew so well. It was then that the Contessa paused. Gently she passed the length of her whip up the sex slit, parting the plump labia to reveal Verenka's famous clit; it stood out straight amid the sombre pubic forest of matted hair, pulsating in its full glory, the hood of dusky skin wreathed back round the base. The woman stared at the thing, prodding it with the doubled-back curve of the lash.

"Dio mio, Franco! Guarda! It's enormous. You'll be able to tie her by it, as you like to do. It beats darling Ashley's! And, look, it throbs, demanding attention. Oh, Franco!"

And with that the Contessa curtailed her whipping, amazed at the size of the stump. Instead, she frictioned the pink protuberance with her whip. Verenka responded as she always did in Paris, jolting and lurching, wrenching on her breast thongs. Her breath became deeper, the eyes closed.

"Oh, yes, yes… please! Punish it, hit it, screw it, please! Suck me, please, please!"

"How dare you say that!" The Contessa was appalled at the begging. "That's Ashley's business, cara, not mine." She swung round to summon Ashley to the centre of the cellar.

She knelt gracefully before her suspended lover, spreading her own thighs wide as the Contessa liked them to be; with her thumbs she drew back the labia by the rings until the cunt was totally splayed in all its drenched, crimson breadth, with the clitoris throbbing in erect anticipation, surrounded by its ring. Ashley looked for a second at the oval gash that she had invaded, chafed, sucked and licked so often. No other genitals were as succulent and vivid, even when the vagina was rancid with male sperm after Verenka had been disciplined in Cell Three… Even that provoked Ashley into wild passion.

Delicately, Ashley took the proud prong of pulsing flesh

into her lips. It felt like gristle that was soft after being left in liquid and deserved a tonguing, a smooth suction along its swart length until Verenka was delirious.

"Ashley darling! Oh, my God, Ashley, Ashley… bite me hard. I'm pouring with love of you. Flick it like the other night… Yes, yes, yes, darling, that's it. On the tip. Please… Now your fingers into my arsehole. Yes, yes! Deeper. Ream it raw, darling… Make me bleed."

The Contessa leaned against the wall of the dungeon, not so much fatigued but rather taken aback by the silky sound of the cunnilingus and the lovely face of her slave glittering with cum and saliva. The agile tongue worked hard and she watched with rapture. The two girls seemed made for each other. And for her. Indeed, she would have both in bed with her the moment they were back in Venice. Chained together.

Verenka came like one of those rare storms over the Lagoon in Venice, heaving herself upwards by the breasts, thrusting into Ashley's face and screaming her relief.

"Oh, God, Ashley, Ashley… I'm dying. You've slaughtered me again. Can you drink up all my cum, darling? It's all yours… I love you, love you. Don't stop… I'm coming again!"

"That will do, girls, thank you," the Contessa Marisa said gently to call a halt to one of the most delightful orgasms she had witnessed for weeks.

On the far side of the dungeon Marina spat. "The dirty whore!" With Marina it had been solely the cunt that had responded, not the voice. She felt strangely angry, outclassed.

Entirely satisfied both with her new acquisition's reaction to her scourge and with the cunt's response to her favourite slave's administrations, the Contessa curled up her whip and returned elegantly but sweating to her seat. Her husband congratulated her effusively. This was money well spent. The slave was gifted, her nudity was stupendous.

It was Gerda who was sent by Vasa to release the flogged, orgiastic slave whom she lowered until the feet rested on the flagstones, the knees bending with difficulty in supporting

169

the weight of the body. Unbinding the breasts, she let the purple masses drop heavily on to the thorax as the flesh gorged with blood, leaving white and violet ridges where the thongs had done their duty.

The pain induced by the breasts' return to normal seemed worse than the recent strokes of the whip, for Verenka cried out uncontrollably as the blood resumed its circulation. She screwed up her features as the surge continued, swinging the globes across her body as if to rid herself of their agony.

"It's quite normal, 106," Gerda comforted her, as she seized the shaking mounds and, as was the procedure at Beaucastel, began to massage them, offering a trace of solace to the trembling nude. Partially and progessively, the breasts resumed their usual form but remained massively marked where the thongs had bitten. Gerda was only too accustomed to the girl's reaction; she had constricted, beaten, tortured with pincers and released scores and scores of pairs of breasts.

Gradually the areoles and teats lost their tumescence, settling back into the summit of each superb, lush hunk of flesh, the rings hanging more or less correctly.

"That's what breasts are for, 106." Gerda offered by way of consolation. "You have to become accustomed to it. For God's sake, stop blubbering you baby, or I'll have you over the trestle."

Almost all slaves at Beaucastel were at some time subjected to the procedure but with infinite care; the discipline not exceeding thirty minutes.

Verenka had hung for close on an hour but that was not Mikhail's concern any more.

Though conscious he was losing her and her flexible, welcoming anus to others, he was proud of her behaviour.

Too bad to discard her but there were always other flesh slaves.

Lalanière released, one by one, the manacles that held out Marina's legs, allowing her to stand, however precariously after the extension, on her own two feet, yet with her wrists still bound to opposing walls. The gesture of liberation was not one of clemency but a sign that her debt had been duly paid to Beaucastel.

The release sent arrows of pain through her limbs after two hours of extension; as the muscular tension subsided, Marina was allowed to teeter drunkenly on unsteady legs. While she swayed, uncertain of her fate, the needles remained in place. The abrupt sight of her scourged and skewered flesh sent a shudder of shock through her head but it was mingled with a curious thrill of sexual pleasure and of pride. What more could be inflicted on a sex slave such as she? Had she not attained the summit of her calling? Only a submissive with her personal and explicit commitment to slavery and her stamina could have braved such a night and found a perplexing gratification at the same time. Subconsciously she felt unaccountably beholden, even grateful, and sexually attracted to the Englishwoman who had worked on her body with such vehemence and obvious pleasure. So different from the crude approach of the bitch Claudia.

Looking at Verenka, Marina felt a swelling need to do precisely the same to her. Take her to tears and then to screams. She wondered again if she herself could be two persons in one, a docile submissive and a dominatrix. Verenka's stretched body had attracted her in just that way. She had learnt much about the whip over the last months. Time would tell.

Yet, with a twinge of remorse Marina recalled Verenka's lusty, extended clitoris at the apex of the magical, soft cunt, the black triangle of luxuriant hair, damp with those incessant oozings from the rose-hued vagina, which now the arrogant Ashley would supervise… Marina switched her recollections off and programmed renewed venom. Somewhere within her, a distant voice encouraged her to hope some perverted dominant one day would slice into Verenka's udders and whip her senseless and… She squeezed her eyes up tight to kill the merciless image.

CHAPTER 16

The guests shuffled and chatted among themselves as the Verenka sequence came to an end. They were more than pleased with what the Master was always able to arrange to satisfy their lust which made their journeys well worthwhile. Many other institutions were far less attractive, employing worn-out whores or members' capricious spouses or dull, gullible mistresses who restricted life to the sobriety of plastic or velvet whips. Beaucastel at least had the mettle to provide sumptuous flesh and torture chambers. Expensive maybe, but good value.

There was again an exchanging of sex slaves during the intermission. Among the servicing females, Katia had to be replaced in view of her exhaustion—for which Vasa would give her on the morrow thirty lashes in the terrible Cell Seven, a mere routine. She was dragged out and her replacement, Renée, entered, full of anguish.

The audience began to thin out. The hour was late and fatigue was taxing the hardiest among the onlookers. Some, however, among them Mikhail and the indefatigable Claudia, now deprived of her lover's wilting cock, stayed on for the final act.

The procedure—slave branding—was short and crisp, far more expeditious than the long floggings dedicated to Marina and Verenka. It lasted barely ten minutes but to Claudia's mind was worth waiting for. One of her deepest yearnings lay in precisely that: to possess, like Juliette in Paris, a reliable sexual slave and to mark and scorch her as her own.

To the far end of the dungeon—the Master insisted that his guests should not be incommoded by fumes—the brazier was being stoked up by the squat Roscoff, masked and wearing a leather apron which, unfortunately for Claudia, concealed his thick cock and hirsute set of testicles the size of billiard balls, luggage that Claudia admired, mainly because they resembled Mikhail's, one hanging lower than its neighbour, and which she prided herself she could roll around together in her mouth.

To the right of the dungeon, the victim hung, spread wide in total extension on the Beaucastel branding grid. The naked woman had her breasts passed through the rods of the grid, bound and sagging beyond. And they were weighted with steel Morgenstern spheres to add joy.

She was the precise type of experienced, middle-aged slave so popular among younger dominants and dominatrices. Despite her age and the punishments she must have endured, to judge by the state of her body, Claudia had to admire the wealth of the rump; bound tightly above over the waist and below round the thighs, the posture and presentation of the massive lumps of buttock meat made them perfect for what was to be done to them. Roscoff first checked and adjusted the direction of the video camera situated in the corner of the dungeon, for Beaucastel to retain complete records... Lifting his apron, the man took hold of his massive cock—to Claudia's delight—and slicked back the foreskin before separating the woman's voluptuous volumes of arse flesh. The anus was bared, already partially open, surrounded by its dark brown, sepia ring, bearing testimony to long-standing, hallowed usage by male erections.

The overseer pressed his vast weapon on to the hole and then bored inwards, tightening his own buttocks, penetrating easily as the sphincter relaxed obediently. For a long moment he shafted the anus with slow, determined thrusts, working diligently and with precise force while the woman jerked, unable in her bondage to respond more freely. Not a sound came from her mouth but the muscles reflected the stimulus of the penetration.

The reaming lasted only a few minutes before the man withdrew, holding back his spunk. He pulled out with a wrench, extruding with his cock the inner anal lining of mucous membrane and circle of muscle, exuding liquids. The aperture, Claudia reflected, was like a mouth blowing out a candle; it remained agape, throbbing for a moment before the overseer released the surrounding meat and the buttocks closed, to clench together with twitching spasms.

To Claudia's dismay, the apron fell back to cover the still rampant cock; she always relished the sight of an erect penis during Mikhail's work on Verenka's behind. But, as compensation, she watched Roscoff extract the first of the two irons from the incandescent cage of coals. He tapped the rod against the torture grid by the side of the oiled body to shake off the ashes. With deliberation, he planted the sparking face of the iron's head firmly into the upper slope of the left buttock. The epidermis sizzled with grey smoke. The female screamed once, grinding her nude carcass into the grating and then sagged. Whether she had fainted Claudia could not guess but when the second iron scarred the right side of the great butt, the naked figure did not react. The peculiar odour of scorched flesh was remote but gradually wafted down the dungeon. The initials, Claudia presumed, of an adored and adoring owner stared out hideously in black on the blanched flesh that glimmered with oil and sweat.

Roscoff then doused the charcoal brazier, removed his apron, to Claudia's relief, and returned to the body. Again he split open the cheeks in order to bore into the anus once more. To take a branded slave was evidently for the man more exciting than to fuck a whipped female; his orgasm came promptly, after only a couple of dozen potent thrusts—a gratifying reward for efficient work. Amazingly, the pallid woman seemed to revive with the distension and vigorous reaming of her rectum, for which she was rewarded with the generous ejaculation the eminent Beaucastel overseer had reserved for her and which he deposited in her bowels as if to endorse the branding, in line with Beaucastel procedures.

When the marked woman had been taken off the gridiron and revived with a bucket of water, Gabrielle, clad only in black stockings, came forward. Lethargically, she first attended to the scars on the drooping masses of rump flesh, smearing in ointments and then turned to Marina, drawing out the

174

collection of needles from the numbed breasts and cunt and medicating the perforations and fissures. She returned the fine steel spikes to their antiseptic receptacles and subsequently, with an air of lassitude, cleaned up Verenka, treating the lacerations and welts casually with dressings.

All three nudes were by now linked by their throat straps into a coffle to be led stumbling out of the dungeon towards their beds in the Slave Hall, towards well-earned respite; they would rest as best they could, nursing their damage gingerly.

The night with all its daunting ordeals appeared to the slaves to be over. At last.

It was at a turning in the last stairwell leading up to the Slave Hall that Lalanière halted the procession.

"I'll take this slave over, Gaby, thank you." The warder unhooked Marina, handing the throat chain to her senior without a word. One slut less to deal with.

Marina found herself being led to a region of the castle that was foreign to her. The corridors were hung with rich tapestries and at equal intervals candles burned in sconces giving off a strange aroma of verbena, or some aromatic herb Marina did not recognize. Under her bare, toughened soles the carpets yielded like silk, the incredible luxury of the place only serving to exacerbate the fear clawing at her throat.

They passed through a cloister into a large, well-furnished chamber.

While Lalanière locked the door, the trembling slave glanced round the room; it was relatively Spartan but in excellent taste. The furnishings consisted of a large table, chairs and a pleasant four-poster bed to one side. To the other, however, festooned with chains, stood a stout oaken flogging stake, reaching to the groined vaulting above and obligingly facing the end of the bed. Behind on the wall hung a row of flesh scourges, neatly arrayed by order of their toughness. Marina at once concluded she was to be lashed to the blood again in an eminently private session to satisfy the overseer's appetite, even before her welts had been given the chance to heal;

accordingly she braced herself, her womb clenching, her nipples puckering with fright and yet the clitoris rigid.

Lalanière however led her to the bed.

"I need to talk to you, Marina." The soft words scared the girl even more than if she had been ordered to stand against the stake. Above all, the use of her name instead of her slave designation, 107, sent a cold shiver through her entrails. What was the man up to? All her danger lights were flashing in her brain..

"We have noticed how appropriately you accept your beatings, yet never seem to abase yourself, like so many others, to abject humiliation. True, you appear resigned and seem to enjoy your whippings but keep your being intact. Am I right? You can call me Pierre."

"I suppose that's so—the whip excites me. I like surrendering to it. I accepted it first on account of that bitch Verenka and grew to love it—the nudity, the exposure as centre of attention, the pain merging into wild sexual pleasure... You know all this."

The overseer nodded before saying: "I watched you carefully while your former lover was being flagellated. Your eyes were hard and gleaming at the sight." He paused before the question came.

"Tell me, would you like to have wielded that whip in the place of the Contessa?"

Marina's heart missed a beat. The man's candid query disarmed her. How did he guess? Should she be honest and declare that other hidden part lurking within herself?

"You mean whip Verenka?"

"I mean just that. Stark naked. To teach her fidelity. But now she's leaving."

A long stillness ensued before Marina could summon up her reply. "Yes, I would have given anything to lash her. Beat her until she begged for forgiveness, the bitch!" She blurted out the words and fell silent for a moment. "I gather she's been bought. Too bad! But yes, Pierre, I should have loved to whip her just as that Janet scourged me. Are you surprised?"

"Not at all. I knew from the start you had it in you. And thus you could pass to the other side of the s/m mirror, Marina. Am I right?"

"Yes. Just give me the chance! I adored watching you flog and then approach slowly in all your handsome manhood with those long flesh tongs in your grasp. Whatever the price in terms of pain, your gorgeous erection and the lash thrill me. I'm sure I could do it." She reached for the throbbing pole of male flesh and beginning to frig it. "I've learnt a lot here."

"As we thought." Lalanière smiled. "You are capable of both roles. You have immense poise. And, for me, you are one of the most beautiful, bewitching women I've seen here. When I flagellate you, I desire you. When I start to fuck you, I want to flagellate you again. And when it's over, I want to have you to myself, right here in my rooms. I suppose, in this strange world, this is what is called love."

Marina felt her throat tighten with excitement. What was happening to her? Was this some sort of subterfuge to trap her in some further predicament, out of which the only issue would be sex torture and caning for endless hours? Yet Pierre enthralled her.

Suddenly the handsome face leaned over and kissed her. "I want you, Marina. Not as in the cells but as an equal." Marina returned his kisses with all the lust and meaning she had in her, instinctively massaging the full length of the cock as if she were a free agent. Her hand slithered intoxicatingly up and down the great shaft; she admired its silky head and the seeping slit that had propelled so much churning semen into her over the last week. The volume of erect flesh was hard and thumped with the man's heartbeats; and her own sex slackened with craving, and then flooded uncontrollably.

"Marina, you have the makings of a dominant female and you know it." The overseer resisted the seductions of the fabulous sexual body next to him; he still had his message to convey. Then they would fuck as never before.

"You've seen them at work, Vasa, Gerda, Gabrielle. This is something you could graduate to and we want you to try." He thrust up his hips to provide the girl with the full gamut of his cock. "The Master of Beaucastel is prepared to offer you a place as a probationary overseer here. You would be under my wing and jurisdiction. Vasa more or less agrees but Gerda needs further convincing, though something tells us that she won't be staying long among us. That would be a slot for you." He gestured to her to seize his balls in her other hand. "Well?"

The girl was now with her head on his chest. "I don't really know, Pierre. Certainly I'll never return to that couple of degenerates in Paris. And not to that damn lycee…"

The shaved head looked up. "Can I have time to think it over, Pierre?"

"No way, delicious. Your proprietors leave today after lunch and the deal, if deal there is, must have been concluded by now. And the payment arranged."

"You mean Beaucastel would purchase me?" Her intestines lurched with elation. "Those bastards didn't even buy me. I joined Verenka for free because I fell in love with her!"

"We are fully aware of how you became entangled with Madame de Clesson and her disgustingly wealthy lover. The Master has already broached the matter with them. It's just the figure that remains to be agreed upon. That's being discussed right now." Lalanière pulled the beauty towards him by the breast rings. He wanted her badly.

"And incidentally your rings will be removed," he added as an afterthought. Marina could not care whether they went or stayed; in a way she liked them. They excited her but basically they were unimportant. What was important was that she knew she was going to be fucked, not whipped at the stake beyond the bed but fucked, and fucked as a free woman for once. She knew the decision had been taken already. The man's arms were around her, drawing her up to slide down on the splendid shaft offered.

As if by way of confirmation, not only of what was about to enter her cunt but of what her future held in store for her, she smiled: "I agree, Pierre. If you will look after me, teach me the rules of the game... And fuck me well. Just as you're going to do now."

The man shafted her with a curious tenderness; to Marina it was totally unfamiliar. And her three orgasms were like none she had experienced over the last months; they came down into her from another world—where some women were free and other women were in chains, unable and unwilling to shuffle them off. And she had decided to liberate herself and join the wonderful, beautiful people of Beaucastel. She would issue forth from Lalanière's quarters a superb flagellatrice, equipped with spiked heels and tall boots to her upper thighs, and breast straps. She would be given, to begin with, an array of whips with which to train on the newly arrived slaves and would be favoured with instructions in disciplining from Lalanière himself. Marina agreed unconditionally. It was a secret dream come true...

Prior to her assumption of office, however, she was ushered into the august presence of the Master for a brief ceremony of formal induction as a member of the community. For the occasion, she was fastidiously prepared; one by one her seven slave rings and five bondage straps were severed. Once bathed, anointed and elegantly made up, Vasa helped her into the high boots and body straps, throwing round her shoulders a long velvet cloak with a high, stiff collar attached by a precious silver clasp embossed with sign of the crossed whips of Beaucastel.

As she entered the holy of holies, her cloak billowing open about her, she recalled the last occasion of such an honour, that moment when her audaciousness had been rewarded with a mouthful of the inestimable semen that was shared by few. Had it helped?

The Master rose from his desk to take stock of the girl he had agreed to promote.

"You are a propitious candidate, my girl. And as such I have purchased you. You have proved yourself with mettle and indomitable faith in your body. Indeed, I have observed your compliance and composure throughout your time here, particularly during your recent tortures, and have no hesitation, now that you belong to Beaucastel through legitimate purchase, in offering you a place here among us as an apprentice overseer. If your conduct—which must be one of complete detachment when on duty with slaves—is faultless during the first month, you will be upgraded to the rank of overseer. Should you give me grounds for complaint, you will be ringed again, whipped and put up for sale."

Marina bowed low. The threat jolted her uterus, making it contract.

"I shall serve Beaucastel, sir, with faith," she murmured, watching the man draw aside his own heavy, embroidered mantle. The thick cock had risen to its full tumescence, the pubis still shaved clean, as she remembered. The Master leaned nonchalantly against the edge of the table, thrusting a pile of papers aside. The pelvis urged forward.

"You may express you appreciation by sucking me to orgasm as the official confirmation of your promotion. Kneel and perform."

In a state of bizarre euphoria, Marina unfastened her cloak and dropped to her knees, naked but freed of her emblems of slavery. She went to work as never before in her life, employing every skill, every resource of virtuosity she had learnt as a sex slave, until the glut of heavy, sluggish spunk swamped and clogged her throat. Desperately she tried not to choke on the massive load; then she swallowed in successive gulps, draining the shaft with all her fingers grasping, her lips tight. Not a drop of the spending was squandered. She felt a thrill of achievement invade her.

She was an overseer of Beaucastel. Inconceivable!

"Get Alana to apply liniments to your skull and eyebrows to ensure rapid regrowth. They are the badge of your past slavery." Astonished, Marina then heard the unimaginable. She could not trust her ears as the words reached her.

"I regret having had to crop and shave you, Marina. You suck with unimpeachable lust and finesse. Go now and render service to our illustrious institution."

Marina had heard her name and the expression of remorse in one sentence and that from the Master of Beaucastel! She bowed, seized her cloak and left to assume her new calling: the profession of a committed and devout flagellatrice in the enclaves of a mighty castle where the whip ruled supreme. For the first time since the night before that obscene slug of a whore had changed beds, Marina was wreathed in smiles though her body ached and smarted with a memory of delicious, atrocious pain now fading into the past.

CHAPTER 17

In the following hours, the castle saw a great deal of movement. Not only were the guests departing, some accompanied by their own slaves, others with their purchases, but a fresh batch of five girls and two youths were being signed in for their period of training under the procedures that rarely varied. One novelty, however, was noticeable to all concerned: Marina was instructed to attend the induction ceremony to learn from Vasa, She sat, a little unsure of herself, at the table as the newcomers were checked.

Mikhail and Claudia were packed and ready to leave under the driving sleet, although the blonde beauty would have gladly stayed on but Mikhail had a bankers' meeting the next day in Paris. Moreover he was loath to leave his mistress under the same roof as Marina after the scene in the dungeon. Claudia had mixed feelings.

Despondently, she stared at the Rouergue countryside drifting past with its inhospitable, endless causses, stone walls and miserably wet sheep.

Mikhail reminded her gently of the price they had negotiated for Marina, for a slave they had acquired almost for free. That, Claudia conceded. Maybe, she thought Juliette could be persuaded to lend them Tansu while they looked round for replacements. Though she doubted it. A docile whore from Madame Flora's establishment could perhaps suffice for a day or two. She couldn't bear to think of the Quai d'Anjou empty, the library unused.

Claudia's mind went back to Gerda, the seductive Gerda who was so capable of pleasuring a woman. But she was a dominant. If the overseer did in fact relinquish her place— and salary—at Beaucastel, she would be worth talking to… But to be bereft of her whipping slaves depressed Claudia de Clesson, a dynamic creature who, she admitted to herself, could not be destituted for long of sleek, female bodies with tender breasts and hungry cunts. Mikhail was of very little help and anyway was fast asleep. Even if he had access to the private Falcon plane from Rodez on, he was of pathetically little help to a damsel in distress. And Claudia hated his snoring. Maybe she was wasting her life with him. She needed a change.

Wrapped in furs, the Master bade a phlegmatic goodbye and a buon viaggio to the group of Venetians at the castle drawbridge. The man had been flattered by the attendance of such noble guests—and shareholders—at the sessions; they had been fed abundantly, accommodated graciously and had paid up promptly when, for reasons beyond the Master's comprehension, they had selected the common slave 106.

Yet he was aware of their gratitude. The slave, number 90, the oversexed English girl, had been stimulated to the maximum, her stamina strengthened and her delicious body flagellated beyond reason. That was what they had requested and the Master recalled the vision of Ashley, hung by the legs, swaying under Vasa's black whip. An exceptional one

He was comforted to see Verenka leave. The young whore had nearly caused bedlam with her sexual appetite for the English beauty and her changing of partners in the midstream of training. The Master recognized the flogging the girl had received from her new mistress as a due. The less he saw of Verenka in the future, the better. Let the Serenissima hang her again by the breasts and carve her gross buttocks, like silver moons, into strips of welted meat.

The two Venetian owners dozed in the warmth of the old Hispano-Suiza forging its majestic path through the slush and the timorous winter light of uncertain day. Verenka felt she was being transported to some allegorical, sexual heaven to be so close to her darling Ashley, despite the flesh smarting with the memory of the beating.

Although medicated with soothing lotions, she lay on her side in the car to alleviate the residual throbbings and pain; the Contessa had gone deep into her epidermis and slit the buttock and thigh flesh. The roots of her breasts still seethed as if the thongs had never been unwrapped; the teats lingered in remorseless erection, tugging at the steel rings, now linked together to conform with the Contessa's wish. She detested loose dugs on slaves. Especially in travel and on safari.

Ashley looked superb in her Russian chapka of white wolf—a present from the Conte after visiting the prison and torture chambers on the banks of the Neva—and a fur coat down to her heels. Verenka wore more or less the same but admired the way Ashley set her cap at an angle; she adored her, like a serf adoring Catherine the Great.

"Tell me about Venice, darling," Verenka implored, kissing her lover's freckled cheek.

Ashley laid a warning finger on the girl's mouth. "Whisper, sweet. Don't wake them. Well, the Palazzo Consenzia is paradise," she went on. "You've never imagined a place as luxurious—our rooms are vast and furnished totally Rinascento. You're going to be spoilt beyond words!"

"Are we the only ones? I mean, just us two, like Marina and me in Paris?"

"Well, not quite, darling, there's another slave but she's kept in the cellars. They're damp as they're below the level of the canal, you see. I've only seen her once when she was brought up for some medical treatment by our dear old dottore, called Raspoli. I like him but you always have to give into him when he treats you. He adores a quick cock suck. Anyway, she was laid flat on the ottoman in the salotto and I could see what they had done to her. She was stark naked, scourged to the blood."

Verenka's eyes widened. "But that's not going to happen to us, is it? That last beating was ghastly even if it excited me when I got used to the first load of lashes."

"Of course not, silly. That's not for us. They thrash us, but with moderation. That whore was just a flesh slave." Ashley smiled and kissed her, her tongue probing deep into her mouth.

"Who are 'they', Ashley?" Whenever Ashley mentioned whipping, Verenka's slit seemed to become tacky as it opened to let her juices seep out and slide down the luscious inner thigh. Ashley sensed the slight quickening of her lover's pulse, enough to encourage her to slide her hand deftly under the furs into Verenka's vagina. And there she kept it while talking softly. On no account should the dozing couple catch a word of the exchange.

"Oh, 'they'?" she whispered. "I mean the guests at the Casa Consenzia. They go down to the nether regions after dinner— you'll adore the dinners in the Hall, hearing all sorts of secrets and confidences—and sexual crud-talk. We slaves are always chained to the table and have to smile all the time. And whatever goes on down there must be exacting because they always emerge flushed and covered with sweat. Fortunato— he's my private fuck, by the way—won't tell me more. And for heaven's sake, don't utter a word of all this in front of the Contessa Marisa. She'd whip me to death for even hinting at the cellars."

Ashley glanced up at the sleeping couple before going on. "And by the way, you can only suck and fuck with those the Contessa designates. Don't ever forget, you're a sex slave and the property of Marisa. Whatever she commands, you do. And when she tells you strip and fetch the thongs and riding crop, run like hell and then slap your belly firmly against the stake. Move fast!"

"Otherwise, darling," went on the ash-blonde, more ravishing than ever in her furs, "one risks finishing up like the one downstairs."

"What sort of things do they do to her?" Verenka wanted the full picture or as much of it as she could get; it gave the unknown Palazzo some reality, and Verenka a lot of strange pleasure she found difficult to control.

"It's pretty fierce, says Fortunato. Apparently the poor girl is chained, all the time she's not in use, to some sort of grating, on her knees, arms above her blindfolded head. The nipples are drawn down to the clit ring with golden chains and she's impaled up the cunt and in the butt on huge iron phalluses to keep her fit."

Her description left a soft smouldering in the elder girl's eye but it came from watching Verenka. Her reaction had been prompt and she would need satisfying very soon. Right there.

Ashley shifted closer on the car's floor of cushions until she was cradling the sultry beauty, her fingers busy from the brown bud of the anus to the pubic bone. To provoke Verenka further, she mentioned casually: "They're thinking of getting rid of the slave, either by public auction or through dear old Beaucastel after a refresher course there. And we all know what that means! In fact, she'll be thrown on to the trash market and sold off for a song. In any case, she can't be worth much after all that wear and tear. And she's only just nineteen. Like you, darling."

Ashley had the stalwart clit-prong firmly between her fingers; it was hot and slimy, set for another journey into the galaxies. She had prepared Verenka well but going down on the swollen, quivering gash was precluded. That, one did not do in a Hispano-Suiza under the nose of one's owners, even if they were asleep.

"You don't think, do you, I'm meant to replace that girl?" Verenka's voice was little more than a waft of breath at Ashley's ear. There was fear in it but it did not seem to impede the building up of a massively complex orgasm, combining pure yearning, wild love and cunt-lust for the milk-fleshed Englishwoman masturbating her under the soft furs, and once again, more coherently than ever—a frantic erotic desire to be put to the whip, abused, hurt and humiliated before this dream of a lover...

"Don't be absurd, honey. We'll live together in the west wing of the Consenzia overlooking the canal. You'll see, it's all fabulous and magical—as long as you obey and reciprocate sexually, even in the torture chamber—and you'll adore it, darling. You get a perfumed bath with oils and massage first." She withdrew her white hand from Verenka's vagina, leaving it gaping and throbbing. "You know I became a trifle soft and

186

needed tuning up, hence my fortnight at Beaucastel. It did me the world of good. Even Vasa agreed!"

Verenka nodded. She too felt toughened and more at ease confronted with a table loaded with instruments of sexual arousal, as Lalanière used to term the things.

Ashley went on gaily. "Of course, one's always under strict surveillance, as slaves must be. But in the day it's all fairly free as long as you're fuori lavoro—I mean, out of session. But things change in the evening… Not every night but most. You're taken into the salotto di preparazione—how's my Italian? You've got to teach me more, I'm hopeless—and stripped naked. It's there that all the paraphernalia's kept: masks, beautiful hoods, body straps, leather corsets, cache-sexes with delicious sharp points all over. And gorgeous, heavy silk cloaks and high-heeled shoes, plenty of chains and weights, and so on… Are you with me, darling?"

Verenka lay inert, her eyes closed. Her vagina was clenching and releasing with lust.

"Yes. Go on. I don't think I can last much longer."

"Well, Sergio and his pretty, sexy wife are in charge, and following their orders, there you're stripped naked, as I say, oiled and loaded with gold chains on all your rings. Often they want you to wear breasts thongs with silver spikes inside to hold you nice and tight. It's simply too erotic for words. And you hear them, if you're not too hooded up, talking about your body and deciding how to chain and flagellate you. I adore that moment, darling. Oh, and I forgot the cunt harnesses. You've got to know about them, treasure. Neat, thin, tight straps round your loins with barbs in them to splay you out wide so that they can work on you to their hearts' content. You spend time after time…"

The older woman then glanced up warily at her owners. They seemed fast asleep still and so she slipped her long, delicate fingers between the furs into Verenka. She found the slit fluid and yet congested and crusted with earlier viscous discharge. The girl was only too ready and needed help.

Skilfully and maliciously, the hand stirred and stimulated the quivering vent of soft mucus. The clit was stiff, supplicating…

"Don't, Ashley, or I'll come." The warning sounded hoarse, intense with a need more urgent than Ashley had ever sensed with her.

"All right. Just because this is not quite the right time and place for you start screaming and thrashing around as you did every night back there."

Verenka was both relieved and frustrated to be rid of the tempting hand.

"Well, the guests gather in the torture chamber." Ashley, all the same, refused to let the girl go. "And it's quite a sight. They appear in sombre cloaks, split down the front—to leave their cocks and cunts free. They're very appealing, at least to me. They always wear that rather frightening bautta, you know, that sickly white mask of the Carnevale under the three-cornered hat. It's sinister, especially when they come up close to maul you and you're stretched naked between pillars. That's when Marisa unlocks my bunch of cunt-rings to free me for the entertainment. And entertainment it is!"

Ashley drew her lover's hand towards her to touch the cluster of metal protecting her major sexual orifice. Verenka felt the rings and tiny padlock amid the superbly furled labia bordering the cleft. The sex was exquisitely wet, drenched with expectancy.

"Then they draw lots as to who should deal with you first. And the evening commences." She paused, enjoying the fingers.

Ashley caught her lover's wide-eyed stare; Verenka really was still a beginner.

"Don't worry your sweet head about anything just now. Our thoughtful Contessa has such a vast array of equipment; you'll never believe it. Fabulous, delicate, beautiful instruments she has had designed for sex torture on sumptuous slaves like us, and rows of incredible whips, all specially made for her and the Conte. You know, everything from those whippy, supple canes for your rump to scourges with twenty thongs for the rest. Even if you're blindfolded, you know them by their effect. You'll love it!" She repeated her enthralled reassurance to which Verenka nodded uncertainly. She was afraid of whips with twenty tails. Even Claudia didn't go that far.

"All the whips are hung in front of you by crimson cords and often the Contessa asks you to decide which you want. And after all that, she is very generous about orgasms—not like those bitches Vasa and Gerda who used to stop us, on the brink of coming and went on whipping. No, Marisa plays the game. None of your three holes is ever neglected and you'll go berserk when they ream your behind with a big, ribbed dildo and mangle your clit to orgasm. You travel up to the stars, darling, and dissolve, well whipped and tortured, into a galactic space of exaltation, dripping with sperm and cum."

Verenka was herself about to spend in the midst of her lover's lyrical effusions. She was erotically outdistanced and Ashley knew it, despite the girl's quite adequate performances she had witnessed at the castle.

"Just follow me, my sweet. You know, when I'm stretched and chained open and naked on the iron grid or over their trestles, I give them all I've got in return for what they give me. What more are qualified slaves like us for? Tell me. Isn't it precisely that you yearn for, nude and breathless in the hands of your mistress or master?"

Verenka nodded, her eyes began to shine like black diamonds as she smiled. "Oh, how I love you!"

The older woman kissed her lover, tonguing her far into the mouth, causing Verenka to clench her vagina again, squelching it in anguish. Closing her eyes, the girl imagined Ashley's clean, neat body spread naked, the ribs standing out, the belly concave, between Venetian lion-crested columns before a hooded, sweating valet with a black whip and a rampant penis, flagellating and flagellating...

189

She opened up, offering her sopping sex to the woman she desired more than anything in the world. And to hell with the sleeping couple. Sergio or whatever his name was could flog her to death, for all she cared…

"I'm coming, Ashley!" The voice was a hushed, choking capitulation. "Rub it hard. Harder! Push into me. Please!"

Ashley cupped her free hand over the gaping mouth, stifling the cry of orgasm.

She came promptly with force under the powerful fingers, not once but several times in a rapid mounting succession of violent spasms, each more maniacal than the previous paroxysm. It lasted a long moment before, with a soft wail of abandon, she collapsed into the protection of Ashley's furs, her cum frothing and spewing out, molten spume over the cakings of the previous discharges that had congealed on her during the journey. Ashley's hand was sheathed in glittering liquids. She was delighted.

"I don't think it appropriate, girls, to make love in a car on a bitter winter's day. Cover up and sleep. You need rest, both of you, and so do we."

Without opening her grey eyes, the Contessa spoke with her customary low-pitched voice that brought the two slaves back to earth, back to the floorboards of the Hispano.

"Scusi, signora Contessa, Verenka was just teaching me some Italian, Mistress." Ashley's rejoinder was almost pert. After all, an orgasm was an orgasm; neither more nor less.

An elegantly stiletto heeled foot reached out and found its way through Ashley's fur coat to grind down on a naked breast. The slave moaned and twisted as the thin point lanced into the soft flesh.

"Well, do it more quietly, darlings, tonight we sleep in Monte Carlo and you can suck and drain each other dry at the hotel. You're unconscionably naughty, Ashley. And you too, Verenka. Now go to sleep."

The Contessa turned back into the warm splendour of rich upholstery while the car slid past Beziers, rippling on to the sets of the autoroute stretching out towards Provence.

Verenka was in quite another geography, hardly aware of the change of speed and different countryside; all she could see were magenta and rose clouds. And Ashley left her in them just as she left her hand, hidden from her owner's eye, deep inside Verenka.

CHAPTER 18

Scarcely able to believe her good fortune and determined to justify it over the following week, Marina attended the changeover of slaves with a mixture of wistful nostalgia to watch her companions leaving and of excitement to see a fresh batch of males and females arriving. Seated next to whichever senior overseer presided over the intake and exodus of slaves, the apprentice took scrupulous note of the procedures; it was she who was given the task on the computer of recording each movement. Gradually, all her former colleagues departed with different coloured throat straps, and some deplorably emblazoned with stripes and welts from their final flagellations in Cell Eight.

The girls, particularly those newly bought, left with delight, a delight blended with a certain apprehension as to what awaited them. Whatever it was, it could hardly be as demanding as Beaucastel, yet they were like strung bows, hoping that their newfound ability to swallow ejaculated gouts and gouts of scalding sperm while under torture would satisfy their owners. Marie-Laure, Marja with her new Belgian owner, Birgit at last re-united with her adoring owners, Krystyna, Katia led away by her septum ring; all left in due course, glancing at Marina with puzzlement and envy.

It was the new arrivals that intrigued Marina; they were to be her victims. Some of the girls were totally unprepared, she noticed, for the initial humiliations that lay in store; stripping naked, marking, manacling. On the other hand, a beautiful, chestnut-haired youngster named Elodie seemed to take pleasure in exhibiting her outsized, double-ringed breasts, one circle of metal hanging from the teat, the second, far larger, pierced deep within the base of the areolas; a girl who boasted her ability to undergo a hundred lashes, attached to the flogging pole by the rings alone. The girl seemed to thrill at her presence at Beaucastel, offering herself immediately to Restif, who hesitated, being in the presence of his seniors. During the induction and for reasons unknown to Marina, Vasa condemned the slut immediately, not to the Slave Hall, not to the cells, not to the Black Dungeon, but the small adjacent chamber where peculiarly cruel sex tortures were performed on over-demonstrative slaves. Elodie merely smiled at Marina, as Vasa introduced the one to the other from which Marina gathered that she would be called upon to deal with the newcomer. This pleased her as the girl had a fabulously attractive body for the whip and for far more sophisticated instruments. And Marina had to train her up.

"This overseer will deal with you, 126, in accordance with your owner's request." Vasa seemed relieved, being grossly overworked, to be able to pass flesh on to someone else and Marina passed an unimaginably erotic hour in Cell Three with the girl, aided by Lalanière who showed her how to rake a female's flesh with a hand-harrow. Then Marina scourged the slave senseless. It constituted her first real flogging and she revelled in it. Pierre had to congratulate her as, fully excited, he fucked Marina against the whipped body. Marina was stirred as much as her lover and came magnificently over and over again.

Marina continued to be nurtured and educated by her lover not only in bed but in every one of the training cells. She made outstanding progress, assuming her routine cell duties with groups of slaves with diligence and truculent devotion to the cause. She seemed to require only summary instruction in handling female slaves and learnt rapidly how best to deal with the bodies and stout cocks of the males. Pierre was a mine of advice, explaining the intricacies of bondage, rump and breast flagellation and the insertion of dildos of dimensions Marina hardly believed would enter, though she herself had received the same in days gone by. To be at the delivery rather than the receiving end was different.

Pierre Lalanière was the first to realize her gifts, not only with the lash, cane or knotted scourge but in grasping the dichotomy—as he put it—and balance of pain and pleasure.

The Master concurred, noting by means of his video, her inventiveness and a sexual imagination—as he remarked to his imperturbable, long-suffering secretary—which was more than could be claimed by some of the senior staff. The secretary nodded, handing him the latest faxes. Together the Master and she listened to the intern's introductory remarks when, for the first time, Marina was put in charge of an induction. She spoke in French, translating now and then the essential phrases into English and German as she explained the three aims of their training. Firstly there was the acceptance and enduring of pain, secondly they would learn to provide pleasure, mostly under the whip for those who used their slave flesh and thirdly they would learn how to derive pleasure for themselves.

She paused to caress the cleft of one of the more luscious females and to frig the straining cock of a youth standing next to the slave; her studded glove slid neatly along the glistening shaft, causing the youth to thrust out his pelvis in hope...

"Bear these principles in mind while you are worked upon during your training here, never forgetting that your distinguished owners are paying generously towards your education. Those of you who do not have owners and are up for sale, should work doubly hard in order to attract potential buyers. We demand of you full co-operation whether you are being fucked, masturbated, sodomised, whipped, tortured or merely kept in bondage. I hope this is clear to all of you."

In the ensuing silence, the Master felt his trust in the woman, shared by Vasa and her three colleagues was well requited. Attentively, he listened as Marina went on to emphasise that complete nudity was demanded at all times unless owners had requested otherwise. And as she ran her twenty thonged whip through her fingers she explained how the Slave Hall was available for any sexual recreation the inmates desired but that any slovenliness, lack of enthusiasm or recalcitrance would be punished at the first instance by a hundred lashes, hung by the ankles. Any further offences would entail the

Black Dungeon.

There were no questions; the slaves were too petrified to utter a word.

Only ten weeks after assuming her duties, Marina was appointed full overseer. Even Lalanière was taken aback by the self-confidence of his protégée and now his official mistress.

One event, however, had contributed towards Marina's meteoric graduation.

Towards the end of January, Gerda resigned, leaving her prestigious position vacant. It went without discussion that only Marina should fill it and she did so like a whip hand sliding neatly into a chain mail glove. Her future was secured.

CHAPTER 19

As the days went by in Venice, where time trickles slowly through the hourglass of history, Casanova's salacious eighteenth century being over, Verenka lived in a sensuous dream of love and sex, despite the heat and the occasional obnoxious smells from the canals. Apart from servicing her owners in their own particular manner, she and Ashley shared all the delights available: outings with gay parasols aloft, expensive dresses and trips in the Palazzo's gondola, guided by the obsequious, well-membered Gino.

But there were unexpected surprises, wild evenings organized by the Contessa, invariably terminating with vicious scourgings. Like the Campanile San Marco and the bulging breast of the Salute, they were part of the scenery.

Verenka was at her best. Whether in the powerful motoscafo on the lagoon or visiting Torcello and other islands—she loved the quiet cemetery and the yews—or strolling round the city or in bed with Ashley and sometimes with Marisa, or even when she writhed and screamed her lungs out at the marble pillar next to the statue of Aphrodite coyly concealing a pristine pubis. Verenka, sometimes to Ashley's discontent, was admired and sought after, particularly by several male guests who candidly demanded her on account of the way she controlled her cunt and sphincter muscles so magnificently, contracting and clenching on the erection working within her and yet at the same time allowing her own climax to gather and explode to the delight of the Contessa and her guests. All found her lewd, depraved and shameless, insatiable in bed and always ready for the whip.

On certain occasions the Contessa and her husband would wake her up in Ashley's arms, take both down to one of the infamous camere speciale to excite them and themselves by handling the instruments and accessories, describing the use of each object in turn—the breast vices and throttling cords, the nipple and labia pincers and clit clamps, the tongs, flesh rakes, needles and screws, hoods, spiked breast cones and the vast array of whips, canes and studded paddles—with which paraphernalia both slaves were fully familiar already. But the perverse inspections by candlelight excited the group prodigiously, especially when the Contessa invited her slaves to select what they would like to have used on them to complete the evening.

Then things began to alter. It was late July. The Contessa maintained that the waning of Verenka's enthusiasm was the result of over-flogging and the unremitting demands made on her flesh by the Venetians with their energy and imagination. She began to dither when summoned by Sergio, the majordomo; during beatings she was seen to clench her buttock meat unorthodoxly; her response and performance became frankly disappointing to her owners. The slave became uncongenial, unentertaining.

True, Ashley had reverted to her former habit of sleeping, if only occasionally, with Fortunato and, to add insult to jealousy, one night Sergio had forced Verenka into the room to watch. Ashley lay on the soiled mattress, bound like an animal in heat, caked with semen and viciously bruised. Her beautiful body was shuddering with wild contentment as the fellow continued to work on her, using both hands—the whip in the right and masturbating himself luxuriously with the left. Verenka was taken aback at the loathsome spectacle and protested. It earned her a dozen lashes from the majordomo there and then in front of the fornicating couple, Ashley in her frenzy applauding crazily: "Ahh… yes… yes, whip the bitch… while I come… Flog me too, Forty, my love… nice and slowly…" Her moans mounted to meet the man's gush of jism over her belly. The sight made Verenka sick.

Ashley's promiscuity was not the only reason of the slave's despondency. She had begun to tire of Venice. A strange pining for Paris nagged at her, for her cosy room at the Quai d'Anjou, the view over the Seine with a gay bateau-mouche sliding by, lit up at night casting chiaroscuro reflections on her ceiling.

And she missed Gemma with her annoying habits. And even Mikhail and the odour of his cigars. He fucked so deliciously with that stout cock. It had made her proud of her orifices.

She was homesick. So much so that she tried once, clandestinely since the telephone was strictly out of bounds for slaves to phone Mikhail or Claudia, preferably Mikhail, if only to sense the air of Paris, of her room and even of the Lycee Charlemagne. It proved to be an agonizing venture. Sergio's wife, the pert, pretty Rosa caught her struggling with the international codes.

She was taken to the lowest cellar, on orders from the Conte Franco to his majordomo, attached by her cunt rings to a hook in the damp wall, and beaten almost senseless over the buttocks. Such was the price of an abortive phone call. The blood welled out of the welts and the dear old doctor had to be sent for once again.

Nevertheless, several days and several whippings later, Verenka tried again to call, despite the risk and the same difficulties with the Italian phone system. She got through to Gemma who only slammed the phone down with a "Putana, vai al diavolo!"

At one moment Verenka thought of Marina and the gorgeous days a year ago in Paris and even in the sinister Slave Hall of Beaucastel where their sweating, naked bodies provided each other with such unbelievable orgasms through the dark winter nights. The sudden image of Marina made Verenka screw up her eyes to dissolve it. All that was past, relegated beyond recall. She crossed out Marina once again from the record of experience. Ashley had been too fabulous to resist. That much was clear. But not so evident was why Ashley's attraction had begun to pall. For a last fleeting second, Verenka recalled how Marina had given up her very career to sleep with her. All that, she murmured, was so much water under the Bridge of Sighs...

One night she was brought to the salotto and her final crisis matured. The Contessa ordered Ashley to flagellate her,

Ashley, of all people! It hurt more than any beating she had ever undergone. That was the end. She sank into deeper lethargy, utterly miserable.

Neither Marisa nor Franco was accustomed to failure with their slaves and they had had many. They encouraged Ashley to reason with the girl, to get to the root of the problem. Ashley's attempts were fruitless. Worse still, their lovemaking was spiritless, without orgasms. The flame in Verenka was quenched.

The family consultation, which included Ashley, was duly convened one stifling August afternoon after siesta. Once the spremuta di limone and cakes had been served the group took up the discussion of Verenka. She had cost a great deal at the outset and her disconsolation was worrying. Whatever, the Contessa claimed, might be Ashley's shortcomings—and her recent offhand manner towards her lesbian lover might well be among them—she was immediately exonerated. For her adoring mistress, Ashley was pure sex and beyond disparagement.

The Conte wondered if stringent measures should not be resorted to, using exceptional corporal punishment to invigorate Verenka. Like the half-conscious slave below in the cellars, she could well be chained and hooded in an adjacent cell for flogging and torture alongside the Kosovo whore every three hours or so and that for, say, two or three days and nights. "At ablution time, she can be hung and hosed down with her sister cellar slave and…"

Gently, the Contessa interrupted him. "Franco, caro, you are incorrigible," she sighed, promptly vetoing the suggestion. "The girl has probably been overused—you know, all those prolonged flagellations for the benefit of Commendatore Undino last week may be partly to blame. I'm sure it's only one of her temporary moods, Franco, and we should not be too, brutal with her, however much she seems to enjoy it. What do you think, Ashley darling, you who know and love the whip?"

The beautiful face was as radiant as ever, despite dark rings under the eyes, as she replied. "Oh, no, Mistress, that's not the way. She'll only ask for more to give herself the chance to spend when she feels the pleasure overcoming the pain. As I do."

"Yes, I know, darling. And you're right." The Contessa thought for a moment. "Perhaps she's homesick or something."

Before the cocktails were brought out the Contessa had taken her decision.

"She must be returned to Beaucastel. An excellent training house for slaves. They really produce excellent, docile flesh."

Sergio was called to fax the Master who, in his immediate reply, felt honoured and sympathetic. An early date of induction was fixed and special therapy was promised.

"If that old bounder of a whore master can't help her over her blues, no one can," the Conte Franco remarked, stimulating his ice cubes. "Of course, if the worst comes to the worst, she can always be put up for sale on the slave market. After all, she's Class A slave material, we should not forget."

With that decided, the gondola was ordered out for an evening's moment of pleasure on the canals. Both Marisa and Franco adored being stared at from the bridges, publicly displaying their girls to plebeian gaze.

Verenka objected to outing but had to accompany them. Throughout the trip, she seemed preoccupied, trailing her hand in the water. Then Marisa told her.

"Verenka, darling, you're going back to Beaucastel for a spell. You need a change and a rest. It will do you a world of good, my sweet, and cheer you up."

Verenka's heart missed a beat. She considered protesting but finally remained silent. A submissive does not argue with her owners. Moreover, Beaucastel was nearer to Paris, to home and to the lycee.

200

CHAPTER 20

Beaucastel looked almost inviting under the sun. When Verenka was ushered in by the grinning Restif, still faithful to his calling, she saw the dogs again on the battlements. As if recognizing an habitué, they growled once and sought slumber again in the shade. The valet led her across the ominous drawbridge, under the portcullis, her gorgeous silks billowing in the warm wind as if she was floating aloft to her destiny but her heart was heavy, her sex tense with fear.

At the entrance to the dreaded castle, Restif clipped a black strap round her throat and attached the customary chain to the forward ring.

"Welcome back, 106." His brusque comment made Verenka glance at his huge cock she knew so well. It was swinging in repose which somehow was a bad omen.

They entered the induction chamber. All was cool and menacing.

The shock was immediate. Directly in front of her sat Marina, the black boots resting on the desk, the heels armed with glittering spurs. Restif bowed to his superior, leaving the girl facing Marina. Verenka's womb contracted again with fear. She dutifully held out her passport, staring in incredulity. It was just not possible that she was faced with whom she saw. Marina! Oh, no!

The leather lash Marina fondled over her naked lap was slender but thicker than the proffered document.

The overseer took the passport and dropped it into the waste bin.

"You don't have to identify yourself, Verenka. I've been waiting for you. Oh, so, so long! And, strike me dead, there you are, in silks!" The blue eyes, those same uninhibited blue eyes, as at the lycee in class, glowed like acetylene. "I hear from Venice that you require some special attention. Well, who would have believed it? And you so sure of yourself with that whore of yours."

The girl saw the heavy whip jerk like an adder disturbed. Her loins conspired against her determination to appear self-composed, as she bowed her head of dark hair in a dread she thought she had long since discarded. Her tongue flicked over the parched lips, adding only an attractive sheen. Sweat broke out over the brow and trickled from the armpits while sex juice seeped from the labia below. Unaccountably, she felt her vagina muscles tighten with a new jolt of warning entangled in ripples of vague desire she could not control. Desire for what? For amnesty, for some word of pardon? Verenka merely sensed her viscera churning within a body that no longer seemed to belong to her but to the magnificent, terrifying overseer before her. After the contractions in her loins, she was aware that her cunt had suddenly slackened as it did when she gave herself to a lover; it seemed to disown her. Yes, it belonged entirely to the other woman and the very same sluggish secretion Marina used to be able to draw out of her, crept down, soft, warm, syrupy. She knew her clitoris was swollen at the apex of her aching cleft but now the labia were throbbing and unfurling and probably Marina could see it all, just as she could observe the flush over the cheeks. Adrenaline pumped and laced through her entire body as she stared wide-eyed at the relaxed figure reclining before her.

The woman was superb, completely changed; the hair had regrown since that fatal night in the Black Dungeon. But then Ashley had been waiting for her. What a shambles it had all become. And now what was going to happen to her? She felt like crying.

Yet Verenka noticed that Marina no longer wore flesh rings, only confirming the fact that the woman must now probably be an overseer with unfettered power to do almost what she wished to a naked slave. Her brain reeled in a vacuum of guilt and helplessness.

As Marina pressed a stud on her interphone, the fair eyelashes flickered with a smile but not the smile of Marina in bed. It was malignant, vengeful.

"Ah, Pierre darling." Verenka could scarcely believe her ears as Marina spoke into the receiver. Not Lalanière, the overseer, the flogger! "She's here, safe and sound. Will you send someone to collect the thing? Yes, Sandra will do fine and tell her to prepare that nice cell next the main cellar, the one with sawdust on the ground for the blood."

The swivel chair squeaked as she leaned back.

"Right, 106, or rather 211/S as you are now—strip nipple-naked and let's have it all hanging out." Marina's command was curt. "By the way, the 'S' is for Special, Verenka, and special it's going to be. As Krystyna used to say, you're going to wish you'd never been born but, then, as you yourself are bound to admit, you deserve it."

Verenka watched the rays of sunshine splinter on the spurs of the gleaming boots poised on the desk between a bowl of roses and the computer. "You see, sweetheart," Marina went on, "it's I who am going to deal with you, which is only just, you will agree, I'm sure. So let's not waste time, off with all that Venetian finery."

The trembling slave had little to discard. She obeyed scrupulously and immediately until she stood in all her unimpeachable, breathtaking beauty, adopting the customary Beaucastel posture of submission, legs parted, hands behind the neck. Marina had to stare at the sight. The breasts were heavier than before and had begun to sag; the vagina seemed to be already soused with the usual silky discharge which she had loved. No doubt the slit was still fetid and curdled with Princess Ashley's saliva but Marina would whip all that out...

The pink, stiff prong of the clitoris was the same, powerful and wet, pouting through the dark hairs Marina knew so intimately. No, Verenka hadn't changed. Still the responsive whore she had been and, to Marina's delight, the insolent, heavy poundage of the rump bore no signs of scars or welts. She would put that right forthwith...

Yet, as she let her eyes rove idly over the flat belly, stabbed with its perfect whorl that she had tongued so often to excite the girl, Marina sensed the odour of the restless, spicy sex. She closed her eyes, invaded with memories of Verenka crying, laughing, and moaning as she lapped, frigged, caressed and sucked, night after night in the room at the Quai d'Anjou.

With a conscious effort, the overseer collected herself. There was work to be done and her whip twitched, reminding her of her duties. She shook herself alert.

"Gracious me, Verenka, you've grown flabby! And there was I thinking they would keep you slim with the whip. Too much pasta asciutta, I presume, you look a sight! You need a taste of dear old Beaucastel, don't you, whore that you are?"

The girl wiped away a tear. She was being humiliated before the real humiliation to come. How many lashes was she going to receive? Fifty? A hundred? More? She felt sick, her cleft awash with thick seepage. She dared not speak to beg for mercy, forgiveness. Instead, she stared at the menace of the supple thing Marina was fondling and at the honed spikes adorning the gauntlets. A rash of gooseflesh pimpled her body just as it had when Claudia came for them to lead them to the library columns. It was the same fear.

"I'm sure you recall the Quai d'Anjou, 211/S." Marina seemed to read her thoughts.

"Yes, mistress." The reply was no more than a whisper. Why didn't the bitch get on with the flogging? Verenka felt the overseer was savouring the agony, as remorse built up.

"And the Slave Hall here where we used to orgasm to high heaven?"

"Yes, mistress."

"And the torture chambers when we hung together, back to back?"

"Yes, mistress."

"Well, 211/S, you absconded,"—Verenka hardly understood—"and gave yourself to a pretentious English whore, didn't you? You really missed your vocation, sweetheart. You're no sex slave. You're a common slut of a whore-bitch."

The nude felt the hostility emerge like a famished beast as Marina went on. "Your owners have asked us to deal with you and you've been entrusted to me. Just a matter of settling an old score."

Verenka's womb tensed: it seemed to be clogged up with terror and a strange excitement, enhanced by the sudden entry of a pretty servant, almost naked but for her service straps and calf-high boots. The girl was a stranger to Verenka who had expected Gabrielle. But no doubt this one was just as expert in the lethal underworld of indescribable pain, hissing whips, the thud and cut of the leathers welting the sweating flesh with blinding flashes shattering the brain. Just as expert in leading her victim slowly and inevitably up the slope towards the wild orgasm that would erupt and heave the submissive body into that incandescent void where pain and euphoria could coalesce at last.

The servant smiled in anticipation. Sandra loved being summoned by her adored overseer to help in a session of sex torture.

"Take this nauseating bitch straight down. No cleansing— just as she is, please. Shave the head and sex. Oil the carcass well, shackle its ankles and hang it for me, nicely open."

Verenka bit into her nether lip, watching the girl grin like a vampire athirst. Yet curiously a thrill rippled through her entrails, stimulated by the girl's savage beauty; the tits were large, the pelvis broad, the skin dark and tawny like her own. The servant's eyes seemed to return her gaze as she sought the clitoris ring in the wet pubis to attach the chain. The flaccid hood had retracted to reveal the unsheathed erection. Sandra smiled.

"She's in full sail down here, mistress!" The lithe fingers flicked at the throbbing prong.

"Let's have less of your impertinence, Sandra, unless you want to take her place. Get the dirty slut out of my sight and down to where it belongs. If the blubber of her fat cunt attracts you, you can have a taste of it later. Now, get moving, girl!"

Clipping two short lengths of chain to the inner labial rings, Sandra opened up the sex and passed the links over the thigh to join them behind over the mass of buttock flesh. Verenka gasped as the chain hauled the tender cowl outwards. She grappled with her still free hands to alleviate the tension that almost tore the metal out of the umber skin. Not even Vasa or Claudia in one of her crazed, erotic moments had jerked that hard.

As the slave staggered after the girl through the Gothic archway, Marina coiled up her flesh scourge in her spiked, suede gauntlets, switched off her computer and followed. Her high heels echoed in the vacuity of the vaulted passage and spiral of steps.

During the descent, the group passed by the body of a naked male slave virtually suspended by the penis to a ring in the rough wall, the distended testicles carrying a hunk of iron. It was as if the spectacle had been organized for Verenka's benefit, to scare and excite her in preparation for what was awaiting her. Though accustomed to such sights and moans, Verenka felt her last morsel of courage crumble. Then the solid oak door slammed behind her. Marina had disappeared, leaving the two girls together.

Verenka found herself in a completely unfamiliar, circular chamber—one of Marina's own innovations with the Master's sanction. The dangling chains, flogging racks and rows upon rows of implements numbed her more than anything she had known at Beaucastel.

"Stretch your body over that slab, cunt upwards!" Sandra ordered.

Shackled backwards by wrists and ankles, Verenka thought her muscles would snap with the strain. It seemed to take an eternity to relieve her of her long locks; the razor rasped over her skull, then over the bulge of the pubis and down the margins of the sex. The smell of soap in the overpowering heat sickened her. Finally she was totally nude.

"You're erotic beyond belief!" Sandra gasped, standing

back. "God, what a body!"

Although Marina, like her colleagues, varied her victims' postures when putting them to the whip, she usually commenced with one of the more classic Beaucastel positions: the nude thrown over a trestle and bound back by the four limbs, which, in the case of males, allowed the erect cock to stand stiff and throbbing above the flat belly for punishment. It was customary for the anus to be impaled deep on a rugged iron spigot bolted to the timber at the appropriate angle to ensure a minimum of movement during the torture and whipping. Another approach was for the body to be crucified, spread-eagled, to present the full expanse of the flesh for the scourge; or else, swinging by the wrists from the beams above—a normal, routine arrangement, used daily in all cells. But Verenka had been designated, at Marina's request, as a 'Special' and thus she was to hang by her ankle shackles, limbs parted almost to the point of luxation, the arms being allowed to dangle loose, unbound, below the obscenely sheared head. The disposition offered Marina the entire area of the bare groin and yawning sex with the stout clitoris delightfully available between the inner thighs; and beyond, the vast expanse of rump flesh that seemed to beg to be welted. Marina's experience had been enriched by her colleagues in two further respects: although the slave would jerk madly during the initial slices of the scourge into the splayed crotch, making her haul her thorax upwards, clawing desperately with the hands, there was no need to tie the wrists; the slave would yield herself up docilely despite the screaming. With open mouth and glazed eyes, Verenka would relinquish all she had to her torturer. Secondly, the reversed position provided a female flogger with interesting interludes: the slave could be forced to perform cunnilingus and, if some measure of clemency prevailed, could herself be sucked and gamahuched into prodigious orgasms, for which the whip never failed to prepare a victim.

Marina had decided to use Sandra for that part of the

proceedings. "I wouldn't allow that cow to touch me even with the tips of her udders, leave alone her pink tongue, chewing the cud she swallowed in Venice." Marina was pure acid. "After fifty lashes you'll clasp the body in your pretty arms and have her suck you off. Mash your sweet sex into her face and make her tongue you."

The serving girl raised her eyebrows in surprise. "Oh, thank you, mistress!"

"And you'll take her lewd clit in your teeth and give her what she'll be pining for. She's like rancid butter when she comes, hardly fit for human consumption but you'll drink her discharge down, Sandra, and like it. I want you both emptied out. Understand?"

She understood at once. She was just as desperately eager to please her superior as herself. The stage was set. Marina's svelte vinyl figure sauntered over to the rack of instruments, the hips swaying above the high boots. And further above, her sex was expelling hot excretions along the inner flanks of her thighs braced with the stimulus of what she was about to do to her suspended victim. At last redress was within her grasp.

Marina had never in her life experienced such a deep thrill of ruthlessness.

It was she who had assembled the incredible array of whips, ordering new leathers, replacing others when worn out. She glanced at the collection lined on the wall: everything from paddles, some studded with steel nails; to bull's hide whips with their dense flanges, spliced at the extremities. Although she knew the feel of each instrument through painful endurances during her own slave days at the castle, she had had months of practice since then in using each on countless defenceless, juddering bodies requiring intensive training to satisfy those who owned them. She was at home.

Then she felt the haft of her own favourite whip in her hand, the terrible lash that Verenka had spied in the induction chamber. What more was needed to commence with?

About to turn, she abruptly caught sight of the alcove, its shelves loaded with other implements. From among the multitude of dildos, rakes, gags, pliers and tongs and she picked up a small object and returned to her victim who by then had been efficiently suspended, sweating, in the centre of the cell. It was a delicious sight.

"Verenka, I want you to enjoy this and what awaits you in the nights to come," she said smoothly, with the irony she was famous for at the castle. "I'm going to flagellate you."

"I know, mistress." The slave's head rose painfully. She knew it only too well.

"And your body will be tortured—as you tortured my affections, you slut!"

"I suppose I deserve it, mistress." The remark was almost inaudible.

Marina smiled. In her gloved hand lay a small, circular clamp of stainless steel, complete with screw, to fit over a stimulated nipple. The pair of them Marina had used recently with great effect on the pert, brash Elodie, something the presumptuous slave and her long teats would not forget for a long time. One such band seemed to Marina perfectly appropriate for Verenka's fleshy clit; it would fit easily and snugly round the base.

Sandra was ordered to rekindle the nub into even fuller erection. A moment later, Verenka lurched as she felt the cold metal slip over and down the famous stump of erectile flesh. Sandra was ordered to take a pair of chromium pliers and seize the twitching summit of the organ between the rugged, plastic jaws.

"Elongate her," Marina hissed between her teeth. "Full length." Sandra pulled on it.

Marina screwed in the wing nut, enjoying each turn as it gradually tightened to bury into the precious organ, once so familiar to her lips, fingertips and the jutting point of her pelvis.

Marina continued to turn the screw until it could penetrate no deeper. As Sandra released the pliers, Verenka drew in her breath with a hiss of pain; the tip of the clitoris bulged out over the crown of the clamp. Marina nodded with satisfaction; it fitted exquisitely and the slave was suffering.

"There we are, Verenka dear. Isn't that erotic? You were always the first to be fucked because of that big clit, weren't you? I'd like to put a couple more on the teats of your great udders but later this week I have other delights for them. A few needles will do you the world of good."

The thing set Verenka's body thudding as the agony seared through her brain, her mouth peeling back as she clenched her teeth. Like the collar, her eyes screwed up tight, trying to extinguish the streaks of pain; she tried not to shriek and offer her torturer yet another pleasure. And to protest would only invite worse. She gathered all her strength.

The steel clamp weighed down the erection, suddenly stimulating her erotically. If only her tormentors would caress the tip, just a few strokes over it, to relieve the stress!

"I can't bear it, mistress!" The superb loins shuddered with erotic pain; she hated and loved it. She felt her whole being as a sex slave stimulated once again. "I can't bear it."

"And you think I could bear your being sucked off by a Venetian whore?"

The overseer stripped down to boots and gauntlets, determined to enjoy her long awaited retaliation in erotic freedom. Professionally, she allowed the thongs of her justifiably celebrated whip to caress the fork of pure sex flesh displayed before her at last. She smiled as the muscles clutched under the graze of the leathers. Her respiration was as short as her victim's.

The flat-braided tails of the whips came away already damp from the girl's vaginal liquids oozing out over the labia and shaved pubis. Marina was accustomed to Verenka's lubricants, but then Verenka was special with special sexual gifts.

The overseer shook out the leather strands straight, took her stance and flagellated.

The slave let out a wild gasp, heaving her thorax upwards

and hollowing her belly as her loins seemed to split in two. Marina allowed the body to regain its breath. Lalanière had explained to his pupil the need for the strokes to be well-spaced in time to permit the pain to invade and sink into the epidermis, compressing the nerves under the whitened flesh before they expanded again into their previous dimension, flaring into welts, dark with the blood pulsing below the surface. Remembering the delicious pain, before orgasm, she herself had felt during prolonged flagellations, Marina dealt deliberately with her victim. She knew the interval between lashes traumatised a naked slave, awaiting the next onslaught. She concentrated on the inner thighs, taut with muscular resistance, until the fork itself was fully prepared; then the scourge bit into the cleft itself, each lash providing Marina with a thrill she had never experienced in her short existence as a flagellatrix.

The screams were unearthly, filling the chamber, the sex rings jangling as the leathers flayed the labia, the oval and, at last, the tip of the clitoris. The shriller the cries, the more viciously Marina cut into the cleft, until dull groans followed. The overseer, with her experience at both ends of the whip, knew what was happening; the slut's orgasm was gathering under the sheets of pain. At the nineteenth lash, Verenka came in a cataclysm, shuddering and howling like a beast.

"Right, that will do for now," Marina panted.

To drive her victim over the brink, Marina crushed the base of her thongs into the apex of Verenka's swollen cunt.

The girl yelled, heaving herself upwards, to come again in a paroxysm of blessed release, the cum jerking out from the vagina to mingle with the sweat on the leather braids grinding into her pulp. The flogging was over.

Verenka drifted like flotsam on the wreckage of her body, half-conscious, while Sandra slowly unscrewed the steel clamp off the clitoris.

The girl jerked back into awareness as the circulation lacerated the tortured prong of flesh. Marina noticed the excessive, almost loving, care the sleek serving girl exercised in removing the tiny ring but was delighted to see the erection still distended, galled, purple and pulsating with spasms among the weals over the shaved crotch. It seemed to be calling for more! What a slut the slave was, what a lascivious whore!

Just sex, nothing more.

Marina had to conform to normal Beaucastel practices, once the whipping was done. Now came the double cunnilingus. She left the two females together while she refreshed her dry throat from a beaker of wine. She relaxed for a long moment on a nearby torture slab to mob her brow and freckled cheeks, leisurely wiping off the sweat and cum from her whip. She was recovering from one of the most satisfyingly erotic beatings Beaucastel had given her the chance to perform. Verenka's crotch was the proof. Revenge was sweet.

So sweet that Marina could hardly believe her compensation.

Returning to the scene, and aware of the video eye surveying all, she ordered Sandra to go to work on the body. Pleasure, alas, had to follow pain in Beaucastel. Even here.

"Take her now, girl! Make her lick you off properly or she'll get another ration, this time with the riding crop." Then, with a trace of remission, she added: "And suck the cum out of her greedy slit, according to rules—though the brazen bitch doesn't deserve it. Get moving!"

Verenka continued to moan, the echoes of pain still intermingling with the onrush of throbbing pleasure, both sensations radiating from the crotch and the quivering clitoris. The confusion and upheaval in her head, after the whipping, were suddenly resolved into a new excitement by the overseer's order. It was almost inconceivable! Sandra was being authorized, even ordered, to pleasure her! Beaucastel was still bewilderingly the same: pain, terrible pain, but pleasure too, out of all mortal proportion...

Sandra hurried forward and embraced the inert body: it felt as if it were seething in a glare of red pain but the bloated lips were clearly begging for relief. Sensuously, as she had been taught, the serving girl went down on the splayed pouch, fully swollen from Marina's vengeance. With a tenderness the girl rarely used on a whipped slave Sandra first licked the surroundings of the engorged nub and then, deflecting the steel ring, took the clitoris into her pursed lips, sensing the ridge left by the clamp. Verenka leapt as she felt the length drawn outwards from the root to tip.

Any whipping was worth this... She gave herself completely to the sweet mouth and concentrated on her own servicing of the girl. Now and then, she varied the suction, releasing the little button of hot flesh to flick it with her agile tongue, licking the curd off the labia. Sandra surrendered to the lips, twisting and moaning as Verenka's fingers circled the very centre of her being, malaxing and crushing into the gleaming, haired triangle at the apex. In return, Sandra left the victim's outsized clit to pulse aloft, while she explored the two orifices, as Verenka did the same on her below. The girl thrust one hand deep into the vagina and with the other probed into the anus; as she did so, the sphincter relaxed to let her in. An unaccountable wave of infatuation enveloped her as she felt Verenka's nimble tongue circling her stub. Rapidly the orgasms gathered as Marina watched the two faces running with slippery juices sliding out of the vaginas. Suddenly, the twin bodies tautened, the buttocks clenching as the initial spasms flowered like rose petals around their stamens. It was wonderful, even for Marina, to watch. Verenka cried out first, as if emptying her soul—if, after Venice, the bitch had one— and voided her boiling spume into Sandra's gullet; the cries echoed among the vaults and chains, reminiscent of the wild, obscene yells during flagellation that had delighted Marina. She herself had responded in her time with equal passion when Claudia had masturbated her, and Vasa too, but not with such abandon. The whore had always seemed to despoil herself while she, Marina, had managed to keep her head. Verenka's spending was lethal; she always died la petite most, as the castle saying went. And in turn, Verenka swallowed the servant's cum, excited by the soft labia and diminutive clitoris. But the servant's orgasm was different: after a harvest of spasms, she culminated in convulsions until a final, ecstatic explosion crippled her, enjoying the mucus stifling and choking in her mouth. Both came time after time, expelling their gorged glut, swamping each other's face with cream sluicing out in hot streams. Repeatedly, Verenka released her own cum that the serving girl lapped up like a bitch at its bowl of feed. Marina felt she must be perverted to enjoy a slave so overtly and that before her august overseer. The girl was evidently unreliable.

The couple gave Marina the clear impression of an amorous relationship. Impossible! Particularly as this was their first genital encounter. But the cunnilingus on both sides had been mawkishly sentimental, something strictly proscribed between staff and slave flesh at Beaucastel which advocated, indeed insisted on, erotic lust not love.

Marina, however, needed her own catharsis imperatively. She was grossly swollen around the labia, in erection and drenched. Dire need—and Lalanière—called.

"Unchain the slut," she murmured to Sandra, wiping off her whip. "And bind her to the flogging wheel for the night."

Sandra, recovering swiftly from her orgasms, glanced at the wheel standing at the end of the chamber. It reared high— an immense, three-spoked circle.

"Tie her tight on it for the night. Hose her down with cold water and have her medicated. You can give her something to drink all the same, but I don't think I'll need you any more for such sessions, Sandra. Tell Hannah to take your place. Understand? You suck too ravenously for your good."

Sandra did as she was told. In tender gratitude towards Verenka for the orgasms and the spectacular session, she gently massaged the marks and tensed muscles after releasing the slave, daubing salve and arnica over the welts that stood out like purple cords around the sex, over the thighs and across the fabulous rump meat. Then she washed her down gently. Verenka yielded to the girl without hesitation and, surrendering to the little hands, something jolted again in her loins under the caresses. She kissed Sandra on the mouth.

But nevertheless the girl was obliged to bind Verenka outstretched to the three spokes of the flogging wheel. She was magnificent. Sandra caressed the body without restraint, licking the breasts and belly sensuously. The naked slave adored it but hung in silence until Marina returned the next day, refreshed and vicious. And the tortures recommenced. Worse than before, with the old-timer Hannah, anxious to assist with the chains and implements. Another night reduced Verenka to prostration, shackled by the four stretched limbs to the wheel, each session visiting atrocious hurt on the curved body but her flesh took it, in a sort of occult defiance of Marina, her orgasms never failing to retaliate.

By the third day, Verenka was humiliated beyond all reason. Taken up to Cell Two, she was spread and strapped onto an enormous inclined crucifix, her three orifices plugged tight with hard, ridged dildos that almost split her, and this before a group of slaves during one of their routine training sessions. Marina ordered each of the female trainees to straddle the slave and drench her with warm golden showers, the male slaves being made to masturbate over her. Only when Verenka was glistening with urine and splattered with lumps of sperm, did Marina proceed with the training course. Verenka's cross was raised to the vertical so that she hung like a side of meat on it, forced to watch the lesson. Almost distractedly, she followed the various beatings, noticing the resilience of the young ash-blonde slave, Elodie, receiving a heavy tawse across her belly and thighs without a murmur. The girl was sturdy and suddenly reminded Verenka of Ashley; with a pain level equally and incredibly high; she also was clearly destined for a conspicuous future, like Ashley. Unlike Verenka who had no future… She closed her eyes as the tears ran down her sunken cheeks. Oh, Ashley, Ashley!

When the next ghastly evening came, an unaccountable halt interrupted Verenka's sufferings, Marina being summarily called to the Master's chambers. He sat in opulence as usual.

"You have done exceedingly well, Marina, from what I have been able to judge from the closed circuit and audio, especially in dealing with 211/S, if a trifle too freely now and then. But I agree the disappointing female requires that sort of tuition and the correction you dutifully administer. But it must stop."

Marina's instinct and intelligence told her that something was afoot and felt obliged to justify the punishments. She reminded the Master of the squalid infidelity Verenka had made her suffer a year before.

"I'm fully aware of her slovenly behaviour, Marina," the gaunt figure conceded, "and of your reaction although, as you know we look askance at exclusive sexual relationships between inmates. All the more so between staff and slaves…"

Crestfallen, she tried another approach. "It's that the bitch requires stern correction, sir. I mean, enlivening, to restore her primal urge." Her hand strayed instinctively to her service scourge, her sapphire eyes flashing. Smooth liquid oozed down her swollen tunnel on to the thighs. The urge to lash Verenka was like a ferret gnawing again.

"That may be so," the Master's tone hardened a shade. "However, I have decided to deal with her in a somewhat different manner. Continued flagellation and flesh torture will only lead her into deeper depression." The voice became more authoritarian. "To revitalize her, I have decided to starve her of any form of sex until her attitude changes."

Marina almost gasped aloud. Lack of response under the whip! What was the man talking about? Even without the help of Sandra's tongue, she had had her roaring in fury to be frigged. Surely he had followed the sessions on his screen. Or had he? The very idea that Verenka needed stimulating was laughable. There was nothing wrong with the slut that Marina's whip could not correct. Depression? Ridiculous!

"My decision therefore," the Master went on, "is to have

her reduced to the lowest level of slavery, totally deprived of attention and above all starved of sex until she craves relief." Marina could hardly believe her ears. "You may not, Marina, be used to such treatment but your senior colleagues, who have been here far longer than you, are fully familiar with it. And with the results. We have employed it on several occasions in the past on lethargic or over-flogged brats."

Again the new overseer stared incredulously at her employer as he elaborated.

"Therefore I have decided with Vasa that the sluggard be relegated to the sculleries and bound naked among the garbage and open drains until she shows readiness to co-operate. Under no circumstances is she to be afforded the least attention or consideration. She will wallow in the filth and her own wastes until she begs to be used again. She'll be made to wait in abeyance, in total solitude, until her spirit rekindles and begs for the scourge and cock, driven by sexual craving to be used. It's a way of reviving a lazy slave by ignoring and distaining her. Moreover, anyone who even attempts to use her in any way, punitively or sexually, will incur punishment to a degree I do not wish to describe. I trust this is as clear to you as it is to your fellow overseers. Vasa will ensure my orders are carried out to the letter. You may leave now, Marina. Amuse yourself with one of the other slaves."

Baffled, the new overseer bit her lip in frustration. Verenka was slipping away from her grasp. Quite apart from the punishment she had delivered recently, Marina believed the bitch needed to be flogged daily. But to be left to marinate in some stinking scullery untouched was completely futile. The lecherous polecat had to pay for her liaison with that cheap English whore, Ashley.

As she left the presence, Marina decided to take matters into her own hands, whatever the risks. Lalanière would help, of course, after one of those torrid sessions together in his rooms where she offered herself in self-indulgent delight to be whipped and fucked.

CHAPTER 21

Dragged naked down the narrow stairwells, Verenka was slammed against the greasy wall by the two valets on service. Made to kneel, the soles of her feet against the glutinous masonry, she was shackled tight, the arms and neck wrenched back and encircled with iron bands cemented into the stonework, the thighs parted to their extreme reach. Simple oval-headed screws were then tightened sufficiently to hold her. The men prized open the jaws to ram in the funnel-gag whereby she was to be force-fed once daily. The open sewer beneath her would slurry away her wastes.

The sight of Vasa crossing the slithery threshold terrified the slave more than the conditions of her prison. Her fear increased as the svelte figure allowed her service scourge to drift over the huge breasts and the quivering belly. Dismissing the valets with a nod, the overseer checked the manacles and throat hoop.

"You've had some of that nauseous excess fat whipped off you since I saw you last, haven't you, bitch? Well, that's the last ration of leather you'll be getting for quite a time." She began to pace the filthy paving. "You're going to remain here in your irons in total solitude—except when you have potage forced into you and that will only take a minute and in silence—until you return to your senses. Until you decide to respond eagerly to whatever's demanded of your body. The longer you refuse to co-operate wholeheartedly with those who desire to flagellate, torture and use your flesh, the longer you will remain here. You will be deprived of sex, the blissful kiss of the whip and any human contact, apart from loads of muck being emptied over your indolent carcass. Get this into your stupid head."

Nonchalantly the chief overseer lifted the slave's right breast with her scourge and let it slap back against the heaving ribs.

"I suggested your torpid ringed crotch and the root of these disgusting udders of yours be bound with barbed wire. You're lucky. They prefer you to suffer stark nude. But if you refuse still to collaborate when you're questioned every three days, I'll have your teats and vulva rings weighted with kilos of iron. You've got plenty of time, whore, to consider your future—days will become weeks, weeks'll stretch, like your labia, into months. So, turn it over in your selfish, sluggish brain, if you've got one."

Relishing her role and aware that the hollow gag prevented the slave from uttering a word, Vasa delivered her sharpest javelin.

"In case you're still not fully aware, your Masters have sold you back to us." She halted before the superbly built mass of whipping flesh, watching the dark eyes widen in alarm. "And I think you know what Beaucastel does to a listless whore slave. Think it over, slag. Before it's too late."

The high heels squelched in the mire, offal and peelings as the bloodcurdling beauty left. Silence descended on the horrendous prison and lasted well into the night when a coarse scullion in clogs and Hessian entered to void a pail of sludge over the victim.

"Give me a hard lashing, Pierre, over all you can reach. I haven't had my clit whipped for a hell of a time. Then lay into my arse and take me back and front…"

Lying on Lalanière's silken sheets, Marina enjoyed these fierce nights with her colleague. Not only did she get the man to tie her legs to the summit of the bedposts but she had him whip her until she came and rode his cock until he pumped her full. Then she told him what she was about to do.

Lalanière's fist halted midway up his shaft as he readied it for further service. He sat up abruptly. "Say that again?"

Marina repeated her decision. "I'm going to fetch that whore 106 or whatever her number is now, and drag her up here and flog her senseless for treason…"

"Are you out of your mind? You heard the Master's orders as clearly as we all did. The stupid bitch is to be left to moulder down there until she pulls herself together. Interfere with her

219

punishment, Marina, and you're courting disaster. Anyway she's just a corpse, covered with filth. Forget her, for god's sakes! You've just been promoted, remember? Don't go and fuck things up! Think of your position."

"Position! All you lot think about is position—positions in the hierarchy, positions for whipping, positions for fucking… I'm going to fetch her and whip her raw. Anyway, at this time of night the whole place's deserted. They're all sleeping off their beatings." She slipped off the bed, mopped herself clear of sperm and discharge and pulled on her boots. "I'm bringing that load of tripe up here so we can both lay into her for an hour or so. Right here. No one will know. We'll thrash her till she wishes she'd never been born."

Her colleague frowned.

"If you want to break house rules, honey, do it in your own kennel. Count me out."

Marina rolled her eyes upward at the man's pusillanimity and made for the door, taking one of the candles burning on the table. "O.K. partner, I'll use my dugout. Thanks for the fuck."

The descent in darkness, despite the flicker of the candle, proved treacherous and slow but the stale odour of cooking guided her. The corridors, where the occasional video eye had long since been switched off, echoed eerily. Sensing her frantic heartbeat over the clacking of her high heels, she tried to distil the motives of the risk she was running: rage, jealousy, hatred, revenge, the desire to dominate and, above all, the sheer joy of whipping the slut's fat flesh. Fear of the consequences was the least of her emotions.

Wrenched back by the iron clamps, the slave girl seemed to be praying on her knees, the arms outstretched sideways as if before some altar beyond the masses of filth. She might well pray, Marina murmured to herself.

"On your feet! We've got another rendezvous together, sweetheart, and this time I want you wide awake." She slapped the locked head twice, dislodging crud from the cheeks hollowed under the thrust of the huge feeding gag. "My god, you're more ugly than ever with that bald head and no eyebrows!" She turned the catches holding the hinged metal braces. "Get that meaty arse moving. We're going for a little walk."

The begrimed figure struggled up, numbed by the bondage and loneliness. As if oblivious of her visitor, she stumbled ahead of the overseer, directed by sharp, premonitory taps of the whip—the precious, tightly plaited riding crop with the loose fangs at the tip, already greased.

It took an age to reach the bedroom in the staff wing but once within, the key turned, events moved fast. Marina hauled the besmirched body up by the wrists until the toes were clear of the rich carpet, the shorn skull thrust back behind the shivering biceps. Marina had to admit that the nude, despite the clotted, viscous slime upon her, was superb; yet the prodigious breasts no longer boasted their former compactness and upturned teats, nor had the buttocks their celebrated camber.

"I'm so glad to have you here in my room Verenka dear, I'm going to give you the belting of your life. I'll whip off all that scum you've got on you and get down into the nerves. You thought by hiding away down there in the garbage, you'd escape this. Well, you're wrong." She paused a second. "You see, one should never change horses—or mares—in mid-stream. Now, as a favour, I'll let you tell me when to start. Just chortle up that tube they've jammed into you."

She watched the rib cage sharpen under the vast, bulges of mammary meat, as a weird groan came out of the distended mouth. Marina cursed her in return.

"Fuck you too, slag!" And the crop slashed into the centre of both breasts at once. It was rare, almost unknown, for the crop to be used on a female's udders at Beaucastel and Marina knew it. As the length of leather flattened the bulges, the victim wrenched her knees up hopelessly and then the body slumped, waiting for the rest.

Marina worked down, as Lalanière had taught her, after sending the slave's breasts slapping into the armpits like sandbags. After a dozen murderous cuts, Marina paused between the lashes to let the pain sink in. The concave belly reddened with heavy welts, then the thighs and sex mound crimsoned. After fifty blows from nipples to knees, Marina found it gave her pure delight to watch the welts swelling like poisoned flowers. There was so much of the bitch to whip... Marina poured herself a drink of Rhine wine and rested a moment. Then she lifted the slave's left buttock; the flesh was flabby.

"As I said, your arse has grown loose and pulpy, hasn't it? I'd have thought squirming on it in a gorgeous gondola with Ashley's fingers reaming your anus would have toughened it. But no. It's like rancid margarine. It needs beating, doesn't it?"

She drove the crop haft deep into the arsehole and left it there.

The long silence that ensued puzzled Marina until she realized her victim had passed out. Even the jolting of the leather handle further and further up into the rectum had no effect. The scourged body hung heavily from the wrist straps until it revived under the slaps delivered across the befouled face streaked with tears. Marina flung the rest of her wine over the head.

"Oh, no, you don't, bitch. You've got a lot more to come now I've given you a rest."

With that, she depressed the spring-loaded clamps jamming the feeding tube behind the teeth and ripped out the gag. The prolonged distension had locked the jaws open, paralysing the slave's mouth.

"Don't gape at me like that, stupid. Don't you think you merit what I'm giving you?"

"Yes, mistress," came the groan.

Then the real flagellation began in earnest. The rump was always the main target at Beaucastel and Verenka knew it.

222

Marina aimed for the previous welts she had raised days before and put all her force into the strokes. As the vast bulges reddened, the screams from the open mouth grew in intensity to a degree that prompted her to ram the gag back into the throat. Although far distant from the inhabited region of the castle, the yells were dangerous. She redoubled the power behind each lash until the sole area of unmarked skin was that down the anal crease and that too she managed to colour. Around the thirtieth crack of the alligator leather, her victim collapsed again in her last frantic writhings.

Marina wiped her scourge clean: it had been the longest and most vicious flagellation she had yet given a naked slave since her promotion. With a pang of regret, she decided to renounce chaining the slut to the summit of the bedposts by the ankle straps to slaughter the crotch; there was little point in proceeding further on a body that no longer responded. There would doubtless be plenty of further occasions, if she played her cards astutely.

The return to the underworld proved more demanding than expected. Marina had to half-drive, half-beat the bitch forward. Several times Verenka crumpled up in the gloomy passages, still trying to come to terms with the harvest of lashes she had received. Finally she was safely hasped in the iron brackets and, having been virtually whipped clean of slime, Marina daubed the form with swill and muck to camouflage at least some of the welts. Marina wiped off her gloves on the underside of the girl's breasts and again cleaned off her crop by running it up between the swollen labia. It came away glittering with curd.

"You're still as devious as ever, Verenka, aren't you? Shamming a lack of libido! Why, you're leaking like a spiked barrel and that great clit's wagging with want. You fake!"

The pathetic face looked up in tears, swallowing hard behind the iron brace. The look was a mixture of supplication, as if imploring Marina to extricate her from hell, and of fear lest the whippings should start up again.

Reading the entreaty in the tear-red eyes, Marina smiled. "Next time it's going to be between those hefty legs of yours, you faithless slag."

The blonde overseer left with a final curse and slipped into her own luxurious bed as swiftly as she could, discounting Lalanière's possible continued availability. She had not appreciated the man's admonitions. She stretched out, gave herself a quick, ecstatic orgasm with the handle of her riding crop and fell asleep. She had eluded risk, if risk there had been and anyway who cared if the dumb slave had a few more welts on her?

Her sleep was the slumber of the requited.

No one really knew who put the match to the powder keg. The spiteful Sandra? Some valet who had taken swill down to the slave?

Urgently, after Verenka's state had been reported, Vasa consulted with the Master. And then events began to tread on each other's heel precipitously.

Marina was arrested the following evening. Lalanière exculpated himself without too much difficulty; true he had fucked her, as usual, but she had left early, seemingly with some plan in mind... what, he did not know, of course. She had just left with a candle.

Marina was put to the rack. Stretched to the limit of her joints, she freely admitted she had "decided to give her former lover a little lesson" but that was all. She had not spoken up as the issue seemed so minor.

"I trusted you, Marina," came the Master's voice, seething with fury, terror invading all his staff. "And you have had the effrontery, the audacity, the impudence to disobey me!"

Marina fought resolutely to defend herself, aware that if the confrontation had taken place in his apartments, face to face, she might well have employed her tongue in a more mundane way and got away with it. But the showdown was public, with authority, jurisdiction and loss of face involved. Inevitably Marina lost out.

"Vasa, you will take this slut down to the Black Cellar,"—Marina's heart froze at the mention of the place—"strip her naked and chain her in the Cage of Retribution to await her punishment. I want her flesh rings reinserted. I want her fully shaved, oiled, gagged and hooded, her sex distended." The man's vehemence scared Marina as much as the sentence that was surely going to be handed down. "And put her under sex torture while she waits… nipples and crotch."

Vasa nodded with relish.

The senior overseer released Marina from the rack, rolled her off the slab and, summoning Lalanière and the squint-eyed Roscoff had her dragged bodily towards the door. Then Marina began to yell. "Please, Master, I didn't mean to disobey… I only wanted to settle with her and… Oh, Master…"

"Take the slut out of my sight before I have her nipples sliced off!" The Master could hardly contain his wrath; it was almost biblical, the quintessence of white fury. His jewel, his favourite, his apple-polisher had played him false. The bitch. How naive he had been.

He withdrew into his inner sanctum with the slim, ominous Vasa to consider the punishment. They went into detail before deciding and then made arrangements for the precise date, time, duration and which guests should be invited, together with the attendance of sex slaves to service them. The invitations went out immediately by fax and coded e-mail.

Long before the dark, limousines began to arrive and park in the castle forecourt

The infamous Black Dungeon had been readied for the night's session. In line with its name, the sinister, subterranean torture hall was swathed with sombre drapes around the viewing area reserved for the spectators. The stage, rising a little above the rest of the cellar, had been fastidiously prepared for the session of slave punishment that would last well into the small hours and even beyond.

The racks of whips and instruments completed the array.

Clearly the trestle and long chains were scheduled for use that night and all eyes were on them.

And yet, as the side curtains were drawn aside, still another piece of apparatus came into view, a comparatively innocent-looking object which several of the more senior members of the Beaucastel circle had seen in use during a previous session organized to punish an equally guilty female some months before. Vasa had insisted with all her power of persuasion that the slave should experience the notorious Breast Plank. Indeed, Vasa derived untold pleasure from beating a pair of well-fleshed breasts painfully anchored to the thing. With some reluctance—Marina still attracted him—the Master finally acquiesced, convinced by his efficient overseer that, since the performance was to be taped, the cassette might well become a best seller. Thus the three items of correction stood in full view promising an interesting night.

Of even greater, immediate significance was the iron-barred cage in which the night's offering had been exposed throughout the day for inspection. Marina's breathtaking nudity hung crucified, a taut X of oiled muscle and tendons, as was the custom, the cunt had been freshly depilated and ringed anew, like the nipples, through the existing flesh slots. The head beneath the leather hood had been shaved clean and Marina's old number, 107, reinstated below the bulge of the left breast.

In addition, the guests could see and appreciate from where they lounged waiting, that the vulva had been wrenched open, golden chains hauling both sets of labia apart to expose the vagina's liquid-crimson oval sheath. The chains encircled the upper thighs and were clipped together beneath the rump. In addition, the engorged, purple teats and rigid clitoris were throbbing visibly and in pain—or, as always with Marina, with lubricity—held in steel torture-clamps screwed tight into the hypersensitive prominences of soft flesh. The pressure was specifically designed to heighten the slave's erotic response to the whips and instruments to come.

Promptly at midnight, to the low, distant background of his favourite Bach cantata, the robed Master entered and bowed gravely to the company of distinguished guests. As he took his seat in the great winged chair facing the stage, his private slave crouched before the splayed crotch, ready to fellate once the performance got under way.

His curt command brought the three overseers from the wings into the dark red lighting of the stage. Their sudden appearance stilled the conversation among the spectators as the figures shed their scarlet cloaks of ceremony to reveal what were almost totally naked bodies—the thorax strapping, gauntlets and even the riding boots had been discarded, leaving only the face veils. Vasa, slim and looking particularly fiendish, had rouged her breast tips and carried a dark garnet jewel in her navel; her sex hair stood out, luxuriously combed, at least that which could seen of it, for she wore a robust black dildo strapped to her pubis and hips. Each of the two men presented a penis even more massive than the dildo, both shafts pounding in full erection, encircled with the usual bristle sleeves.

Deprived of sight, Marina sensed the overseers' ominous presence and guessed they differed from their usual appearance. They were set to enjoy the night just as the onlookers would and as their nude victim was meant to, insofar as she could bear it. Further, she knew her orgasms were not only permitted but encouraged. In whatever fashion her torturers were arrayed, she hoped against hope she would be able to take her punishment staunchly and that it would indeed trigger her orgasms as during her training and whipping sessions in the other cellars. At the prospect of climaxing, her breathing began to shallow and quicken. Apart from her masturbations, she had not come on a phallus or under a female slave's tongue for at least twenty-four hours and needed sex.

The ill-favoured, squint-eyed Roscoff flung open the gates of the cage and unchained her. Roughly he dragged her out on to the centre of the stage where she stood quivering with a mixture of blind fear and excitement—the same as when, in

227

the past, she was led down to the cells or taken to a guest's room for flagellation and sexual duties. Now on stage, naked, hooded and gagged, she tried to show off her body to its best advantage before it was blighted by the whips. The series of admiring comments rising from among the invisible spectators gave her a fleeting tingle of pleasure, knowing her resplendent curves were glinting under the lights as each visitor readied his or her attendant slave for service while she was prepared for whipping.

Vasa, as senior flogger in charge, unscrewed the clit clamp and loosened the metal teeth crushing the teats. Marina staggered with the pain of the removal as the circulation took up again in the flesh nubs but at least she was accustomed to that, as she was to the display of her stretched cunt. If the nipple and clit clamps were gone, hopefully they would release her labial chain. But there she was mistaken. She was to remain sexually splayed throughout the session.

Then the overseers began to work on her. What followed as her first ordeal was not only a terrifying shock but something that lay far beyond her range of experience and imagination. At least, she could not see the preparations or implements...

She was hauled blind and naked towards the contraption some guests had already identified as the seldom used Breast Plank. There Vasa calmly passed a thong through the slave's nipple rings to wrench the breasts up to the collarbones where she tied it off on the forward ring of the throat strap. The slave felt herself being forced to her knees before what seemed to her to be a crescent-shaped edge of a horizontal board; her thighs were then chained rigid to the metal uprights, the trembling arms stretched to hooks in the cellar's vaulted ceiling. Sensing the three overseers' hands on her and feeling the cocks slapping against her as she was chained, she froze in dread, her throat desiccated behind the gag. In the past, her trepidation became entwined with spirals of voluptuous, erotic longing to be whipped naked and fucked before connoisseurs. But what she was being prepared for now seemed different.

Once in position, unable to move more than her masked head, the sweating nude felt her breasts being released. As she lowered them, Vasa hooked her fingers through the rings and hauled hard; the umber cones and nipples elongated unbearably at the extremity of the distended, tube-like mammaries. Suddenly Vasa released the tension to let the flesh drag back on the surface of the board. With a ghastly jerk, the slave felt the undersides abruptly speared on a crop of small, angled spikes.

It was only when her entire body lurched madly, almost tearing the bench from its floor bolts, the enveloped head flung back with a choked yell, did Marina realize in frenzied horror what was being done to her. Alive with minute steel barbs, slanting forward like claws, the board speared into her breasts mercilessly; each tug only embedded the slender tines deeper into her lymph. An explosion of white pain streaked through her reeling brain when Vasa crushed the flesh down on to the surface; Marina ceased to struggle, moaning into her gag, sweat crawling down her face behind the stifling hood. The chain splaying her cunt by the rings seemed to tighten hideously as if about to rip the labia. Then it eased.

The old-timers in the cellar knew, better than she, that the curved spikes were honed needle-sharp, for they had seen the plank used before, with hallucinating effect, on nude females. This part of the evening alone justified the journey to Beaucastel and they watched with fascination, trusting the victim would already be leaking her preparatory discharge, as slaves put to the plank always did. Whether later in the session she would be fucked and allowed orgasm remained to be seen; in any event, she was now ready for the whip. For the guests it was flagellation that really counted. After verifying the victim's position and satisfied with the grip of the myriad pin points, Vasa turned to the Master to receive the fatal nod.

When it came, her black quirt swung back, paused and hissed, thudding into the quivering breast flesh. Shlack!

The breast meat rippled and flattened. Shlack! Again. Again.

Then again she slashed, the tongues of leather reddening the pale flesh, each stroke driving the curved points deeper into the epidermis. Blue and white flashes seared through the slave as the gagged throat yelled and yelled until her lungs shrank within her. Yet, despite the crippling pain, some hidden instinct made Marina restrain her lunges. The slightest tug from the chest in desperation would only tear the underside of the flesh.

She let the tiny spears sink in completely until her breasts seemed to become part of the plank. Marina knew that breast beating was part of a female slave's predestination but surely, her spinning brain told her, not under such vicious torture… But then she was not merely a female slave. She was a condemned female slave with breasts.

Varying her lashes, the overseer pounded harder into the masses and then struck the ringed areoles and teats jutting out beyond the margin of the board. Purple from the previous torment in the holding cage, the extremities swelled up as the overseer flayed them with professional exactness. Vasa then sashayed over to the instrument rack and returned with a thin bamboo rod to complete the task; with that she sliced down across the tips again, sending the rings pitching and tossing as though they no longer belonged to the body. Only when Marina had passed out, her head drooping, saliva trickling from under the hood, did Vasa receive the sign from the chair to desist.

Lalanière and his brusque colleague freed her in much the same manner as Vasa had jagged and blooded her— sadistically, enjoying her suffering. Vasa's sex was leaking copiously down her inner thighs for all to see and the men's blue-veined erections jolted, the slits oozing long filaments of bright sap.

Her feet trailing behind her, the slave was dragged by the armpits over to the second apparatus, the hideous trestle, for her second instalment of retribution. As always, she too was awash with longing, despite the shock and pain she had just endured.

Amid delicious groans of spending among them and their slaves, the guests sat back to be served refreshments. So far the evening was living up to the castle's renown. And there was a great deal more still to be enjoyed.

The hooded body was thrown backwards over the sharp crest of the trestle, the flat belly cinched with a broad strap while the legs were bent, raised and parted wide, the feet chained halfway up the joists, exposing the gaping, drenched sex still chain-splayed. Roscoff then bound the wrists to the lower rung at the rear of the timber pyramid. The two men then stood back to allow the onlookers to take in the sight; the entire room could clearly discern the stalk of clitoral gristle pulsating at the apex of the distended oval gash. Less visible were the scarred undersides of the breasts hanging behind towards the head.

"Proceed." The order was no more than a sibilant lisp as the Master depressed the head of the tireless slave down to the root of his cock.

Revived with a bucket of water over her head, Marina felt the adrenaline pumping through her as she waited. What she could not see was Vasa selecting from the instrument rack the pair of flesh tongs destined for the cunt and Lalanière taking hold of the notorious nipple wrench, the latter equipped with flat jaws. Both instruments were designed to lock on to, and wrench at the tender flesh sending a slave into sexual delirium.

"Prepare her first, Roscoff."

The brute Roscoff, a consummate flogger of women, grinned at his colleagues. Now it was his turn. Only when he had brought the slave to a sufficient level of erotic pleasure through being whipped naked would the steel appliances be employed. He shook out the slender six-thong of knotted leather and took his stance over the dangling head. Loosening the hood and prizing out the gag, he jabbed his cock into Marina's throat. Then he whipped down into the outspread fork of the thighs. Ten lashes sufficed to set the slave's head jerking, sucking arduously on the penis as best she could. At the same time the body heaved with each stroke.

Clearly, despite the pain, the slave was stimulated.

Suddenly the muscles tensed as the crotch reddened and bloated; Marina shuddered and went rigid, freeing herself of the fellation. And in a crescendo of yells she came stupendously as the whip thrashed across the clit. Roscoff thrust back into her gullet and emptied all he had stored up over the last hour. Then the gag was plugged back into the throat, choking and clogged with sperm, and brutally the man strapped the hood back.

A ripple of applause, mingled with cries of other orgasms, reached the stage as the Master nodded to Vasa.

The two overseers knew the slave was ready without his signal.

Through the waves of her orgasm, the slave felt the chill grip of Lalanière's pincers close over each of her inflamed teats in turn; as her body froze stiff, the neck taut against the rung of the trestle, Marina knew it was her sex partner gripping the dark, purple grapes he had sucked and mauled so often in bed. She offered herself up to the thrilling pain with a strangled shriek of euphoria when suddenly Vasa's steel entered her, snapping at the walls of the swollen vagina and then seizing the base of the clit. The twists sent the slave into three more successive spasms that startled even Vasa, the veteran, the specialist of work on the female genitals.

It was the Master who restrained the enthusiasts. Marina sank back on to the trestle, consoled that the pain had turned so easily into pleasure. Yet she still had her two other orifices begging for penetration and, for that matter, her mouth again, if need be.

From the couches and cushions in the cellar's penumbra the sound of suction, groans and long drawn-out sobs of sexual relief filled the air.

"Now, Vasa, if you please…" the voice of authority again, "Kindly string her up…"

The slave girl was released. Staggering drunkenly to the

centre of the stage, Roscoff's scourge guiding her, Marina fell to her knees, her freed hands grasping her crotch and breasts. She was given little opportunity to soothe them as she heard the clatter of chains being run down from the upper extremities of the stage; desperate not to disgrace herself before her Master and the company, she struggled to her feet to have the chain hooks inserted through the rings in the wrist manacles. Slowly the slack was taken up on wall sprockets and drums until the still resplendent volume of nudity was stretched before the dazzled eyes of the spectators. As if crucified, not on the flogging cross Marina had experienced so often in her earlier days of slavery, but in a void, she undulated sensually between the tug of the long chains, astonished her ankles remained unpredictably free for her to waver in all her beauty. Her outstretched arms, offering the entire body to the whips, seemed to welcome the prospect. At last what she most desired had come.

Instinctively, she sensed the two senior overseers discussing and selecting their leathers before taking their stand. From the hushed remarks and heavy breathing, she had the presentiment that Vasa stood before her to the right, having attributed to herself the targets she was partial to—the breasts, belly, open sex and the thighs. Pierre Lalanière, Marina knew, would want her back and slim buttocks as in the past. A feeling of relief quivered through her as she realized the repellent Roscoff with his strabismus was not summoned to participate. Presumably he had had his ration of pleasure; she still tasted his acrid spunk coating her teeth and throat.

Marina readied her sleek nakedness for the flogging, but what ensued, at the Master's guttural command, overpowered even Marina's resilience. Each side of her elegant body received the fifty-five lashes ordained. Tottering forward, as far as the long chains would permit to dilute the shock of Lalanière's riding crop, she merely offered Vasa an even greater plenitude of breast and abdomen flesh to add to what the overseer had already devastated and it was the thrashing across the hollowed belly and elongated labia that ground down her stamina and drove her to the limit of her strength. The two overseers, obviously by dint of long partnership, had raised double flagellation to a fine art: the alternate lashes threw the body forward and then back. Marina shrieked and sobbed into the dank leather of her hood but by the thirtieth lash she gave in and let them slam into her body, swaying but rooted to the spot. Then suddenly pleasure welled up in her, breaking over her like a tidal wave as she felt her vagina clenching and then dilating as her orgasm became imminent and urgent. Her muffled cries changed into moans of craving. Had she been ungagged she would have yelled to them to lash directly into her clitoris...

Lalanière welted both buttock mounds until there remained no trace of unwhipped flesh; somewhere in her crazed, floundering brain, Verenka's huge, rich arse came back to her. It sufficed to set her vagina firmly on the highroad to orgasm.

Then Vasa slammed hard into the belly again. Her whip had knots enclosing lead weights but it was the shredded tips that carved a gash below the navel and set the slave writhing and yelping once more, the path to her climax becoming mired with pain.

Oblivious of what followed the white-hot explosions, Marina tried to come but then surrendered and passed out in a convulsion of misery laced with jolts of approaching pleasure she was unable to harness. She sagged by the wrists, her legs trembling.

Suddenly her body resurrected, alive and vibrant, Lalanière's rigid cock and bristle ring were boring into her and had passed the compliant sphincter. She recognized it spontaneously as he slid in deliciously, despite the crusty circle of bristles; ramming hard, the prodigious shaft butted against the thin membrane high up within her, while her anal muscle clutched the root of the penis, as Lalanière himself had made her practise night after night; the man's pelvis ground into the blood trickling from the broached buttock. Marina spread her legs, bending forward in rapture to enjoy the gift out of the blue.

Then, almost more inconceivable was the sultry breath on her cheek as Vasa in turn locked horns with her, grabbing the two nipple rings in one hand, the huge dildo in the other, to drive the rubber-ribbed monster up into the soused, swollen vagina. The hard rod gouged Marina to the maximum of her elasticity, until it was butting against the cervix, jousting with the thrusts of the male cock behind. Marina rode the two insertions with a fury that dissolved whatever pain remained of the floggings and tortures. Brought divinely by Vasa's lunges to the first of four superb climaxes, she came almost simultaneously with the scalding discharge Lalanière spumed into her bowels. And then Vasa herself orgasmed formidably; brought off by the surrounding base of the dildo bearing on her clitoris. As she came, Vasa seemed to release thick liquid up into the slave's innards, juice she pumped in both directions, into Marina and into herself, by squeezing on the dangling ball sack of the artefact. Marina could not believe her good fortune as she raved through more orgasms. After the blinding flashes had destroyed her, she admitted the crescendo was worth the whole maniacally rigorous welter of the session.

Without warning, Marina was relieved of her hood and gag. The sweat pouring down her shaven brow at first impeded her from taking in the scene. Then her eyes adjusted to the red glare—in fact only a glow—of the stage lights and the semidarkness of the cellar.

The voice from the chair seemed to issue from outer space.

"Do you now regret your crime, slave? Or should we flog you further?"

Gathering what saliva she could, Marina strove to reply. She was weak from her yelling and more so from the orgasms that had ripped through her.

"I apologize for my disobedience, Master. As a common slave again, I shall obey and try to work my way up again into your good graces. Thank you for punishing me."

The gaunt face smiled from the chair. "You took it well. Be cautious from now on."

Hours later, Marina found herself in Cell Three, chained by the ankles, head down, to a ring high up on the masonry, her cunt chains removed. With an indelible pen Sandra was busy inscribing fresh digits on the ribs just below the damaged breast.

"There, they've given you a new number, bitch." The girl's insolence stunned Marina as though she had been given a jolt from the cattle prod. "You've got to start life from the foot of the ladder again as a flogging slave. You'll have to heal up a trifle before your next bout of sex torture, won't you, whore? You look atrocious. No one will even take a second glance at you as you are. And, by the way, you have to obey me from now on. I'm in charge of your botched pigpen of a body. One mistake, honey, and I'll give you a taste of the flesh rake, as you used to say."

Relegated finally to her bunk in the Slave Hall after cursory attention from the newly inducted nurse, Marina grew disconsolate, her once sparkling blue-green eyes like pebbles deep in some distant mountain stream, awash with tears of loneliness. None of her former colleagues, leave alone the fresh intakes and trainees, would approach her; many had suffered hell from the compulsive flogger's hand prior to her disgrace. Not even Pierre Lalanière made the effort to console her or even whip her, replacing her once superb body by Sandra's, who in fact fucked and fellated just as commendably.

It was well into the small hours several nights later that Marina felt a warm, well-fleshed female body, naked and ringed, insinuating itself into her bunk. As the creature cuddled up beside her, the skin had a strange but familiar texture and pungency. Whoever was risking her life by slinking in between a disgraced slave's sheets at such an hour must have some motive or be sex starved. The body was actually offering itself in complete darkness to a discredited slave only just recovering

236

from a public flagellation.

"You have forgiven me, haven't you, Marina darling? I'm so glad you're back here in our old dorm again. They made me watch you being flogged and tortured down there the other night and I was so proud of you. You were so brave, so beautiful…"

The voice gave Marina a shock that deprived her of breath. Verenka! Verenka, naked in bed next to her, kissing the bruised nipples… Verenka, of all living creatures!

"Let me lick you down there, darling, where they whipped you." A manacled wrist was already straying to Marina's sore crotch. It was the same hand and the same husky, bewitching tone that had haunted the Quai d'Anjou and groaned in endless ecstasy.

"I'll do it so, so gently, darling," the voice murmured. "Oh, how I love you…"

"I can't believe it, Verenka!" Marina whispered. "I'm sorry, darling, I whipped you like that I don't know what got into me. You'll just have to forgive me. Only, you did leave me high and dry, remember."

"Dry! You were never dry with me on top of you, darling." Then it was Verenka's turn to pause. "I'm going to make love to you. I'll do it ever so gently but first I want to ask you something, something very special."

She hesitated again. "Would you whip me again, naked and chained like the other night? I loved it, darling."

Marina's heart missed a beat and then accelerated. "You did? Really?" Her throat had tightened. "Well, I can't. Because I'm no longer an overseer."

"Yes, of course. But one day… For now at least you can make love, no?"

She made Marina reverse in the bunk to soixante-neuf herself under her. Each set of trembling fingers fumbled a moment among the other's rings to unglue the swollen vulvas.

"For Pete's sake, don't wake the others, darling." Marina's whisper was lost as she lapped ravenously into the orifice.

237

Intoxicated with an odour and taste she had almost forgotten, she pursed her lips over Verenka's superb clit and slid down to the ring.

Nothing Beaucastel had to offer could possibly rival this legendary stem of sexual lust.

Puritan Punishment

By Caroline Swift

London under Oliver Cromwell was not the haven of temperate sobriety history has led us to believe!

These diaries, kept by a young maid who was left in the care of her drunken aunt and uncle, reveal a hotbed of lust and depravity. As Janet, cast out by her relatives for refusing to submit to their desires, soon discovers, London is a dangerous place for a pretty ingénue.

Refuge under the roof of the dominant Lady Postell comes at a high price, but it is one Janet finds she is willing to pay. Journeying to Maveringham and Winscombe Abbey she encounters a host of dominant lovers but foolishly is persuaded into attempting to escape. This is a dangerous course of action when recapture could expose her to the full force of Puritan Punishment!

This is Caroline Swift at her erotic, graphic and eloquent best.

There are over 100 stunningly erotic novels of domination and submission in the Silver Moon catalogue. You can see the full range, including Club and Illustrated editions by writing to:

You will receive a copy of the latest issue of the Readers' Club magazine, with articles, features, reviews, adverts and news plus a full list of our publications and an order form.